HER RODEO RIVAL'S RETURN

REBECCA CROWLEY

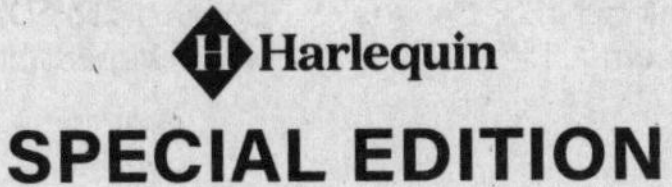

Recycling programs for this product may not exist in your area.

ISBN-13: 978-1-335-47270-0

Her Rodeo Rival's Return

For questions and comments about the quality of this book, please contact us at CustomerService@Harlequin.com.

Harlequin Enterprises ULC
22 Adelaide St. West, 41st Floor
Toronto, Ontario M5H 4E3, Canada
www.Harlequin.com

HarperCollins Publishers
Macken House, 39/40 Mayor Street Upper,
Dublin 1, D01 C9W8, Ireland
www.HarperCollins.com

Printed in Lithuania

1 2 3 4 5 6 7 8 9 10 LIT 28 27 26 25

"Kenzie." His cold command snapped her back to the present.

She was pressed against Jesse's chest, his hands holding her wrists.

Hot damn, he smelled good.

Barn-stored leather, earthy and soft. That first frost of autumn, fresh pine and raw bark and crisp grass underfoot. The long shadows of an early-setting sun, twilight hastening in ambers and golds, chased by the velvety hush of darkness.

Kenzie gaped at him like she was trying to catch a mouthful of flies. His grip on her wrists was firm but careful, the sneer wrinkling his nose not totally convincing. Dark lashes fringed his narrowed eyes—eyes that dipped to her lips and stayed there.

Does he taste as good as he smells?

Dear Reader,

I'm thrilled to be publishing my first book with Harlequin Special Edition! As a rodeo-loving Kansan (currently transplanted to Texas), these characters are close to my heart, and I can't wait to share the Singer Pro Rodeo dynasty with readers.

Former corporate raider Jesse Singer assumed the helm of America's oldest—and only—Jewish rodeo dynasty after the death of his older brother. The family's fifth-generation stock-contracting outfit is on the brink of bankruptcy, and he's determined to save Singer Pro Rodeo—especially from Kenzie Wallace. Born to nothing but deprivation, Kenzie Wallace fought her way to second-in-command at Singer Pro Rodeo, and she'll never forgive Jesse Singer for firing her. Now she's back in action at a new ranch, and she's made it her mission to run Singer Pro Rodeo into the ground.

When a fake-folksy billionaire launches an unsanctioned, unregulated league to siphon their athletes and their audiences, Jesse and Kenzie will have to quit stink-eyeing their way around the circuit and work together to protect their sport—and hope their hearts survive the ride.

Happy reading!

Rebecca Crowley

Web: rebecca-crowley.com

Instagram: @rebeccacrowleybooks

Facebook: facebook.com/rebeccacrowleywrites

Rebecca Crowley loves to write stories about imperfect people finding their perfect match, and never tires of the happily-ever-after. She's married to the charming Brit she met while studying abroad and has two daughters she hopes will love romance, too. Having pulled up her Kansas roots to live in New York City, London and Johannesburg, Rebecca currently resides in Houston.

Books by Rebecca Crowley

Harlequin Special Edition

Singer Pro Rodeo

Her Rodeo Rival's Return

Visit the Author Profile page at Harlequin.com.

To Kev, who always believed I would get here,
and to Joss, who showed me the way.

Chapter One

Two thousand pounds of muscle, bone and downright bad temper landed with such force that clouds of dust billowed beneath the floodlights. Not Nice kicked his rear legs nearly vertical and the cowboy riding him went flying, executing an Olympic-quality aerial somersault before landing flat on his face.

Crammed into the metal bleachers, the crowd held a collective breath as the bullfighters surrounded the bull. Before they could intervene, the cowboy sprang to his feet, prompting relieved applause. He managed a sheepish wave as he hobbled bowlegged back to the fence, the fringe on his chaps fluttering as he walked.

Kenzie Wallace watched Not Nice trot out of the arena, his gait loose and calm, his eight-second workday finished. He was the relaxed, jovial opposite of the mean-as-hell monster who'd just launched one of the top-ranked cowboys in the Pro Rodeo League so high that she half expected a call from NASA.

Not Nice was Kenzie's best bet for Bull of the Year at the League finals in December, and the points—and the payday—he'd just earned got her one step closer.

She should be delighted. She should be over the late-summer moon hanging high above her head. She should be bumping fists and slapping palms and clambering down from the platform behind the chutes, basking in this moment of glory.

She glared at Jesse Singer instead.

He stood at the other end of the line of chutes, arms crossed, boots planted, surveying the proceedings with an imperious lift of his chin, like he was the freaking king of the rodeo.

Which she supposed he was. Singer Pro Rodeo was one of the oldest stock contractors in the history of the sport, and for over a hundred years had bred bucking bulls and horses on their ranch outside Stillwater.

And just like real royalty, the Singer family had their admirers—and their critics. Much of the rodeo community held them at arm's length, the Singers' legacy, dominance and individually pleasant overtures never fully penetrating the fog of rumor and speculation that swirled around them.

The Singers weren't dishonest, or disloyal, or anything but perfectly respectable people good at their trade. What the Singers were, was Jewish. And even in this day and age, in this specific segment of American life, some folks simply didn't trust a family that didn't go to church.

She narrowed her eyes at Jesse from across the platform. His gaze was fixed on Repeat Offender, the speckled, five-year-old bull waiting patiently while his high-ranked rider tightened a rope behind his shoulders.

Repeat Offender was the jewel in the Singers' ornate crown, a diamond among a stable of precious stones. His intense athleticism and easygoing temperament made him dangerous on the scoreboard, yet safe and workable after the whistle. More than anything, though, he had that innate drive to perform that would one day seal his name in the history books alongside Bushwacker, Panhandle Slim and Little Yellow Jacket.

She should know. She'd raised him.

Kenzie watched Repeat Offender peer through the bars of the chute, his ears flicking as he took in the noise of the crowd. He should've been a shoo-in for Bull of the Year at the League finals in Vegas—and if Jesse Singer wasn't such a pompous idiot, he would've been.

Instead, he had Not Nice nipping at his hooves, vying for the most coveted accolade in American roughstock.

The cowboy nodded and the gate sprang open, unleashing Repeat Offender into the arena. The animal bucked high and hard with his head low, his back legs flinging up. The cowboy leaned over Repeat Offender's shoulders—a sensible move to stay balanced on any other bull—but Repeat Offender instantly jerked up, rearing his head back and throwing the rider off-center. The cowboy worked to regain his purchase, but his control deteriorated, his free hand flailed, his legs scooted off his rope. Repeat Offender twisted left, and that was it—the cowboy went sailing through the air, landing on his backside with his elbows in the dirt.

Yanking off his helmet, the cowboy shot Repeat Offender a look of pure, dazed bewilderment. The bull stepped out of the rider's loose rope and, as he calmly strutted out of the arena, Kenzie could've sworn that beast looked mightily self-satisfied.

She stifled the affectionate smile that had crept onto her mouth and returned her attention to her nemesis. That was the last ride of the night. Both their star bulls had buck-offs, so they'd wait to get their animals' scores from the judges. Meanwhile the winning rider would take his victory lap around the arena, standing in the bed of a shiny pickup provided by a local dealership. The crowd would file out into the clear, mid-August night, and the rodeo in Hobbs, New Mexico, would be over for another year.

Not for her. She'd be in Nebraska next week, South Dakota the week after, hauling cattle, tying flank ropes, visiting corners of America lots of people never knew existed. She loved this sport, this community, this lifestyle. She'd worked hard to be where she was, and she finally had the life she wanted.

Almost.

Kenzie cleared her throat, flipped a couple pages in her notebook and charged across the platform, pausing only to sidle around a cowboy kneeling in prayer.

Her movement caught Jesse's attention. He watched her approach, his sharp gaze nearly—but not quite—making her falter. All the Singer siblings had the same black hair and peacock-blue eyes, but Jesse was the only one on whom that color was disconcerting—as if being obnoxiously handsome wasn't enough. Lee's eyes had been warm, tropical seas. His sisters' reminded her of turquoise jewelry.

Jesse's eyes were death lasers.

He aimed them straight at her, their intensity undiluted by the shadow from the brim of his hat. A small hole in the straw permitted a sliver of the floodlights' glare to slash across his face in a way that was suddenly, urgently familiar.

"Are you wearing Lee's hat?"

Jesse regarded her as impassively as if she'd asked him the time, his mouth a flat line. "What do you want?"

That was definitely Lee's hat. She recognized it, with the big turkey feather in the band. It was too small for Jesse; it sat too high above his ears.

Lee Singer, Jesse's older brother and her former boss, had launched a charm offensive unlike any other in the Singers' multigenerational history, showing his face at every event he could squeeze in. He pumped hands, slapped backs, cracked corny jokes and dazzled some of the family's harshest detractors with his big smile and bigger personality.

Then a distracted driver ran a red light, and all that energy and brightness and gale-force enthusiasm was reduced to a little granite square in the fenced-off field where five generations of Singers slept for eternity.

Kenzie glanced down at the toes of her boots, weathering the wave of grief that still rolled over her when she thought of Lee, even two years later. He'd been more than her boss. He'd been her mentor, her friend and her biggest cheerleader.

Then Jesse had come home and fired her.

Anger was a welcome alternative to sorrow, and she wrapped it around herself like a blanket as she refocused on Jesse. He'd taken everything from her the day he tossed her out, all the dreams and goals and wild ambitions she'd worked toward since old Mr. Singer hired her as a bottom-rung ranch hand.

"That hat doesn't fit you," she informed him.

His eyes flashed with deep dislike before he reined himself back to indifference. Kenzie permitted herself a tiny smile of triumph. Iceman Jesse was a tough nut to crack, but she carried a big-ass hammer.

"I jotted down some chute notes for you. You might try Storm Watch out on his left—he's stronger on that side. Hobgoblin had a nice performance, but Bad Omen is a problem. He really went for those bullfighters, and it wastes everyone's time when the pickup riders have to rope a bull and escort him out. You need to socialize him. Have lots of different people around him every day, being nice to him, showing him there's no need to be on the offensive. He's young enough that you can turn this around, and you need to. Sending cowboys to the hospital is bad for business."

She ripped a page from her notebook and handed it over. Jesse didn't read it—he'd barely blinked while she spoke.

Without a word he ripped the paper into pieces, shredding her careful observations and constructive ideas into indecipherable scraps, then dropped them into the space between their feet.

"Thanks," he said dryly.

Kenzie looked down at the ragged segments of torn paper, scattered like a half-hearted snowfall between the toes of their boots. She glared up at him, squared her palms on his chest and shoved him. Hard.

Unfortunately, Jesse Singer was about as tall as a redwood and just as sturdy—so sturdy she was momentarily surprised by the strength concealed in his lean build. He arched a brow at her with the weary impatience a bobcat might give a bee, and the anger that had fueled her since that horrible day she met him bubbled up and boiled over.

"I'm trying to help you. Why do you always have to be such an ass?"

"If I wanted your help, I'd hire you," he replied.

Kenzie fisted her hands. She prided herself on her toughness, her thick skin, her ability to succeed as a woman in an almost exclusively male industry. She'd learned to ignore even the lewdest remarks and get on with her job, proving herself again and again until the only whispers behind her back were about when that Bull of the Year plaque would have her name on it. She was levelheaded, unflappable, and as strong as the bucking stock she raised.

Yet Jesse Singer set her off like a cheap firework.

Kenzie had grown up just twenty miles from the Singer ranch. But she'd been born into nothing but deprivation, her single mom's work ethic as much of an inheritance as she could claim. The man who'd stepped outside his marriage to conceive her could barely look at her, never mind embrace her as his own. Whatever she had, she'd earned—including her new job at the Broken B, run by an old farmer with new wealth and a penchant for the rodeo.

The Broken B was a small outfit, a fresh-faced entrant to the cutthroat world of stock contracting. Under anyone else's leadership it would've grown slowly, cautiously, collaboratively, and barely been a fly on the rump of the Singer empire.

But Kenzie was determined to rip that throne out from under Jesse Singer's entitled ass.

"One day you'll realize you made the biggest mistake of your life when you fired me," she told him, pointing her index finger. "You're only where you are because you've got my bulls, the ones I chose and fed and trained. But even the best athletes have to retire eventually. You'll be stuck with a stable of bad decisions who'll do nothing except drain every last dollar you have, and your big-city career and fancy education won't save you. For someone who's supposed to be so smart, you sure act mighty stupid."

Jesse's expression was infuriatingly neutral despite the growing audience of onlookers Kenzie's tirade had attracted. A cluster of cowboys hesitated at the bottom of the platform. Hands from the Broken B and Singer Pro Rodeo watched their bosses nervously. The spectators seated closest to the chutes halted their departures, bright-eyed at the prospect of postshow drama.

Kenzie didn't care. Every word she'd said was the truth. She wouldn't apologize—not to the spoiled, self-righteous idiot standing in front of her.

Jesse tilted his head, one side of his mouth quirking in a patronizing smile. "Like I said, if I wanted your opinion, I'd pay for it."

The gate snapped open on the chute restraining Kenzie's temper. She shoved him again, and again, the utter failure of her efforts to move him even a fraction of an inch only stoking her fury. He'd taken everything from her. *Everything*, and it was only through sheer grit and determination that she wasn't back in her mother's guest room, setting off at midnight for her graveyard shift at the truck stop. He was a disgrace to his family, a disgrace to his *name*, and if his brother could see—

"Kenzie." His cold command snapped her back to the present. She was pressed against Jesse's chest, his hands holding her wrists.

Hot damn, he smelled good.

Barn-stored leather, earthy and soft. That first frost of autumn, fresh pine and raw bark and crisp grass underfoot. The long shadows of an early-setting sun, twilight hastening in ambers and golds, chased by the velvety hush of darkness.

Kenzie gaped at him like she was trying to catch a mouthful of flies. His grip on her wrists was firm but careful, the sneer wrinkling his nose not totally convincing. Dark lashes fringed his narrowed eyes—eyes that dipped to her lips and stayed there.

Does he taste as good as he smells?

Kenzie snatched that brazen thought halfway through its zigzagging trip around her brain and stuffed it back into the Naughty Box where it belonged—along with all the other sinful fantasies featuring a post-personality-transplant version of Jesse Singer. She planted her feet to wrench out of his grasp—but then a lasso swung down and tightened around their waists, pressing them even closer.

"Sorry, kids, no fighting in the arena." That evening's champion tie-down roper pulled them toward the exit, grinning as the people in the bleachers whistled and cheered.

Kenzie's face burned as they scuttled to the edge of the platform, desperately trying to ignore the warmth of Jesse's body in the cool desert air, or the subtle way he held her elbow as he helped her down the stairs. She would never live this down, and it was all his fault.

As usual.

The roper cut them loose with a wink and they jerked apart, glowering at each other as employees of the Broken B and Singer Pro Rodeo gathered at a safe distance. The ranch hands' allegiances were indistinguishable, their battered cowboy hats and dust-streaked jeans as uniform as their guileless, wary expressions. For a moment, Kenzie considered how petty this was. Their tit for tat was a waste of time and energy, and she was as much to blame as Jesse for keeping it alive.

Jesse turned his attention to his operations manager—his *new* operations manager, who she knew he paid two thirds of what she'd earned when that was her job—and all that twisted-up rage and resentment rushed back, fresh as a blizzard and twice as deadly.

"Load 'em up, Pickens. We're done here." He turned his back and walked away.

Kenzie knew she should do the same. Should've done it a long time ago.

But Jesse Singer had destroyed her livelihood, her lifelong dream, and her one chance to prove her worth to her absent father. She'd never forgive him. They'd never be friends.

And she'd stop at nothing until she destroyed what he loved, too.

Chapter Two

"Look who's back." Billie, Jesse's sister, slid her phone across the diner table.

Jesse set down his fork and picked up the phone. The screen showed a social media account belonging to Casey Custer, the fake-folksy son of a tech billionaire who'd finally been cold-shouldered out of the Pro Rodeo League last year.

Ready to rodeo like never before? Big news coming your way. Stay tuned!

Jesse flipped through the photos above the caption, his scowl deepening. Disassembled cattle chutes stacked in a large indoor arena. A close-up of a bull rider's mud-smeared helmet, the grille obscuring his face. An artsy, shadowed shot of a bull Jesse recognized as Petunia, the animal whose potentially lethal aggression—and Custer's refusal to do anything about it—had resulted in his informal expulsion from the League after even the smallest-budget rodeos declined to hire him.

Jesse's twin sister, Mae—an emergency-room physician who worked rodeos part-time as medical staff—had made the initial complaint against Custer to the League, submitting a letter detailing the frequency and severity of injuries caused by his animals. The League commenced a formal investigation, but the wheels of frontier justice moved faster, quietly canceling Custer's contracts until he was nothing but a spoiled brat with an expensive collection of cows.

At the time, Custer pointed a very public finger at Singer Pro

Rodeo, claiming they'd made false accusations to gain competitive advantage. In the flood of badly punctuated social media tirades that followed, he'd called the Singers conniving, greedy, immoral cheats, flirting with an anti-Semitic conspiracy theory about their links to the pharmaceutical industry.

Jesse and his sisters had assured each other no one would believe such unhinged lunacy—but the supportive comments beneath his ramblings were hard to ignore.

"Just what we need." Jesse passed back the phone.

"What do you think he's up to?"

"Nothing good."

Billie frowned at the screen and Jesse picked up his fork, but his worry over Custer's next vanity project—and his limitless financial resources—soured his appetite for what had been the best breakfast quesadilla of his life, right here in small-town New Mexico.

He sighed and sipped his coffee instead.

Jesse hadn't expected an easy transition when he stepped into his late brother's boots. The Singers had always chosen power over popularity, and much of Lee's relational progress had died right along with him. Not to mention Jesse had inherited his father's shrewd mind and sharp manner, as innately cold and aloof as Lee was warm and ingratiating.

He hadn't guessed it would be this hard, though. All of it: concealing his brother's disastrous financial decisions, gaining the trust—and contracts—of the community to rebuild the Singers' crumbling empire, and single-handedly preserving a rodeo dynasty that spanned five generations.

He glanced at his sister as she rolled her eyes and resumed eating her pancakes. When she wasn't overseeing their bucking-horse herd, Billie was a pickup rider for Singer Pro Rodeo, one of the best in the League—and the only woman. All three of his sisters relied on income from this business to keep them fed and housed. So did the rest of Singer's employees, including his parents, who'd retreated to a two-bedroom house at the edge of the property.

The house where Lee had been born.

Jesse took off his hat—Lee's hat. He ran his hand through his hair and put it back on, sucking in a breath against a stab of grief.

Growing up, he'd idolized his older brother, living for the praise Lee was quick to hand out. When Jesse got into college, when he finished his MBA, when he was hired in the New York City office of an elite, global strategy-consulting firm, Lee was in the figurative front row, clapping his heart out.

That was why no one could know what Lee did to the business. Years of uncontrolled costs and reckless spending had put the hundred-year-old operation deep into the red. Kenzie Wallace, sweetheart of the stock-contracting world, had been at Lee's elbow the whole time, watching him bleed money and not doing a damn thing about it.

He thought he'd solved that problem when he fired her, but she'd turned up at the Broken B like a bad penny—and she had Singer Pro Rodeo in her crosshairs. She'd humiliated them both with her tantrum last night, which was already being spun in her favor. After all, who would side with the corporate cowboy wannabe, who'd been too good for the family business that was the envy of the entire industry? No one, not when the alternative was to root for homegrown, church-raised, bootstrap success story Kenzie. Rich versus poor, the tyrant versus the rebel, and although his middle name was David, he was definitely Goliath in this tale.

Which was why Kenzie's appearance in the diner's doorway made him groan out loud.

"Don't look," he warned his sister, but it was too late. Billie twisted around, the movement drawing Kenzie's attention.

Kenzie's bottle-green gaze landed on Billie, then bounced to him. Her whole face underwent a seismic shift, her pleasant expression darkening to a scowl, her fair skin reddening against her pale blond hair.

It used to be pink, he realized with a jolt. Pink as bubble gum, frivolous and fun, the lone splash of color in what felt like acres of black at the funeral. He'd stared at it during those hours she'd sat shiva with his family, clinging to the impressions of county-fair cotton candy in the pouring rain, a lipstick love note on a truck-stop bathroom mirror, a favorite teddy bear retrieved from the backyard at midnight.

It was pink the day he'd fired her. Blond when he saw her again a few months later. He guessed she'd had to dye it to get rid of it. Color that bright didn't fade quickly.

One of her henchmen—okay, *ranch hands*—asked her a question, disrupting their hostile staring contest. Jesse sighed and looked at his quesadilla. Prize money aside, this was worth coming back for.

Maybe next year he'd manage to eat it.

"Time to roll?" Billie asked.

Jesse nodded and, in an effort to avoid eye contact with Kenzie, took the long way around the small dining area and paid the bill at the register.

Glancing back at Kenzie, who now sat at the head of a table of hands like the big shot she aspired to be, Jesse smirked. She might be a good judge of cow flesh, but given her track record, she'd bankrupt that old fool at the Broken B before he booked his hotel for the League finals in Vegas.

Comforted by that thought, he stepped outside. Billie waited by the truck, her nose wrinkled unhappily.

"Battery's dead. Must've been that cold snap last night." She sounded as weary and exasperated as he felt.

Of course it was. And of course, the crew had gone on ahead of them, getting an early start on the eight-hour drive back to Oklahoma.

"No problem. We'll find someone to give us a jump."

Together they glanced up and down the semirural stretch on the edge of town, which was totally abandoned this Sunday morning. Aside from their own, the only vehicles were a couple of beat-up sedans that probably belonged to the diner's waitstaff, and the gleaming fleet of pickups with the Broken B's logo emblazoned on the doors.

Jesse shaded his eyes, squinting at a slumped building across the street. "Maybe that welding place is open?"

Billie rolled her eyes. "I'll go back inside and ask. Kenzie doesn't hate me as much as she hates you."

"I'll do it. It was my idea to have breakfast before we left."

"You sure?"

"I'm sure," he confirmed gloomily.

"Shout if you need backup. Those Broken B guys look tough, but I could strangle them with the jumper cables."

"I admire the creativity, but let's resolve this without violence."

He headed back in the diner, resolutely keeping his gaze away from Kenzie and her crew. He approached the nearest waitress, attempting his best version of a charming smile.

It hadn't worked in the boardrooms of supranational public companies—and his bosses had quickly learned he was best deployed as a bad cop—and if the waitress's grimace was any indication, it didn't work now.

"Sorry to trouble you," he began, shrugging on the homegrown Okie accent he'd spent years working to shed. "Truck battery's up and quit on us. Any chance we could get a jump?"

She winced. "My car's on its last legs, but I could ask our cook. Might be a while, though. I just dumped a big order on him."

Be nice. Be patient. It'll take as long as it takes.

He tried the smile again, drumming his fingers on his thigh. "It'll only take a minute. Surely he can step out real quick?"

He was aiming for good-natured cajoling, but it came out like a demand—as usual. The sympathy vanished from the waitress's eyes, and he cursed silently. At this rate he'd be lucky if they got over the state line by dinnertime.

"I'll give you a jump."

Jesse closed his eyes at that familiar voice, pinching the bridge of his nose. When he reopened them, Kenzie Wallace was at his elbow, a hand on her hip, a smug smile on her heart-shaped face.

"Appreciate the offer, but this helpful lady—"

"Needs to get on with doing her job," Kenzie finished.

"I'll wait for someone else."

Kenzie rolled her eyes. "That's awful petty, even for you. Come on, my coffee's getting cold."

She shoved through the door of the diner, leaving Jesse no choice but to slink along behind her, sheepish and pissed off.

Outside, Billie was about as pleased to see Kenzie as he'd been. They'd been good friends when Kenzie worked at Singer Pro Rodeo—so good that Billie hadn't spoken to him for a week after he fired her. Once it became clear that Kenzie was determined to beat Singer in the race for Bull of the Year, however, Billie's loyalties had changed.

Billie was far more hurt by Kenzie's vendetta than he was. Jesse was used to wielding the ax, being reviled, having hateful whispers tail him down hallways. He'd made a lot of people a lot of money by being a ruthless bastard, and he'd adjusted to the isolation that went hand in hand with his success.

Billie, though… She had a good heart.

Not that anyone would guess from the glare she shot Kenzie as the two women exchanged curt nods—or the way she mimed thrashing her with the jumper cables when Kenzie went to move her truck.

"I know," he muttered. "Trust me, I know."

Kenzie aligned her truck's hood with theirs and popped it open. Billie attached the cables, Kenzie started her engine, then the three of them stood in silence, staring at the red and black cords trailing between the vehicles.

"Are you sure that's on right?" Kenzie leaned over their engine and inspected the cables, while Jesse found himself inspecting the fine shape of her backside in her snug jeans.

"Of course it is," Billie snapped.

Kenzie straightened. "Just checking."

"Your breakfast must be ready by now. Go on and wait inside. We'll let you know when we're done." Unlike when he spoke to the waitress, this suggestion was meant as a demand—which Kenzie completely ignored.

"And leave you two to sabotage my truck? No thanks."

"Sabotage your truck?" Billie laughed. "For real? You're losing your marbles, girl. The only one trying to sabotage anything is you."

"And how exactly am I doing that?"

"You damn near pushed my brother off the platform last night, and you're asking me how?"

"He's a big boy. He can handle a tiny little thing like me. Can't you, Jesse?" The smile she slid him was downright serpentine.

He stared at her, cool and detached, refusing to let her see how much she rattled him—how much space she occupied in his overfull, overstressed brain.

Because it was a lot.

Billie, on the other hand, jumped headfirst into her resentment and showed no inclination to swim out.

"To think I used to like you—used to trust you. Do you have any idea how often I went to bat for you with Lee? Angling to get you promoted, to get paid more, to have more responsibility."

Kenzie's eyes flashed, lightning on sea glass. "No one had to back me to Lee. He was in my corner every minute of every damn day."

And you sucked him dry, Jesse thought on a sudden swell of fresh, hot betrayal.

He didn't know whether Kenzie was stupid, selfish, or both, and he didn't care. She'd exploited his brother's kindness. Spent his money so she got what she wanted today, without a care for tomorrow. Destroyed a hundred years of hard-won prosperity with a flick of her wrist and a flash of that pouty smile.

She'd pay for it. However he had to, whatever it took, he'd make her pay.

"Try the truck," he commanded his sister.

Shooting Kenzie a look so full of sharp promise it practically ricocheted off the diner, Billie climbed into the cab and tried the ignition.

The engine purred like a cat, traitorous and unapologetic.

Without a word Jesse unclamped the cables and slammed the hood shut. He avoided Kenzie's glance, his hand on the passenger-door handle when she barked his name.

Her green eyes glittered with threat, and if she hadn't been the one thing standing between him and securing his family's future—if she hadn't been the cause of its downfall in the first place—he might've noticed how the brightening morning lit them up. How they beckoned him, crystalline beacons promising respite and safety, and an end to his long, long loneliness.

Mermaid eyes.

Siren eyes.

And he knew how that story ended.

"This isn't over," she informed him, the words trembling with anger.

He swept his gaze from her blond hair to her booted toes and back again. His lips quirked into a patronizing smile—one that came naturally.

"Yes, it is."

He hauled himself into the passenger seat and shut the door, gazing at nothing but the horizon as Billie pulled away.

* * *

"I should get back to town. Early shift tomorrow." Jesse's twin sister, Mae, pushed back from the thick-hewn dining table their great-grandfather, Hugo Singer, had hand-carved from a blackjack oak a tornado ripped from its roots and deposited at the ranch house's back door.

Or so the story went.

It was one of countless tales handed down through generations of Singers since their distant forebears, Hedy and Fritz, came to America from Austria in the 1880s. No one knew exactly why they'd decided to plunk down in Oklahoma rather than continuing west, especially since Fritz was a leatherworker who'd never farmed so much as a blade of grass, but it proved a good choice. Fritz opened a saddle-making shop in Stillwater, and thanks to a couple of fortuitous visits by passing cowboys, Singer saddles became a staple of the nascent sport America would eventually call the rodeo.

Hedy and Fritz's son, Hugo, bought the family's first bucking bronc. By 1910, he'd bought the ranch, too. Just under a thousand acres of wild prairie, perfect for grazing equally wild roughstock.

The two World Wars were tough on the rodeo and on the Singers, but there were stories about that, too. Stories about the prisoner-of-war camp that opened in Tonkawa in 1943, and the captured German soldiers sent to labor on local ranches. Supposedly some of them came to work the Singer fields. And supposedly, not all of them returned.

Though if any Nazi ghosts haunted the property, they kept quiet, Jesse considered, looking past his sister to the darkness-shrouded hills on the other side of the double-height windows. Maybe they understood it was a fair trade—their lives for his great-uncle's, the Jewish boy gone back to fight for his people on the shores of the continent his grandparents had fled. Maybe this was their penance, doomed to reside forever among the

Jews they'd sought to exterminate, captive witnesses to their triumphs and their success.

Or maybe they were just cowards, keeping to the shadows, loath to rouse the wrath of the family at whose hands they'd already suffered so brutally.

Fingers snapped in his face. Trixie, the youngest of the Singer siblings and the League's reigning barrel-racing champion, regarded him with an amused smile.

"You look happy. What're you thinking about?"

"Revenge." He picked up his empty plate and rose from his chair.

The four siblings filed into the kitchen and began cleaning up. Billie and Trixie had their own small homes on the ranch, and Mae lived in Stillwater, but they'd been convening for dinner at least once a week since he'd returned. He was pretty sure it was their way of keeping an eye on him, checking he wasn't getting prairie madness from too many hours spent alone, listening to the wind howl at the windows of the rambling ranch house.

Jesse appreciated their concern, but he enjoyed his own company. He'd never been a people person. Not in high school, where he was too brainy and bookish to be popular; and not at his Ivy League college, where he was a slow-talking hillbilly no one took seriously. Work, on the other hand, was where he'd thrived, freed from the pretenses of affability, his quick mind and sharp demeanor assets instead of hindrances.

He'd been an outsider his whole life. Why not get paid for it?

"Wyatt said they're going cake-tasting soon. Any chance the maid of honor gets to tag along?" Trixie asked.

Billie shook her head, smiling at the mention of her pickup-rider partner and longtime friend.

"I wish. You know Bettina's mom will find the fanciest, most expensive cake maker in the state."

Mae winked. "Only the best for the former Miss Rodeo Oklahoma."

"Runner-up for Miss Rodeo Oklahoma," Billie clarified.

Trixie rinsed one of their grandmother's hand-painted china plates and passed it to Jesse. "Didn't know fourth place was considered runner-up."

The three of them snickered good-naturedly at Wyatt's future mother-in-law. Bettina was sweet as pecan pie, but her mom couldn't leave a store without speaking to the manager.

"Speaking of which, you owe Wyatt an RSVP, big brother. How many seats do you need at this shindig, one or two?"

Jesse shot Billie a chiding glance as he stowed another plate in the dishwasher. "One, obviously."

"Why obviously? There's a whole wide world of eligible ladies out there, just waiting for a handsome, successful stock contractor to roll in and sweep them off their feet. By which, I mean you." Trixie pointed a soapy spatula at him.

"Is that right? And which of y'all will be bringing a date, while we're on the subject?"

Billie, Trixie and Mae all took sudden interests in their tasks, scrubbing cutlery and wiping down counters with never-before-seen vigor.

Jesse smiled affectionately at the most important women in his life. He didn't know why the four of them were still single—well, he had his own reason, which was that he had no business worrying about his own future until his family's was secure. But they'd had good marital examples in their parents and grandparents and uncles and aunts, they were all employed, and they all had clean criminal records, a quality not to be underestimated in their line of work.

Never mind—he had bigger problems than his sisters' romantic woes. He had a long list of overdue bills to juggle, one of the toilets in the bunkhouse was backed up, and he'd already declined several offers of a redneck repair from his loopy ranch hands. As his sisters gathered their bags and moved toward the door, he decided to call the plumber and save his staff from themselves.

"Drive safe," he told his twin, who squeezed him tightly before walking out to her car. Trixie and Billie followed suit, leaving him on the wide porch, waving as their three vehicles trundled single file down the long driveway.

When their taillights disappeared behind the slope, he turned back to the house—and stopped.

He knew what he'd find inside: echoes of his boisterous childhood reduced to the ticking of the grandfather clock in his office—Lee's office. A single lamp illuminating fine print until his vision blurred and his head ached. Drop-dead exhaustion becoming alert anxiety the moment his head hit the pillow, then a view of the shifting shadows in his bedroom until he gave up on the prospect of sleep. He'd return to his desk, pick up where he'd left off, and eventually fall asleep in his chair with a pen in his hand.

He couldn't change that—but he could delay it.

Jesse grabbed his keys and drove his pickup to one of the horse barns. The minute he stepped inside, Bounder poked his head out of his stall, snuffling a greeting as if he'd been waiting on Jesse's arrival. Jesse walked the buckskin quarter horse into the aisle and tacked him up.

It was a slow process, especially considering it used to be second nature in an upbringing spent largely on horseback. But that was a lifetime ago, and a version of himself he wasn't sure he had much claim on anymore.

Jesse led Bounder into the hushed evening and mounted, steering the gelding away from the lights of the barn. It never took long to find the middle of nowhere on the Singer ranch, and soon they were crossing fields and cresting hills, the buzzing insects and late-summer moon their only companions.

He hadn't been allowed to ride this late when he was a kid. Too dangerous, his dad said. Too hard for the horse to see obstacles, too few people moving around the ranch to hear a cry for help.

But he was an adult now, and this was his horse—his land. And this was the only time he really felt part of it. In the darkness, unobserved, he could melt into the place that made him. Let all those years in between lose their edges and dissolve into the shadows. Forget his difference, forget everything holding him at arm's length from what he'd always known. Stand in his birthright like he deserved it.

Like he belonged here.

Don't wait too long to come home.

Jesse jerked Bounder to a stop and twisted in his saddle, certain he'd heard his brother's voice over his shoulder—but there was no one. Only the faint clink of metal, the creak of leather, the muted thump of Bounder's hooves as he shifted his weight, and the ferocious pounding of Jesse's heart.

He urged the horse on. Lee's words echoed from the day Jesse had left for college, two minutes before their mom fretted aloud about missing his flight, fifteen years before Lee was killed and Jesse finally returned.

Jesse had grinned at him, confident he was only a plane ride away from a life so much bigger than the one he'd been leading. Lee's smile faltered for the briefest of seconds, then he'd winked at his younger brother and slammed the tailgate shut.

"I'll leave the light on for you," he'd promised. He'd rejoined Billie and Trixie on the porch, lifting his cowboy hat in farewell as the pickup eased away.

Jesse swallowed hard, his throat tight with sorrow as he pulled Bounder to a halt at the top of a slope. Acres upon acres of Singer land spread out before him, its undulating vastness rivaling the star-scattered sky overhead. He'd been born here, was heir to five generations of ambition and toil and victory, and of an American dream not yet extinguished by the harsh light of day.

Lee had warned him, and he hadn't listened.

He'd waited too long.

He owned this ranch, but that didn't make it his. That didn't mean he deserved it.

And he had no idea if he ever would.

Chapter Three

"One more," Kenzie advised.

Her foreman, Ramon Flores, threaded another rope through the top of the practice chute, adding to the spiderweb already in place.

The bull calf shook his head, snorted and attempted to buck—only for his rear end to come in contact with the rope, preventing him from kicking too high, encouraging him to stand still. She watched him for another few minutes, but the calf didn't make another attempt, just peered curiously through the slats at the empty arena.

Kenzie nodded. "Better. We'll keep working on his chute etiquette. He's got the blood of a champion, but he needs the manners, too."

Ramon motioned to the hands to remove the ropes, then turned back to his boss. "You want to see that other one we've been working on? He's standing real good now, nice and calm and patient."

She shook her head. "You've got it handled. I'm supposed to meet my mom in town, but I'll be back midafternoon."

"Don't hurry." He grinned.

Kenzie returned his smile in equal measure.

Ramon was a gem. All her staff were fantastic. Loyal, hard-working, and never so much as sniffed at taking orders from a woman.

Of course, it helped that she'd hired most of them herself.

Bob Boyd's family had owned the Broken B since the 1890s—or, more accurately, had nabbed it off Native Americans in a land run. For generations, they'd been little more than small-scale crop farmers until Bob took over, squinted at the pumpjack that hadn't moved in decades, and decided to make a few calls.

Now the Boyds were oil-rich and time-rich and everything-rich. Bob had decided to pay people to do his farming for him, then invested his own energies—and a significant amount of his money—into his true passion: rodeo.

The Broken B was glossier than Singer Pro Rodeo on all levels, Kenzie considered as she left the arena and climbed into one of the ranch's six-month-old pickups. The equipment was high-end, the buildings were brand-new, and the roughstock's bloodlines uniformly elite. Kenzie had been at Bob's elbow as he pulled the operation together and made almost all the decisions from the beginning, so there was little—if anything—she would change.

Yet as the pickup bumped down the gravel road leading to the highway, she couldn't help thinking the Broken B was a bit...boring.

It was crisp and fresh, yes, but it lacked Singer's stately maturity. While the Singer barns were old, the fences sagged, and there was always something needing repair or replacement, its flaws were trivial in the context of its history. The Singers were a founding family of American rodeo, and their legacy quietly insisted on itself in every square foot of that property.

A legacy that would end with Jesse, she vowed, scowling as she passed the turnoff that would take her straight to him.

As she drove into Stillwater, she tried to put mental, as well as physical, miles between them. Her mom still lived in Perry, where Kenzie had grown up, though her mom had traded their trailer for a pretty three-bedroom house when she married her longtime boyfriend last year. Stillwater was a good halfway point between Perry and the Broken B, plus it had more places to eat and shop, so every couple of weeks she met her mom in town to catch up.

The black pickup baked in the mid-August sun, which refused to let the mercury drop below three digits. Kenzie found a shaded parking spot near where her mother had parked outside the boutique and rushed inside, hurrying through the cowboy boot–shaped planters flanking the door.

Irlene Ruedlinger—née Wallace—was hard to miss, even among the shelves packed with clothes, jewelry and gifts. Not because of the bright blue streak dyed into her short, gray hair, but because her sunny disposition and perpetual smile created a magnetic field of sheer delight. Kenzie had always admired her positive outlook, undimmed by an unplanned, teenage pregnancy, years of hand-to-mouth subsistence, and an ugly court battle to finally prove Kenzie's paternity. Through it all, Kenzie's enduring memories were of her mom's optimism, her compassion and her unshakable belief that most people would find their way to goodness, if given enough time and encouragement.

Kenzie must take after her dad in that respect, she thought grimly.

"Hey, there, sweetie, look what I found." Irlene whirled toward her, wearing a pair of bedazzled aviators.

"Stunning." Kenzie gave her mom a quick hug, then plucked the sunglasses off her mom's face and put them on.

"Gorgeous!" Irlene exclaimed. "But look, they also come in pink."

They moseyed through the store, idly examining everything from wildflower-patterned dishware to bright orange chandelier earrings, ready for the start of college football season. Irlene chatted about her now-husband Ned's nursery, regaling Kenzie with the most sensational gossip highlights—par for the course in such a small, rural town, where rumors were always more fun than reality.

"She's convinced Satanists have taken over that old shed by

the cemetery. Bought a whole bunch of garlic plants to hang around her front door. I was halfway to telling her that's for vampires, not devil worshippers, but if it'll make her feel better, who am I to spoil it?"

Kenzie snorted. "Please send me a photo of her house decked out in garlic."

"I will. Anyway, better this Satanist thing makes the rounds now so it'll fizzle out by October. People get a whiff of the devil too close to Halloween and it kills our pumpkin sales."

Kenzie smiled as she thought of mild-mannered, sweet-tempered Ned wringing his hands about his beloved pumpkin patch. His shy, deferential courtship all those years ago was one of the best things that ever happened to her mom, especially when he encouraged her to file for child support. That money didn't erase fourteen years of hardship, but it put Kenzie through college, paid for a safe car and allowed her mom to quit her second waitressing job.

It also vindicated Irlene in the eyes of the community, reframing her from a promiscuous young woman who didn't know who'd fathered her child to the naive girl who'd fallen for an unfaithful older man. Though, to be fair, Irlene had long stopped caring what other people thought of her.

Unlike Kenzie.

"How was New Mexico?" Irlene asked.

Kenzie set down the snow globe she'd been admiring. "Fine. Not Nice earned a good paycheck."

"Were the Singers there?"

"They always are."

"And did you take my advice and kill them with kindness?"

Kenzie examined a turquoise necklace. "Not exactly."

Irlene said nothing—she didn't have to. Her disapproval had been palpable since the day Kenzie shared her plan to lead a one-woman revolution against rodeo's royal family. Irlene told her to pursue excellence for her own sake and nothing more, because hitching your happiness to hating someone else was a short road to misery.

Maybe her mom was right. Maybe snatching Bull of the Year out of Jesse Singer's hands wouldn't give her more than a fleeting sense of fulfillment before the competition started over. Maybe she'd even feel a little sheepish about her single-minded pursuit, peppered as it was with public skirmishes and sniggering bystanders.

Or maybe watching his face fall as her name was read out would make every second of frustration and resentment and white-hot anger absolutely worthwhile.

Only one way to find out.

Irlene hefted a ceramic pumpkin with OSU printed on one side—almost certainly a gift for Ned. Turning it over, she read the price and put it back down. "I'm all set. Should we check out?"

Kenzie nodded. "I'll bring this stuff up to the front. Could you check those trucker hats back there, see if they have one that says Go Pokes? I might get one for Ramon."

As Irlene moved away to look for the hat Kenzie knew didn't exist, Kenzie swept up the ceramic pumpkin, hurried to the register and handed over her credit card.

"I couldn't see—oh, Kenzie, you didn't," her mom chided, arriving at her elbow.

"I sure did." She signed the receipt, then passed the tissue-wrapped pumpkin to her mom.

Irlene tilted her head. "You don't need to take care of me. Save your money for yourself, and what you need."

"What I need is to spoil my hardworking mother. Fair?"

"Fair." Irlene planted a kiss on Kenzie's cheek. "And thank you. Ned'll love it. I'll put it in the car. Go grab us a table."

Kenzie made quick work of the short walk to the café down the block—it was too hot to dawdle. She ducked inside, then grinned when she recognized the barista from their freshman year at Oklahoma State.

“Kenzie, how you been?” Twyla practically threw a salad at a customer and rushed over to the register.

“Real good, thanks. What’s new with you?”

Twyla held out her hands to indicate the café, and Kenzie smiled. Twyla was bubbly and outgoing, but she’d never been able to commit to much, and she’d changed majors so often Kenzie had eventually lost track.

“You’re employed. Could be worse, right?”

“Sure could,” Twyla agreed. “Hey, that hot boss of yours was in here yesterday.”

Kenzie blinked. Bob Boyd was a nice man, but a centerfold he was not.

“Isn’t he a little old for you?” Kenzie asked.

“No—he’s our age. Isn’t he?”

Kenzie shook her head. “He’s almost seventy.”

“Jesse Singer is almost seventy?” Twyla half screeched.

Kenzie’s eyes widened as the pieces clicked together. “No, no—you’re right. Jesse is about thirty-five. But I don’t work for him anymore. I thought you meant my new boss, Bob Boyd at the Broken B.”

“My bad. And here you had me thinking Jesse was the sexiest senior citizen ever to walk this planet.”

“Not quite.”

“Anyway, I can see why you quit. Hard to stay focused with those blue eyes on you.” Twyla pointed her index fingers on either side of her nose.

“I didn’t quit—he fired me. And he was a real dick about it.”

Twyla considered. “Well, that’s a fact to keep in mind. But let’s say, hypothetically, your girl just wanted a nice dinner and a roll in the hay. Think he’d be up for it?”

“Ain’t got the first clue.”

Not that she saw Jesse as anything but a hard-hearted ass

who deserved what she'd give him, but the turn of this conversation left her unsettled. Just the thought of him and Twyla… Him and anyone…

Her stomach shifted uneasily, and she changed her mind about the rich, melty-cheesy sandwich she'd been about to order.

"Put in a good word for me, if you can," Twyla said.

"I'll try," Kenzie replied, not in the mood to explain why she was the last person from whom Jesse would take advice. She placed her order, and as she paused to let Twyla catch up on the till, she sensed someone's attention on her from the corner of her eye. The man's head whipped around when she glanced over, and she squinted to study him.

Seated at the table nearest where she stood, his back to her, he was accompanied by another man in a near-identical suit-and-cowboy-hat combination. Kenzie took in the fringe of gray hair beneath his hat, the shiny black boots, the gold wedding ring—and froze.

Jay McCutcheon. Small-time rancher, former Perry city council member, and the man who'd cheated on his wife with a waitress thirty-three years ago.

Her father.

She wrenched her attention back to Twyla, forcing a smile despite the freight train roaring through her ears. Encounters like this weren't frequent, but they weren't rare. Stillwater wasn't that big, and Perry was even smaller. She'd had over twenty years to get used to these chance run-ins, and since they never amounted to more than an awkward glance and a cold shoulder, they really shouldn't ruin her whole day.

Yet this one already had—especially when she realized she'd just reminded Twyla that she'd been fired from Singer Pro Rodeo.

Kenzie cringed, imagining her father's silent disappointment as she confirmed out loud that his money had done nothing but finance her failure. His two older children were married with kids and had solid careers. They were golden-haired, bright-smiled, and always perfectly put together. She bet he was thinking of them right now, thankful his legacy lived in his preppy progeny and not this ball cap–wearing loser with ragged nails and dirty boots.

"Which dressing did you want with the Caesar?" Twyla's finger hovered over the button.

"Sorry, one second." Kenzie looked at her blank, silent phone, then gave Twyla an exaggerated wince. "Damn, I'm so sorry, it looks like I need to rush back to the Broken B."

She raised her voice as she continued. "I'm running the whole show over there, building the stock-contracting business from scratch. Lots of responsibility, lots of staff needing my direction. Sounds like there's been a small, uh, fence emergency—a problem with the fence. They need me back there right away. So many grown men getting paid so much money, and still they can't make a single decision without me."

McCutcheon's back was still turned, but Kenzie made her smile extra self-effacing, shrugging as if she had no idea how someone like her could be so essential.

"Well, dang. I'm glad we got a second to catch up. Sure you don't want something to go?"

Kenzie glanced through the glass front door and spotted her mother on the opposite side of the street. She shook her head as the situation gathered urgency. "I'd better bail. Let's grab a drink soon."

"I'll hold you to that."

Kenzie gave Twyla a hasty goodbye, then all but threw herself out the door and across the street, intercepting her mother just in time.

"Their panini press is broken. Let's try that diner down the way instead."

Irlene craned her neck toward the café. "Is that Twyla behind the counter? I haven't seen her since—"

"I told her you said hello. Come on, I'm starving."

Another lie, Kenzie thought unhappily as she guided her mom around.

She hated that her father could do this—hated the way she let him undermine her self-confidence when he was the one in the wrong. Yet she'd never been able to shake that drive to impress him and show him what he'd missed.

To prove that he should want her. That she was worthy.

As they walked away from the café, she tossed a final glance over her shoulder and caught one last glimpse of McCutcheon through the window, his body twisted toward the door, his gaze pointed in her direction.

He was smirking. She just knew it.

Chapter Four

"Thank you to Miss Rodeo Nebraska and Miss Teen Rodeo Nebraska for the presentation of the colors. This flag represents our great nation, the United States of America. We enjoy many freedoms in this country, and perhaps the most precious is the freedom of religion. And so, ladies and gentlemen, I ask you to bow your heads and join me for the invocation."

Jesse had already removed his hat, as was customary when the American flag was carried around the arena on horseback. He held it over his stomach and took a subtle step backward, as those around him closed their eyes and bowed their heads.

"Heavenly Father, thank You for being with us tonight. We ask for Your blessing over this arena, and that You be with all our athletes and keep them safe—the cowboys, the cowgirls and those who walk on four legs instead of two. We thank You, God, for all You have given us, but especially for Your son, Jesus Christ, who died for our sins."

Jesse stared straight ahead, his chin high and his spine stiff as he tuned out the rest of the announcer's words. The opening prayer was a time-honored rodeo tradition, as standard and unquestioned as the eight-second buzzer. A few of the big, urban rodeos like Fort Worth and Houston had flirted with religious inclusivity, but only because they had enormous local audiences and could afford the backlash.

And backlash there was.

Rodeo was the Singers' livelihood, and to an extent they

had to get along to go along. Some things in life were beyond compromise, though, and the invocation fell into that category.

Jesse had just turned five the first time he was permitted to travel with the crew, so excited he had his backpack ready days in advance. He couldn't remember where they'd gone; that event blended into the hundreds of small-town rodeos of the busy summer season. Jesse had obediently ducked his chin at the announcer's instructions, only for his grandfather to prompt it back up with a roughened finger.

"We bow to no one but God," his grandfather told him, his touch warm and firm.

That night, and every night thereafter, Jesse held his hat low and remained respectfully silent, but he never looked down again.

The invocation wrapped up with a collective amen, and a girl from the Albion High School Junior ROTC stepped forward to sing the national anthem. Jesse held his hat over his heart through her performance, then squared it on his head as the rodeo queens reappeared, galloping around the arena flying flags emblazoned with sponsors' logos. The announcer introduced the pickup riders—his sister Billie and her partner, Wyatt—and the bareback cowboys got into position.

Jesse jogged down the steps of the platform behind the chutes, stole around the corner of the elevated announcer's stand and ducked into the shadows between two of the trees lining the side of the arena.

Autumn came early this far north, and the cool breeze cut through the late-summer evening with taunting promises of crackling leaves and bonfire smoke. Only a handful of insects danced half-heartedly in the glow of the floodlights, and as a squirrel skittered along a branch overhead, it was easy to imagine the frenetic summer schedule had already concluded, giving way to the long, homebound stretch before the League finals in December.

Jesse used this last moment of calm to close his eyes and briefly murmur his own prayer. Bookended with his minimal Hebrew, he asked God to protect his animals, protect their riders and protect his family.

Then he stepped out from beneath the trees and nearly tripped over Kenzie Wallace.

Heat rushed into his ears as he thought about how he must've looked, skulking in the shadows. He righted himself, bracing for whatever she was about to fling at him.

Instead, she took a stumbling step backward, her lower lip between her teeth, her expression bordering on…sheepish?

"I didn't see you there. Am I interrupting something?"

"Just taking a breath before it all kicks off."

"Sure. I get it."

They stood in awkward silence, gazes sweeping in ridiculous trajectories to avoid connecting. He should walk away, but her unsure expression indicated she wanted to say something else—something he wanted to hear, for reasons that could only be stupid and self-destructive.

"Were you—was that Hebrew?" She lifted her eyes to meet his.

So, you were *spying on me. That's a new low.*

The acidic barb was on the tip of his tongue, paired with a haughty saunter past her, close enough that their arms brushed.

Which was why he was probably more surprised than she was when he replied, "Yes."

"All the Jesus stuff must get a little weird for you. It gets weird for me sometimes, and technically I'm a Christian."

"Technically?"

"My mom grew up in church, but they weren't huge fans of unmarried single mothers. We didn't go often. Anyway, I don't mind the invocation, but slapping Bible verses and crosses on every spare surface is too much. I can't hardly find a pair of jeans these days without Psalms number whatever stamped on the pocket."

He shrugged, unable to hide his amused smile at her indignation, which she'd punctuated by slamming her hand on her hip. "This is a dangerous sport. People get hurt. People get killed. If their faith helps them get on that bull and ride for the win, I don't begrudge them."

Kenzie snorted. "Guess you're nicer than I am."

Jesse laughed. Not the polite chuckle and tight smile that were usually the most he could offer, but a real laugh, born of surprise and delight. "I doubt that very much."

Kenzie's grin mirrored his own, and they fell into comfortable quiet again. The trees muted the pounding music and the roaring crowd into muffled thumps and faint voices, as if the arena was small and distant, and the conflicts and stakes played out upon its dusty ground were someone else's problem. His greatest trial right now was dislodging his gaze from the way the twilight threw shadows across Kenzie's shoulders and turned her blond hair to silver. She looked so ethereal he fought the urge to touch her just to convince himself she was human, and not a wayward wood nymph who'd stolen a tight T-shirt and ripped jeans.

As the audience's cheer rose, Kenzie said, "Sounds like you brought the carousel horses by mistake."

Reality hit him so hard he rocked back on his heels. Her tone teased, but her words cracked through Jesse's brain like a bolt of lightning. What the hell was he doing? Lurking in the gloom, making friendly chitchat with the woman who'd spent all season slicing his rankest bulls' earnings in half, muscling her way into contracts that had been Singer exclusives for decades.

He was losing his damn mind, that's what he was doing. Letting her loom way too large in his thoughts when he should be focused on his family, his animals and the legacy her incompetent mismanagement had already half buried.

Jesse arched a brow. "Didn't know you were an expert on champion bucking horses, since you've never raised a single one."

A swing and a hit, as Kenzie's eyes narrowed and she crossed her arms. The Broken B's bulls were excellent, but their horses were terrible, no doubt because Kenzie had only worked with the former at Singer. "Neither have you, unless Billie's seen the light and found a new job."

"Billie and I work together—we all do. We make decisions as a team, and we spend money as a team."

The last of the late-August sunlight had nearly disappeared, but enough remained for him to make out the flush rising in her cheeks.

"Lee gave me a budget—"

"And you spent it. All of it. I know."

She rolled her eyes. "I don't know how things worked in your fancy, mile-high office in New York City, but down here in the real world, things cost money. Feed bills, vet bills, farrier bills... Bulls are expensive, and stuff adds up."

"Funny you mention adding, because you didn't seem to do much of it when you worked for my brother. Lots of subtracting, though. Money out almost every day."

She took a step forward, so angry now her finger vibrated as she poked it in his chest. "Screw you, you stuck-up prick! I would never, *ever*, steal from your brother. And if you believe he was stupid enough to get taken for a ride like that, then you didn't know him as well as you think."

Jesse clamped his back teeth together, the sinister, secret truth shifting uneasily in the pit of his stomach.

She was right. In some ways he hadn't known Lee at all.

Jesse didn't really believe Kenzie was dishonest—he believed she was incapable. Elevated to a position beyond her scope and given way too much autonomy, because Lee wasn't savvy or sensible. He'd been foolish and flailing, and no one had any idea.

Nor would they.

"Or maybe he overestimated your potential." He bit down hard against the molten fury rising in his gut. "Maybe he thought he'd take a chance on you. Invest in someone hardworking and loyal. Give you his trust, his support and his money. And maybe you failed him."

Kenzie's head jerked back as if he'd hit her, and he had a fleeting flash of guilt, a sudden and overpowering distaste for striking such a low blow. Then he reminded himself it was the truth and let his chin rise on a wave of vindication. She'd dug this hole. He was just pointing out its depth.

Kenzie stuck out her hands and shoved him like she had in New Mexico, only this time he was prepared for the donkey-like strength belied by her short frame. He caught her wrists and held them, but instead of wrenching away like he'd hoped, she used their proximity to kick him in the shin.

Hard.

"Christ's sake!" He released her and wrapped his hands around his throbbing leg.

"You can call him all day, but I'm pretty sure it'll go to voice mail."

"It's a colloquialism." He dragged up his jeans and inspected the damage. At least her boots weren't steel-toed.

"It's a what?"

"A secular phrase that—never mind. You're lucky you didn't break my leg and spend the rest of your boss's money fighting a lawsuit."

"Should've known you'd hide behind lawyers instead of squaring up like a real cowboy."

"I'm not—" The sentence died in his throat as he realized he wasn't sure how to finish it. No, he was no longer a suit-wearing assassin who destroyed billion-dollar companies with a cold glare and carefully worded paperwork, but that was how most of the rodeo community still saw him.

Which was ironic, considering his colleagues had teased him about being a cowboy since the first time he opened his mouth. They'd viewed his return to the family rodeo empire as inevitable, coming full circle, reverting to who he was—who he'd always been.

"Let me see." She moved to his side and yanked off his boot.

"It's fine."

The indignity of her hand probing above his sock overrode his annoyance and the dwindling pain. Her grip on his ankle and her fingers on his shin were at once tender and firm, and despite baring a mere inch or two of flesh to the great wide world, he felt half-naked. As if Kenzie's clever hands were a whisker away from exposing him entirely, her bottle-green eyes poised to assess the results.

His chest tightened, his cock stirred, and he jerked his leg out of her grasp, barely staying upright as he hopped toward his discarded boot.

"I think you'll live." She straightened.

"And I think you need to keep your—"

"Y'all playing nice?"

Tucker Ramsey and Sage Sterling, two high-ranked bull riders who traveled together, lounged at the edge of the trees' shadows, the light from the arena illuminating grins as wide as the chaps draped over their legs.

"Just weathering another assault from Miss Wallace like a gentleman." Jesse took a subtle step away from her.

"He's a jackass. He deserved it."

Tucker and Sage exchanged a knowing smile.

"If you two can call a truce for a second, Tucker and I were glad to catch you both at the same time. What do y'all know about this project Casey Custer's cooking up?"

Jesse's attention sharpened, and beside him, Kenzie stiffened.

"Not much," he said. "What do you all know?"

"Not much, either," Sage replied. "Custer texted both of us last night. Said he wanted to talk, but we were hoping we could get some more information first."

"He can be real persuasive," Tucker added.

Jesse nodded. He'd grown up around cowboys like Tucker and Sage, many of whom had little education beyond cobbled-together high schools in tiny, rural communities. There were no salaries for these guys, who earned only what they won. They had to calculate which rodeos to go to, in which order, taking into consideration the prize money, the bulls, their likelihood of winning, plus the travel costs. Some excelled at maximizing their earning potential, but plenty of others barely made enough to survive.

Kenzie shrugged. "Whatever it is, you know it's bad news. That man doesn't have an honest bone in his body."

"Most likely his dad rented an arena so he can run some animals around and feel like a cowboy," Jesse said.

"Maybe. Thing is, though, he's got a hell of a lot of money," Sage ventured.

Kenzie's and Jesse's gazes locked in alarm.

"You can't seriously be thinking about riding for him," Kenzie replied.

Jesse shook his head. "The whole reason he's out of the League is because he didn't care about competitors' safety."

Tucker and Sage looked at each other again.

"Look," Sage said, his tone reluctant. "It's hard to imagine any kind of bull-riding event being worthwhile if bulls like Repeat Offender and Not Nice ain't in the mix—"

"Which they won't be," Kenzie interjected.

Sage continued, "But y'all know as well as we do that lots of these rodeos haven't upped the prize money in years. Haven't increased y'all's fees, neither."

Jesse and Kenzie kept quiet. This was a cyclical problem in rodeo, a sport that required a lot of expensive infrastructure yet catered primarily to occasional, local fan bases, usually in areas where people couldn't afford significant hikes in ticket prices. That put pressure on rodeo organizers to keep costs low—costs that included the fees paid to stock contractors and the cash prizes paid to competitors. Meanwhile the price of gas, grain, labor and everything else it took to pair that bull with its rider for eight seconds increased, eroding everyone's margins, and their will to carry on.

Sage shrugged. "If it's a good paycheck, I'd think about it."

"And climb on a bull that'll hurt you so bad you're out of the League finals, or worse?" Kenzie said, taking the words straight out of Jesse's brain.

Thank God she had, too. They'd listen to her. They wouldn't trust him.

Sage grinned again, lazy and lopsided. "That's every ride. Ain't it, Tuck?"

Tucker nodded. "Can't let that worry get you, or you've ridden your last bull."

Jesse opened his mouth to say something about calculated risk, then changed his mind. Bull riders were as stubborn as they were fearless, and he'd known some who'd do eight seconds on a grizzly bear if it paid enough.

He couldn't blame them for wanting an easy payday. He just hoped that was all Custer had in store. The League couldn't lose its best cowboys, not when their names and stories drew more sponsors and fans than even the rankest bull. But surely Custer wasn't playing a long game. He was making a lot of noise over nothing, as usual. Whatever he was cooking up, it would be short, silly and swiftly forgotten.

"Come on, you two." Sage gestured toward them. "Let's get y'all separated before you end up in time-out."

He'd put it all behind him, Jesse decided as he and Kenzie joined the bull riders in the short walk back to the arena. He'd squashed bigger ambitions than Kenzie's and Custer's combined in half a day's work. By the end of the year, Singer would be back on top, and these ragtag challengers would go the way all insects do when summer ends and frost bites.

He had no choice. He *had* to win.

For the family.

For Lee.

Chapter Five

"Sorry 'bout that, folks. We got so many people tuned into the live stream we just about broke the internet."

Kenzie rolled her eyes at Casey Custer's fake country accent as she maximized the screen on her phone. Everyone knew his dad was the former CEO of a major software company and he'd grown up in a big-ass mansion near San Francisco. Why he insisted on this phony hillbilly act was beyond her.

"And now, the news you've all been waiting for."

She sat back against the headboard, took a sip from the beer bottle on the nightstand, and propped her phone against her knees. It had been a long day of travel to South Dakota, and she'd been looking forward to an early night before this weekend's rodeo began tomorrow. A hot shower, a good book and a long sleep in a comfortable bed.

Then that little twerp Custer had posted that he was revealing his new project tonight, and she'd been tethered to her phone, tense and unhappy, as she waited for the live stream to start.

The motel she was staying in was down the street from the fairgrounds and adjacent to fields where people could tie up their horses, and every room was occupied by rodeo professionals. She could practically hear the collective breath they all took as the image of Custer dissolved and was replaced by a medieval-style crest with the silhouette of a bucking bull in the center.

"Custer Productions and Custer Pro Rodeo are pleased to

announce the launch of the Supreme Rodeo Series—rodeo like you've never seen it before."

The logo shimmered and faded, then the screen burst into a montage of shadowy, slow-motion clips: a cowboy tying on spurs, a bull pawing the ground, an American flag whipping in the wind.

Custer's voice continued over the top. "The best cowboys in the world will take on the meanest bulls and the toughest bareback broncs in America's biggest indoor venues, and they won't just be competing for buckles and glory. You ride, you earn. Simple as that."

A knot of concern tightened in Kenzie's stomach. He couldn't afford that—could he? Normally, prize money was awarded only to the top finishers, meaning plenty of cowboys stuck their eight seconds and still walked away empty-handed. But if they had a near guarantee they'd get paid…

The key would be the schedule, she considered as Custer droned on about preshow entertainment and a complicated points system that added up throughout the season. Since he was revealing this toward the end of the regular rodeo season, his league would probably run counter to the traditional schedule. Made sense—give audiences and riders something to do in the offseason.

"You can catch all the SRS action year-round, as it tours every corner of America."

A list of locations and dates scrolled on the screen. Kenzie picked up her phone and squinted at the small type, then dropped it on the bed in horror.

"Oh, crap," she said. "Crap, crap, crap."

Every one of his events coincided with the biggest rodeos on the circuit, and each one was scheduled within touching distance of its competitor. Calgary, Cheyenne, Pendleton, Fort Worth—the list read like a carbon copy of the Pro Rodeo League calendar. That meant the best cowboys and stock contractors would have to choose one or the other, and it sounded like he had enough money invested to make that decision easy.

Kenzie recovered her phone and stared wide-eyed at the man now back on the screen, his smile self-satisfied as he shared some made-up story about what inspired Supreme Rodeo's origins. She killed the live stream, queasy at the sight of him.

He could say whatever he wanted. This was nothing more than a vanity project.

No—it was worse than that. This spoiled, vindictive child had finally found something he couldn't have, so he'd decided no one else should have it, either.

He was declaring war on the whole damn sport.

Her phone rang. Bob Boyd's name flashed on the screen, and she snatched it to her ear. "Hey, boss. How're you?"

"You see this Custer thing?"

"I saw it."

"What do you make of it?"

Kenzie frowned at the lack of outrage in her boss's tone. He was new to the rodeo game. Maybe he didn't understand the implications.

"It's bad for us, bad for the whole sport."

"How do you figure?"

"No one can be in two places at once. He's trying to draw the stock, the riders, and the audiences away from the major competitions. Plus, he's only doing the two most dangerous events, bull riding and bareback. No roping, no bulldogging, no women's anything. No respect for the history and traditions. All Custer cares about is money and attention."

"You think it'll work?"

"I hope to hell not."

"We wouldn't want to miss a good opportunity."

Kenzie swallowed several bitter retorts, reminding herself that Bob wasn't Lee, and her honest counsel wasn't always what he wanted to hear. "I'd never let that happen. With Custer's track record, though, I'd want a lot more information before I put my—*your*—animals at risk in his hands."

"I hear you. Hey, hang on a second." He fumbled with the phone, prompting a few random beeps, then came back on. "Pete from Black Creek Rodeo is on the other line. Keep your ears open. We'll talk in the morning."

Bob hung up and her phone immediately rang with another call, this one from Ramon. They spoke only briefly before they both took other incoming calls.

The rodeo tended to attract outdoorsy, low-tech people who viewed phones as unpleasant necessities, but they all figured out how to use the call button that night. She spoke to most of the senior ranch staff, several of her stock-contracting peers, quite a few conflicted bull riders, and even a couple ropers with whom she had only a passing acquaintance but who were so worried about the future of their events they reached out anyway. She offered everyone the best assurances she could muster, which weren't great—especially when she reflected on her conversation with Bob.

Bob was a rodeo fan, but he was primarily an investor. He didn't have Lee's passion—any of the Singers' passion, including Jesse. She got it. They were born into rodeo, and Bob wasn't. He wouldn't have their same level of awestruck obsession with the art and science of the sport, and unlike them, he hadn't dedicated his entire life to the preservation and progression of an iconic piece of American culture. He hadn't taken his first steps in the back of a cattle hauler, hadn't studied equine biomechanics alongside his multiplication tables, and didn't bear a name synonymous with rodeo since the sport's early foundations.

Then again, neither did she.

Point being, she could've relied on Lee to find Custer's venture as offensive and menacing as she did. Bob was trickier to navigate and harder to predict. She had to tread carefully, which sucked, because she wanted nothing more than to stomp around and commiserate.

She could do half of that, at least. Go for a walk and get some fresh air. Especially since the sleep she'd so eagerly imagined would be a long way off, now.

Kenzie pulled on her boots and jacket and crossed the parking lot toward the road instead of the fields behind the motel. She couldn't deal with any more stressed-out riders and ropers. She needed space to think.

The two-lane country road was virtually empty at this time of night, and she reached the fairgrounds in a few minutes. She cut through the grassy stretch that would be packed bumper-to-nose with vehicles by this time tomorrow, rounded the brick building where the 4-H ribbons were awarded, and reached the dark, silent arena.

Kenzie laced her fingers through the chain-link fence, taking in the perfectly raked dirt and the empty announcer's stand. She'd expected this place to feel poised. To vibrate with the anticipation of thundering hooves and snorting bulls and hollering fans.

Instead, it slumbered. Restful and unstirred. Not indifferent to the thrilling unities of man and beast that would occur on its soil, but calm and at peace.

A distant bleacher creaked. She peered at the darkened corner and caught the subtle shudder of a shadow, the pale brim of a hat, those long legs and dark hair too familiar to ignore.

Lee.

Kenzie didn't hesitate, and she wasn't afraid. She'd grown up with enough kids from the Rez to believe that life and death weren't as straightforward as her mom's church liked to insist. She scaled the fence and dropped down on the other side, then jogged across the front of the bleachers toward the apparition.

She didn't dare say his name. Her only fear was disrupting this moment, whether it was real or imagined or a dream. Yet as she approached, he turned, alerted by the sound of her boots. She slowed, but he'd spotted her. He watched her from beneath the brim of his hat.

Lee's hat.

Jesse.

Kenzie stopped short, fighting a swell of humiliation. How stupid could she be? Thinking Lee could come back to help her. To offer the advice and reassurance she wanted so badly.

She swallowed hard. Lee was gone.

And his awful brother was here to stay.

"Howdy," Jesse called down from the top row.

She exhaled shakily, telling herself to walk away instead of wasting energy on an argument.

The bottle of Tennessee whiskey beside him changed her mind.

"Howdy, yourself." She clomped up the bleachers, cataloging the differences between him and Lee as she came closer. Lee had been stocky and cuddly; Jesse was long and lean. Jesse's eyes were quicker, his smile slower, and while Lee's face was as wide-open as a barn door in the wind, Jesse's was impenetrable.

Everywhere Lee was blunt and soft, Jesse was sharp and hard.

And sexy.

Kenzie plunked down next to him, banishing that notion as she picked up the bottle without asking. She was one of a very small circle of people who'd known Lee was gay—a circle he'd spent most of his adult life cautiously widening, hoping one day he'd feel safe sharing his identity with the rodeo community. There'd been nothing between them except sibling-like affection, so for Kenzie's libido to suddenly wave hello at the thought of Jesse was unsettling.

She took a swig. The whiskey's blooming heat instantly dissolved her tension—including the tension between her legs.

She'd expected Jesse to scowl at her arrival, or make some sniping comment, or straight-up tell her to leave him the hell alone. Instead, he took the bottle and matched her shot with one of his own, then held it aloft.

"To Casey Custer." He saluted. "May his last sight on earth be Petunia's hooves."

"Too heroic. Let him get hit by a bus like regular people."

"Not fair on the bus driver."

"Heart attack on the toilet?"

"Heart attack while jerking off on the toilet," Jesse slurred.

Kenzie held up the bottle, assessing how much was left. "Big bottle for one man."

"One man about to spend the night in an RV with all three of his sisters. The same RV he drove for ten hours today."

Kenzie smiled and passed the bottle back to him. "Maybe not big enough, then."

He grunted an assent and took another pull.

As he lowered his chin and the brim shaded his face, she remembered what she'd seen.

Who she thought she'd seen.

"This'll sound wild, but for a second I thought you…" She trailed off, deciding he might not be as drunk as he sounded. They might be in the same boat as far as Custer was concerned, but that didn't mean Jesse wouldn't seize whatever advantage came his way. "Why do you wear your brother's hat?"

He sat back, propping his arms on the bleacher behind him and extending his legs. "You're the only one who's noticed."

"Or the only one not afraid to ask you questions."

"No one's afraid of me."

"Your staff are. I still know people at Singer. They tell me what they can't tell you."

"Such as?"

"They're intimidated by you. They feel like their jobs are always on the line. They're worried you'll sell the ranch to investors in New York City and run it like a corporation."

"That's ridiculous. I'd never do that."

"I don't think you would. But you're a mystery to them. They don't understand where you came from, and that makes them nervous."

"I came from Oklahoma. From the ranch," he insisted.

She shrugged. "Maybe you did at one point, but not for a long time. Not now."

"Bull." He raised the bottle to his lips.

She took in his troubled expression, his hunched shoulders, his white-knuckled grip on the bottle, and for an instant she felt sorry for him. It must suck to feel like a stranger in the place you were raised.

Then she remembered the high-handed way he'd waltzed in and changed everything without so much as asking a question. She snatched the whiskey and chased away her sympathy with a big swallow.

She set the bottle down so hard it clanked. "You haven't answered my question."

"Which was?"

"Lee's hat."

Jesse sat forward, propping his elbows on his knees as he turned that royal-blue gaze on her. Even in the dark his eyes were luminous and intent.

"You know why," he said softly.

"Because you miss him."

He smiled, his pain so fresh and familiar it overwhelmed her animosity. She reached for his hand.

"I miss him, too."

Jesse didn't snatch his hand away, or sneer at her grief, or slice her in half with a jagged reminder that she'd only lost a boss while he'd lost a brother. He squeezed her fingers, then raised his other hand to her face, gently cupping her chin and tilting her gaze to meet his.

As her heart rate kicked up, Kenzie felt as cautious and excited as if a bobcat stared at her from the edge of the yard. Jesse's eyes were softer than she'd ever seen them, their ice melted to reveal the bathwater-warm sea beneath. Her chaste grip on his hand seemed pornographic when she realized the edge of her palm rested on his hard thigh, barely inches from another hardness she'd imagined more often than she cared to admit. She had the urge to reach for it, to satisfy months of fantasies and hold him in her hand, velvety and throbbing and powerless.

Her fingers twitched and her breath caught, her nipples so tight against her bra that every inhale was torture. Jesse sized her up, a decision flickering behind his eyes like a candle on the other side of stained glass. She knew what he was thinking—she was thinking it, too. And if he wanted her permission, he could have it.

"Yes," she whispered.

His mouth was on hers with the hiss of that word still on her lips.

He wasn't tender, and he wasn't sweet. His kiss was greedy, possessive, and she was glad. Kenzie had no interest in romance, was mistrustful of people who carried on about their feelings, and prided herself on having never been sweet-talked into disaster like her mom. She had sex when she wanted and walked away, and Jesse's unapologetic lust was both alluring and a relief.

She pried off his hat to kiss him square and hard. Her hands moved to his shoulders. One of his moved to her nape, the other snaking around her back and pulling her in tight. He tasted good and smelled even better, whiskey and leather and frost, and when she opened her mouth, his tongue found hers with all the confidence and command she'd expect from the heir to the Singer throne.

Singer.

The word broke the surface of her lust like a shark fin, sleek and fast and just as threatening.

I'm kissing Jesse Singer.

I despise *Jesse Singer.*

She moaned against his mouth, hot desire and cold rage twining together in a sizzling knot that traveled down her body and lodged at the apex of her thighs. She fisted her hand in his hair and let her teeth catch his lower lip. He growled and yanked her closer, sliding his palm to her ass and squeezing so hard her toes curled in her boots.

Kenzie lost track of her surroundings, lost track of her limbs, and her world became a frantic kaleidoscope of fractured impressions. Jesse's tongue in her mouth, pushy and strong. His sandpaper stubble rasping her cheek. His fingers gripping her chin, holding her, guiding her, refusing to let go. She pawed him, sought him, pulsed with wild need and incandescent disdain. She willed him to be sober enough to stop this before they made a huge mistake, because she couldn't.

She wouldn't.

The clink of glass against aluminum startled them apart as the whiskey bottle rolled off the edge of the bleacher. They both dove for it, but they were too late. Their heads cracked together, and they each jerked back in pain while the bottle thumped onto the grass below.

"Damn, that whiskey gave me a headache and I'm not even drunk." Kenzie rubbed her forehead where their skulls had collided.

"I can go down and fetch it. Make the headache worthwhile." Jesse's smile was broad, but his expression had closed, as if curtains had been drawn over his stained-glass eyes, that bright candle from moments ago reduced to a faint glow.

Instantly she was wary, hauling shut her defenses like the heavy door on a tornado shelter, but she wasn't fast enough. There was still a tiny gap left open when he spoke again, plenty of space for his next question to pull her up and out of safety.

To suck her into his swirling funnel of betrayal and deceit.

"Has Custer made you an offer yet?" he asked.

Jesse's tone was so light, so jovial, so calculated and inoffensive that she recoiled.

So that was what this was about. Throwing her off guard and mining her for information. Playing nice so she'd say something she shouldn't.

Kissing her until she trusted him, then brutally grabbing the upper hand.

What was wrong with her? God, she was stupid. She'd fallen for the oldest trick in the book.

Almost fell. She hadn't told him anything—yet.

She teased her lips into a defiant smile, tamping down the indignation roiling in her belly.

"It's late. I'm going to bed, but you should stay. Give yourself a hangover so bad it'll feel trivial when Not Nice outscores Repeat Offender tomorrow."

Jesse's smile never faltered, yet his eyes iced over. "See you in the arena."

"You sure will." She flashed him a wink and waggled her fingers in goodbye, then sauntered down the bleachers like she had all the time in the world. Hips swinging, hair flipping, breasts bouncing as much as she could manage.

Her stride was light and easy, but with every step her self-recrimination grew harsher and louder.

Jesse Singer was not her ally. He was not her friend, and he was absolutely not her lover. No matter what he said or did, she had to remember they were on opposing sides. They were rivals. Competitors.

Enemies.

She climbed over the chain-link fence and jumped down, then picked up her pace, confident Jesse had lost sight of her. She shivered in the rapidly dropping temperature, remembering what had drawn her there in the first place.

No, there'd been no benevolent spirit pulling the two of them together, no spectral hand guiding them to their destiny. Just the devil himself, pretending to be drunk, pretending to be kind.

Pretending he wanted her.

Kenzie exhaled in disgust and moved faster. She should've known. Jesse was conniving, ruthless and entitled.

Just like her father.

She broke into a run, desperate to put as much mileage as possible between her and that evil bastard. As if she could get far enough away, she'd forget it altogether—forget his smug smile, his phony good humor and his pathetic attempt at wooing her into his control.

Kenzie ran hard and long, ran until her boots hurt her feet, ran all the way back to her motel room. She slammed inside, sweat-soaked and panting, and pressed her back against the door like he was on the other side, ready to push it open.

He wasn't—but he might as well have been.

Because her body still burned everywhere he'd touched.

Jesse wove through the hushed maze of campers and trailers, reduced to vague lumps in the darkness. Singer Pro Rodeo's RV was at the far end, bigger than all the others, the gap with its nearest neighbor significantly wider. Whether that distance was respectful or superstitious he didn't know, but it was always there.

He shucked off his boots and snuck inside, less worried about depriving his sisters of their beauty rest than having to explain why he was creeping back at one o'clock in the morning. He'd waited on the bleachers far longer than necessary to ensure Kenzie didn't think he was chasing her. He was dead sober, though pretending he was drunk might be simpler. Truth was stranger than fiction on this occasion.

No one stirred as he shut the door behind him. Trixie and Billie shared the bunk beds in the back, Mae took the sleeper sofa, and he had the pull-down bed in between—which, of course, he now had to set up.

He eased past Mae and felt around for the latches before deciding he'd just put his sleeping bag on the floor. Then he stepped out of his jeans, mindful of his clinking belt buckle, and sidled over to the plastic tub beside the sink that served as a makeshift medicine cabinet. He found the bottle of aspirin, unscrewed the cap, and tilted it with painstaking slowness so the pills wouldn't rattle—then missed his own hand, sending the bottle's contents cascading onto the floor.

"What was that?"

"Who's there?"

"Jesse?"

He cringed, imagining his sisters' heads popping up like prairie dogs.

"It's fine," he whispered. "Go back to sleep."

As usual, no one listened to him. Lights flicked on, and within seconds, he was surrounded by three dark-haired women blinking at him in disapproval.

Trixie propped her hands on her hips. "And what sort of time do you call this?"

"Have you been cavorting?" Billie chimed in. "You smell like you've been cavorting."

"I've been drinking." He stooped over and gathered the pills, then dropped them back in the bottle. "Now I have a headache, and I want to go to bed."

Billie gazed up at his forehead. "With a bruise like that, I'm not surprised."

Jesse winced. Great—he and Kenzie would have matching bruises. Thankfully his would be covered by his hat, saving them from awkward questions.

"I banged my head. Height hazard."

They rolled their eyes in unison. His sisters hated being reminded that he'd gobbled up all the tall genes.

"Your sister the doctor should look at it." Trixie smirked at their inside joke about their mom, who never missed an opportunity to announce Mae's profession.

Content to leave Jesse in his twin's capable hands, Trixie and Billie filed back to the bunk beds. Mae motioned him over to her bed, turning off the bright overhead light for a smaller reading lamp.

She touched the sore spot on his head gently, then patted his arm. "You'll have a nice goose egg tomorrow, but you'll live. I prescribe two aspirin and a lot of water."

"Thanks, Doc. What do I owe you?"

"This one's on the house. Friends and family discount." She winked. "I can pull that bed down while you get the pills."

He shook his head. "I'll be fine on the floor. Go back to sleep. We've got a big day tomorrow."

"We always do. Are you okay?"

Jesse hesitated. His bond with Mae was the strongest of all his siblings—no surprise, considering they'd been roommates in the womb. He never told anyone everything, but he told her the most.

What happened with Kenzie, though… No. That had to stay with him.

He shrugged. "Just worried about this Custer thing."

"It's a low blow. But we'll figure it out."

"We always do." Jesse swallowed his aspirin.

Mae flipped off the light, leaving him alone in the dark on the hard floor, his head pounding and his mind reeling.

He was an idiot—that was the bottom line. He'd been stressed and tipsy, and she was so pretty he'd lost his damn mind.

Then he'd made it worse. He'd overestimated their sudden alliance and asked a question that was too honest and too exposed. Only she hadn't seen it for the vulnerable, risky misstep it was—and he should be grateful for that.

Yet her withdrawal—the way she'd read malice instead of

a mistake, and that appalled, damning look she'd given him—hurt more than the throbbing in his skull.

That was Kenzie. She always assumed the worst about him, when he was just trying to do his best.

Jesse shifted onto his side, willing himself to forget their kiss, that fleeting moment of connection. He was lonely, that's all. He hadn't been with a woman in, what, two years? Two and a half? Not since Lauren. At the thought of his last girlfriend, he rolled onto his stomach and smothered his groan in his pillow.

Lauren hadn't broken his heart because he'd never felt safe enough to hand it over. He'd been close, though—close enough that her parting lines about the impossibility of a long-distance relationship still stung.

She'd liked him when he was a hotshot M&A consultant—loved him, she said. She liked that he was Jewish, liked his preference for cheap beer over fancy wine, and liked that he was modest and low-key amid their professional cohort of ostentatious spenders. His rodeo upbringing was a novelty, an amusing anecdote when she introduced him to her close friends or her parents. She told them about his subscription to a rodeo-streaming app, and how he refreshed bull-riding standings like other people checked baseball scores.

And because he'd been alone so long and was desperate for someone to finally embrace his contradictory identity, he thought that meant she got it. Got him.

Then his brother died.

Lauren didn't come to the funeral. It happened so suddenly, and Oklahoma was so far when she was angling for partner at her law firm. She couldn't take the time off. He understood. He didn't blame her.

In the days following, though, he found himself reaching for her support and coming up empty. She was compassionate and kind, but she kept turning the conversation to his return. She couldn't comprehend why he'd want to hang around somewhere so small and remote any longer than necessary. She chatted about a backstabbing colleague and the new restaurant down the block, and he'd stared out the window at the Singer acreage, the lush summer green slowly giving way to autumn's brittle brown, and his life in New York City felt as distant as a star.

Jesse did fly back to New York, but only to pack up his apartment. Lauren came over and stood among the cardboard boxes, her eyes damp and her posture resigned.

"Oklahoma," she'd kept repeating, as if she couldn't believe it was a real place. "You're seriously going to live there forever?"

"It's where I'm from." He'd pried the key to her apartment off his cowboy-boot key chain.

"I know, but I never thought you'd go back."

Part of him hadn't thought so, either. That felt like a betrayal too grave to admit out loud.

"I'm sorry, Jesse, but I can't do this if you're out there. It's too far, and it's too…"

"Different," he'd supplied. "I know."

"But if you ever change your mind and come back—"

"I won't."

Mae sighed in her sleep, drawing him out of that empty apartment and away from the click of the door as Lauren shut it behind her. He turned onto his back and blinked into the darkness.

Jesse was ranch-tough and Wall Street hard, but he was a sucker when it came to women. Lauren had smiled benevolently at the Stetson in his closet, and he practically threw himself at her. Kenzie let him kiss her, and he was ready to disclose his whole competitive strategy.

He had to get his guard up, particularly around Kenzie. Until the ranch was on an even keel and this Custer nonsense put to bed, his love life would stay at the bottom of his priority list. He couldn't afford another slipup. Not with so much on the line.

And maybe one day, when Singer Pro Rodeo was thriving and his sisters' futures secured, he'd meet a nice Okie girl from a small town who'd always wanted to live on a ranch. She wouldn't be Jewish—even his imagination couldn't stretch that far—but she'd love rodeo and love his sisters and choose him over Jesus.

She'd have dyed-pink hair and a strawberry-sweet mouth. She'd be clever and funny and smart. She'd kiss him fiercely and give him good advice. He'd know her body better than his own, mapping every curve with his hands and his mouth, learning exactly how to make her gasp, when to make her moan. They'd have two kids with bottle-green eyes, he'd remind her not to cuss around the babies, and they'd drink whiskey after bedtime.

Jesse yawned and fell asleep, his lips curled in a contented smile.

Chapter Six

"And over here we've got a yearling bull, sired by three-time league champion, Spilled Milk. You should see this guy spin."

Jesse made notes in the margins of his auction catalog. The bull rider turned stock contractor who owned this ranch, Justin Pitland, was relatively young and extremely eager. This was his first production sale, and although Jesse appreciated his desperation to send one of his bulls to Singer Pro Rodeo, he wished Justin would stop talking and leave him alone.

"Now this guy's a two-year-old." Justin moved to the next of what felt like a patchwork quilt of pens set up behind the fenced practice arena.

A born showman, Justin had accumulated an impressive number of eight-second paydays during his career. What his southeastern-Oklahoma property lacked in size, it made up for in atmosphere. When his visitors weren't perusing the animals for sale, they could escape the early-September sun beneath a row of canopies and enjoy free coffee, free doughnuts and free, branded koozies. Tablecloths, fall-colored bunting and decorative gourds set this event miles apart from the production sales Jesse had attended as a kid, where a root beer–flavored lollipop and a warm Dr Pepper were the pinnacle of the snack scene.

Jesse understood what Justin was trying to do, and he respected it. A black-and-white auction guide and a microwaved cup of Folgers weren't enough anymore, not with the amount of money involved, and not with the ever-increasing competition.

Justin was getting people into a good mood, giving the sale a sense of occasion. He'd discovered new ways to do old stuff, and Jesse admired him for it.

That was why Jesse was here in the first place.

Singer Pro Rodeo rarely bought bloodlines. They had such a long history of champions they'd hardly ever needed to.

Jesse wanted to change that.

Repeat Offender was a once-in-a-generation animal athlete, and, barring any calamities, would be inscribed in the annals of rodeo's rankest bulls—hopefully to the exclusion of Not Nice.

But he was only one bull, and so precious that Jesse was extra conservative when it came to shuttling him around the country to compete. He had his minimum qualifying rides for the Pro Rodeo League finals, and would almost certainly be on the list of bulls selected for that competition when it released next month. Other than a couple of trips to particularly high-paying rodeos, Repeat Offender would spend the next ten weeks luxuriating at the ranch, eating and sleeping and frolicking in the pasture—and whatever else seventeen hundred pounds of beef did for fun.

Without Repeat Offender stealing the spotlight, the rest of the lineup looked pretty beige. They weren't bad bulls—most were very good, and some had potential for greatness. But Lee had spent so much money on short-term fixes that he'd neglected the future pipeline, and their bench strength got thinner every day.

That was Kenzie's doing, Jesse had concluded after she resurfaced at the Broken B. That was why Bob Boyd had gone from a nobody to the owner of Repeat Offender's biggest challenger in less than two years. No one could be that good at training or identifying talent. She'd simply bought the best animal she could find, and she'd probably used half of Boyd's riches to do it.

That wasn't Jesse's play. He intended to spread his risk, invest carefully in a few choice yearlings, and hope a hundred years of Singer magic could shape them into winners.

In fact, there was only one animal here that interested him, but he didn't dare let on—not when he'd already heard whispers about Singer showing up. He identified where he could place red-herring bids to drive up prices, both to divert attention from the yearling he wanted and give Justin's earnings a little boost.

Although if Justin kept jabbering, he might not feel so magnanimous.

"Now, this one might look familiar," Justin said. "Recognize him?"

Jesse squinted at the white yearling. "Should I?"

"You don't see the family resemblance? His grandsire is Singer Pro Rodeo's Pony Ride."

"So he is." Jesse smiled, remembering the snow-white bull as he reached over to scratch the cow's head.

"That bull scared me half to death once, sticking his head out of the pen to sniff me in the pitch-dark." Justin laughed. "I swear I jumped about a foot in the air thinking it was a ghost. Thought your daddy might never stop laughing. I got that sucker rode, though. Eighty-nine points to win Ellensburg. Your dad and I were both laughing that day—all the way to the bank. How is he, anyway?"

"Pony Ride, or my dad?"

Justin grinned. "Both."

"Enjoying retirement in the peace and tranquility of central Oklahoma."

"Glad to hear it. Give him my best. Your dad, that is. I ain't forgiven Pony Ride."

Justin slapped Jesse's shoulder, finally moving on to speak to someone else. Jesse stayed another minute with Pony Ride's grandbaby, remembering when his dad had been commanding and wisecracking and fun, instead of hollowed out by grief. Before he collapsed at the funeral, before he retreated into a fearful fragility that should've been decades off.

Three years ago, Jesse never could've imagined his authoritative, decisive and wickedly intelligent father admitting he'd grown nervous about merging onto the highway.

Then again, three years ago Jesse couldn't have imagined running the ranch in Lee's stead. All their lives changed that day, and not for the better.

Not yet, anyway. Jesse would bury the secret of Lee's catastrophic finances so deep in profit and growth that no one would ever find out—or if they did, they wouldn't care. It'd be an inconsequential dip on a skyrocketing line graph, and only he would know how close they'd come to losing it all.

Jesse wove through the remaining pens, sketching out his strategy in coded notations. He had his eye on a black yearling with no name yet, sold as lot number twelve on the list. Unlike most of the animals up for auction, this one wasn't sired by Justin's most famous bull—in fact his lineage appeared mediocre on paper. But after watching videos of him bucking the lightweight dummy box, twisting and kicking and diving like a submarine, Jesse knew this animal had immense potential. His age and build would make him the perfect addition to the Singer stable—a bet on a future Jesse was nearly destroying himself to secure.

Cash flow at Singer Pro Rodeo was tight, and he didn't want to pay over the odds. He took his seat on one of the folding chairs lined up in rows inside the tent, crossed his arms and set his expression to underwhelmed and impatient.

"Singer. Good to see you." Bill Jessup, who'd been breeding bulls longer than his own father had been alive, lowered himself into the next chair and stuck out his hand.

Jesse shook it firmly, wondering if Bill knew his name. He was probably the fourth Singer to run the ranch since Bill started, so he didn't blame him if he couldn't keep track.

"What do you like?" Bill opened his catalog.

Aware that several nearby conversations had paused to listen, Jesse let the Singer halo effect do its work. "Three, eight, nine, and I'm thinking about eleven."

Pages flipped and cattlemen murmured, revisiting those animals in the context of Jesse's interest.

Justin sat at the table facing the audience, joined by an auctioneer. He thanked everyone for coming, told a thirty-second version of his transition from bull rider to stock contractor, and was halfway through a joke about naming bulls when he paused, his attention flicking to the back of the tent. Jesse joined everyone else in following the direction of his gaze—and instantly regretted it.

Kenzie Wallace smiled an apology as she took a seat at the back—until their eyes met and her expression hardened in distaste. Jesse whipped around, but the damage was done, and as the auctioneer began with the first calf on the list, his mood sank to the floor.

Forget her, he coached himself, like he had every waking hour since he'd kissed her five days earlier. He'd barely slept in two years, changed careers faster than most people changed outfits, and was single-handedly executing a financial turnaround that would make the best CEOs he knew stand up and applaud.

So he'd drunk some whiskey and kissed a pretty woman. Birds didn't fall out of the sky. The sun didn't turn red. The earth continued to turn, indifferent to two petty mortals pressing their faces together on an empty bleacher at midnight.

Neither he nor Kenzie would gain anything from the wider world finding out about their momentary lapse in judgment, so for all intents and purposes nothing had changed.

Nothing except the intense, recurring and extremely naked dreams about her that ruined what little sleep he got.

Jesse shifted in his chair, planted his boots on the ground and summoned that ruthless detachment that had made him beloved and reviled in equal measure in the country's toughest boardrooms. He had no problem being brutal and heartless on behalf of his paying clients. He could sure as hell do the same for his family business.

"All right, y'all, that's enough from me," Justin said. "Each of these animals is ready to bring what their daddies gave 'em, so I'll turn it over to George."

George adjusted his camel-colored felt cowboy hat and leaned into the microphone. "For lot one, we've got a two-year-old bull. Nice action on this boy."

He launched into the rapid, rhythmic cadence of an auctioneer, his eyes darting around the crowd as he noted the bids and ramped up the price. Jesse lounged in his chair as people twitched their fingers or jerked their chins to place bids in the coded and almost imperceptible commerce of livestock, where thousands of dollars were spent with barely a nod.

"Sold, number three twenty-one." George paused while he and Justin recorded the winning bidder's number and price. Then he moved on to the second lot, and his musical chant started up again.

Jesse bid twice on the third lot, giving his pre-auction assertion credibility. He bid more aggressively on eight and nine, feigning indecision, then irritation, scribbling nonsense on his catalog as if he was annoyed with himself for letting a good opportunity get away.

When lot eleven came up, he sat up straight and narrowed his eyes in determination. He bid early and high, prompting a flurry of challengers. He nodded again, and again, pushing the price slightly higher than he deemed fair.

The next bid came in, and George turned to him, brows raised expectantly.

Jesse let his gaze fall to the catalog in his lap and sagged in his seat.

"Sold, number four-oh-four," George announced.

Jesse caught the winning bidder's triumphant smile in his peripheral vision. He'd bought a good animal for a decent price—and more importantly, he'd gotten one over on Singer Pro Rodeo.

Bill nudged him. "Tough luck."

Jesse shrugged, exaggerating his disappointment. He sensed the mood around him shifting, exactly as he'd hoped. Sympathy undercut competitiveness. People remembered his father, his brother, and the tragedy that had brought Jesse here in the first place.

He's doing his best, he knew they were thinking. *This ain't his world, but he's trying.*

George opened the bidding for lot twelve. Jesse waited through a couple of low offers, squinting at the catalog, then gave a half-hearted nod. The next bid was hesitant, almost reluctant.

What the hell, he imagined the other rancher saying to himself. *This bull ain't no great shakes. Let him have it.*

George called out, "Can I get eighteen hundred, eighteen hundred, can I get—"

"Two thousand."

Every head in the tent turned toward the woman's voice, defying protocol by chiming into the auctioneer's chant. Kenzie Wallace had moved to a seat parallel to Jesse's and was perched on the edge, wearing a polite smile.

"Two thousand," George confirmed.

Jesse nodded, raising the price.

Kenzie upped her bid and Jesse countered, his adrenaline surging as he fought to keep his expression impassive.

His self-imposed limit was thirty-five hundred dollars, and they were still a long way off. She was just antagonizing him. She couldn't possibly see the bull's potential.

Yet, as the numbers climbed higher, so did his agitation.

Kenzie hadn't put in a single bid, and now she was desperate for this one animal? No chance. This was personal.

He glared at her across the row, and she scowled right back.

Jesse sat forward, dropping any pretense of uncertainty. Kenzie's obsession with him was petty and childish, but when it posed a real threat, he had no choice but to fight. He'd protect his family if it killed him.

They bid against each other fiercely until every person in the audience stared at them with slack-jawed astonishment. George's chant picked up speed, his eyes bright as he glanced between the two of them. Back and forth, his head swung as though watching a tennis match. Jesse refused to look at Kenzie, hardening his jaw and his resolve, ignoring the queasiness that worsened each time he nodded.

"Twenty-five hundred… Twenty-seven hundred… Three thousand…" The black-and-white numbers poked their heads out of George's spiel like squirrels popping up in a tree. Jesse's mind twisted with mathematical gymnastics as he revised his budget, pictured his P&L spreadsheet, and frantically tweaked his numbers and expenditures until the total resettled where he wanted it.

The bidding hit thirty-five hundred and he held his breath, praying Kenzie would drop out. Instead, she nodded them up to thirty-six, then thirty-eight. When she inclined her chin, bringing them to four thousand dollars, Jesse's pulse thundered in his ears.

He grasped for rationality amid the heat flooding his veins, scrabbling for the cool, corporate side of himself that knew better than to let pride overrule sound financial decision-making. Overspending on a bull was no victory at all. Kenzie knew that, and in all likelihood cared more about emptying his wallet than denying him this animal.

Still, he nodded again, and again, and soon they hit forty-two hundred dollars, prompting a wowed murmur from the crowd.

Jesse stole a glance at Kenzie. She hunched forward, her lips thin, her expression as stubborn as he'd ever seen—and that was saying something. For a split second his determination stumbled, replaced by bone-deep weariness.

He was tired. Tired of confrontation, tired of this uphill battle, tired of locking horns in some stupid game of revenge. There'd be other bulls. Let her take this one.

She's already taken enough, whispered a vicious, vengeful voice, and his attention snapped back to the auctioneer.

He wouldn't back down. Not today.

"Forty-two hundred… Forty-three hundred… Forty-three and a half…" The numbers became meaningless bunches of syllables as their one-on-one bidding war raged. George shrank the intervals, clearly aware the prices had become reckless.

Justin's eyes rounded with disbelief. Still, he and Kenzie pushed higher and higher, the depth and ferocity of their feud laid bare for all to see.

Until a new voice piped up from the back of the tent.

"Seven thousand."

Simultaneously, Jesse and Kenzie turned toward the newcomer.

Casey Custer stood with his hip propped against a chair and his Stetson tipped back, revealing his sandy-colored hair and ruddy cheeks. He wore a tailored suit, shiny boots and a sense of self-satisfaction so thick Jesse could almost smell it.

Custer's bid had stunned George into silence, but like a true professional he picked up the curveball and ran with it. He offered the new price of seventy-one hundred, his gaze locked on Kenzie and Jesse as he spoke.

They swapped a contrite glance across the aisle, their mutual animosity eclipsed by Custer's outrageous intrusion. The man was about to pay double for that bull, and Jesse was in no position to stop him. He slumped in his chair, stewing over his defeat.

"Sold, seven thousand dollars to number—what's your buyer number?" George asked.

"Didn't know I needed one. Don't worry, I'm good for it." Custer winked.

Jesse dropped his head into his hands, dread settling on his shoulders.

He'd lost it. That single-minded drive, that relentless clarity of thought, that glacial indifference that made him who he was—it was gone. He'd been given a run for his money by a formerly pink-haired incompetent, then beaten by a spoiled brat.

When he was away, when he was the interloper in a world that never quite understood him, wading through a life that was alien to everything that reared him, he'd been a winner. He'd known nothing but success.

Now he was home, back where he belonged, and everything he reached for slipped through his fingers.

He had to pull himself together. The stakes were too high, the potential damage too great. He'd been so focused on Kenzie and the Broken B that he'd missed the biggest threat of all—the one that could tear the entire sport apart.

Bill's hand closed on his shoulder, giving him a paternal squeeze.

"Can't win 'em all," the old rancher said, his gravelly voice kind and sympathetic.

"Maybe not." Jesse hauled himself upright. "But I can try."

Kenzie watched Custer over the rim of her coffee cup, his goofy grin as fake as his dumbass accent. He'd swept through the second half of the auction like a tornado, outbidding anyone who dared raise their finger, and paying absurdly inflated prices for middle-of-the-road roughstock. At first, she thought he was even more of an idiot than she'd imagined, but as the auction ended on a ripple of shaking heads and disappointed grumbles, she decided he'd done this on purpose.

He didn't want those animals. He wanted to take them away from everyone else.

Now Custer stood by the arena fence like visiting royalty, surrounded by fence fabricators, insurers, outfitters and a bunch of other rodeo-adjacent service providers eager to get his business.

She actually needed a new fence guy, but the way this one brushed her off and beelined for Custer meant that was one more problem she wouldn't solve today.

Speaking of problems, her gaze swung to Jesse Singer, standing off to the side, frowning into the distance.

Her heartbeat skittered and she turned away, draining the last of her lukewarm coffee. Kissing Jesse was one of her top three worst decisions of all time, right up there with her ankle tattoo and the mascara she'd shoplifted from Family Dollar. Every time she thought about that kiss, her face burned with humiliation and regret.

And arousal.

She crumpled her cardboard cup on a disgusted exhale. Her sex drive had been simmering on the back burner for so long she'd almost forgotten it was there. No wonder that long-legged, laser-eyed douchebag made her boil.

Kenzie worked around men all day—too many men, felt like—yet there was a dearth of truly appealing options. Among those whose personalities didn't put her off right away, there was always some other disqualifier. Too short. Too young. Too churchy.

Jesse, on the other hand, was well built and very pretty, his angular face and thick hair nearly making up for his perennial sneer. He was smart and sexy and he smelled fantastic. Who could blame her for sniffing in his direction? If she asked every barrel racer on the circuit to pick the hottest men in rodeo for a naked calendar, she bet she'd come up with twelve solid months of Jesse Singer.

Kenzie sniggered as she tossed her cup in the trash, then wandered into the long shadows of the late-afternoon sun.

Three hundred and sixty-five days of Jesse in the nude—now *that* she'd like to see. Naked Jesse in February, with a strategically positioned, heart-shaped box of chocolates. Naked Jesse in April, wearing bunny ears and holding a basket of eggs. Naked Jesse in July, saluting America with his big, thick, star-spangled firecracker.

Or fully clothed Jesse, standing right in front of her.

She dragged her gaze from his belt buckle to his eyes. It took a while—he really was tall—but the hint of impatience tightening his expression was worth it.

"Yes?" she greeted him dryly.

"You were staring at me with your tongue half out. Thought I should make sure you weren't having a seizure."

"I was not," she insisted, belatedly realizing that was, in fact, exactly what she'd been doing.

Nearby, Custer guffawed so loudly they both turned in his direction.

Kenzie clucked her tongue. "Look at those vultures, climbing over each other to get a piece of the man who just wasted a small fortune on a second-tier bunch of bulls. You'd never know Custer used to be a pariah."

"Pariah," he repeated mildly. "That's a big word for you."

"Shut up." But her words were as half-hearted as his jab had been.

They watched Custer in silence, their bidding war over the high-potential yearling now seeming downright juvenile. They'd been so fixated on scoring points against each other, they hadn't noticed the whole game had changed.

Kenzie narrowed her eyes. "I bet he doesn't even want those bulls. He just doesn't—"

"—want anyone else to have them," Jesse finished.

They exchanged a swift, knowing glance.

At least there was one thing they agreed on.

"We need to do something, Kenzie."

She wasn't sure whether it was the gravity in his tone, his use of the word *we*, or the sound of her name in his voice, but every nerve in her body snapped to attention.

She peered up at him, searching his face for any hint of deviousness or dishonesty. She came up empty. Those blue eyes of his were steady, sincere and genuinely troubled.

Then again, she'd thought he was being real last weekend, with his sweet smile and his whiskey kiss.

"Do you have any ideas?" she asked.

"Not yet."

Neither of them spoke as another stock contractor walked past, pausing close to where they stood and plucking a mini packet of cookies from a snack bowl. He moved on, and Kenzie angled toward Jesse.

"We should find time to talk. Will you be in Albuquerque this weekend?"

He shook his head. "It's Rosh Hashanah."

"Jewish New Year. Lee told me about the different holidays."

A faint smile curved Jesse's lips. "Rosh Hashanah was his favorite. He was big on starting over."

"God, that's so true. He never used notebooks, even when we went to stock auctions. He said he wasn't the type to go flipping through old pages. Didn't like looking backward. He did everything on blank pieces of paper he took from the printer tray. He had a whole constellation of them on his desk. No idea how he kept track of it all."

Kenzie laughed, but Jesse's expression hardened.

She sighed, in no mood to retread this old ground. "I know you think Lee did everything wrong, but—"

"I didn't say that."

"It's true, though."

Jesse shook his head. "No. I think Lee did the best he knew how to do. I should've…" He shook his head again. "Whatever. Doesn't matter now."

Since Kenzie was pretty sure he was about to finish that sentence by saying he should've fired her earlier, she was inclined to agree.

"How about the end of next week? We might be able to grab time on the phone before then, but you know what it's like this close to the end of the regular season. Feels like I barely take a shower without someone needing to talk to me."

Heat flashed in his eyes, as quick and electric as lightning. Was he thinking about her in the shower? Oh no, now she was thinking about him in the shower, his skin slick and wet, water dripping down the line of hair on his stomach toward—

He cleared his throat. "Thursday's good."

"Thursday. Good. I mean, that works. I'll—"

"You two look cozy. Have y'all finally let bygones be bygones?"

Casey Custer wasn't just a bucket of cold water on her sizzling thoughts—he was the Arctic Ocean. Everything about him was an offensive parody of her cherished profession, from the spurs strapped around his designer boots, to his turquoise bolo tie. Just being near him sent a grossed-out shiver down her spine. She inched closer to Jesse, who was at least the devil she knew.

"You wrote some big checks today," Jesse said, his tone icy.

Custer grinned. "Like they say, you have to spend money to make money. Supreme Rodeo performances are already selling out, and you know as well as I do how many animals these events demand."

"You need a lot of riders, too. Uninjured ones," Kenzie said, recalling a particularly gruesome injury inflicted by one of Custer's bulls before he was booted out of the League.

"Despite the rumors spread by a certain member of the medical profession—" Custer looked pointedly at Jesse "—my bulls are as harmless as yours, Miss Broken B. In fact, that's what I want to talk to you about. Both of you."

Kenzie glanced at Jesse, but his gaze was fixed on Custer.

"Although I'm building my own roughstock breeding program, having some animal headliners would give the Supreme Rodeo Series a big boost. Only, I won't be doing traditional stock contracting like the League does—coughing up fees for outfits like yourselves to supply pickup riders, bullfighters, chute staff, and certainly not a medical team. I'm offering individual slots for individual animals—with individual payouts."

"That's so inefficient," Kenzie argued. "The whole point of the inclusive package is to create economies of scale. It costs the same to haul fifteen cows as it does to move one or two, plus then the event organizers aren't hiring each and every—"

"How much?" Jesse asked.

"Two thousand per ride, plus a bonus for points."

Kenzie's jaw dropped. That was more than double the average in the Pro Rodeo League. She'd have to run the numbers, but suddenly the expense of transporting just a couple of bulls didn't seem quite so prohibitive.

She searched Jesse's face for a reaction, but his expression had the dead calm of a lake on an overcast, windless afternoon.

"The rosters are filling up quickly, but I'd gladly make space for the top animals from Singer Pro Rodeo or the Broken B." Custer gave them a smug grin.

Part of her wanted to tell Custer where to shove his slots—but another part begged her to be pragmatic. Jesse was a rodeo heir, beholden only to himself. She had an employer and a salary, both of which relied on her producing results. She was confident Not Nice would be selected for the League finals in Vegas, but could he beat Repeat Offender for the top prize and the purse it carried?

Bob Boyd didn't share her passion for the history and artistry of rodeo, and her attempts at explaining the masterful skills his animals displayed always ended on monetary terms. If he were here, he'd say yes. He'd tell her to snatch this chance away from Singer, and shove Broken B bulls into the lineup.

Except he wasn't here, because he paid her to be here instead.

She turned to Jesse, silently making a deal with herself. If he threw her under the bus and grabbed Custer's offer, she'd fight him tooth and nail to claim it back.

But if he refused to be bought—if he defended their way of

life and chose the integrity of tradition over an easy payday—she'd stand beside him. It was what she would do if she could afford to.

What she couldn't do alone.

Jesse tilted his head. "You can call these shows whatever you want. They aren't rodeo. I raise roughstock for rodeo. Not novelty acts."

Kenzie's heart zoomed into her throat, fit to burst with delight and thrill and relief. She'd deal with Bob somehow, find a way to translate ideology into dollar signs. Right now, though, she focused on facing down her enemy—the one in front of her, not the one at her side.

"Bull and bareback riding *is* rodeo," Custer argued. "I'm just skipping the boring events. No one's going to pay the kinds of ticket prices these arenas require to watch some loser tie a calf's feet together."

Jesse shook his head. "Rodeo is a sport. Not a spectacle."

"A sport *is* a spectacle. Guess a Yale education isn't what it used to be," Custer sniped.

"Sport is about tradition and talent and pushing the bar higher and higher. Spectacle is strapping desperate cowboys to dangerous animals because the audience wants to see someone get trampled."

"Lots of people watch sports because they're dangerous," Custer countered. "Look at boxing, or NASCAR."

"But you're *only* showing the risky, chaotic events, because you're pandering to those viewers," Kenzie interjected. "Those should be hooks to get people into the stands. Then we hope they fall in love with barrel racing, or breakaway roping, or even the rodeo clown. Whatever it takes to get them excited, look a little closer, follow the athletes, and come back next year."

"Which is noble—and unprofitable. I'm not interested in subsidizing whiny farmers riding expensive horses in the name of *tradition*." He put the word in air quotes. "If you two want to bankrupt yourselves to save a bunch of boring rope throwers, go ahead. I think we'd all be better off if we stop pretending anyone cares and let those events die."

"Then we're lucky you're not in charge," Kenzie muttered.

Custer's grin returned, and so did his hokey accent. "I sure am in charge, Miss Wallace. And I want you two to believe me when I say there's no hard feelings here. Especially you, Singer."

Jesse stiffened. "Is that supposed to be an apology?"

"For what?" Custer's eyes widened in mock confusion.

"Posting that garbage about the pharmaceutical company that happens to have been founded by someone with my last name."

"I never said you were related."

"You implied it."

Custer shrugged. "I just shared news articles about the allegations against the company, and a few theories about its ties to political figures. I'm interested in current events. Don't take it personally."

Jesse laughed, bitter and disbelieving.

Custer raised a contrite palm. "You're right—I have a big platform, and I should be more thoughtful about what I post. If my followers made a connection where none existed, and if that offended you in any way, then I'm sorry. I hope you'll consider what I've suggested. Singer bulls would really pull in a crowd—as would their peers at the Broken B. My offer stands to you both. Until it doesn't."

Custer raised his hat and executed some version of a bow bastardized from black-and-white Western movies. Spinning on his heel, he sauntered away, whistling as he walked.

Kenzie and Jesse watched him depart, then turned to each other.

"You went to Yale?" she blurted, the question so random, even she hadn't seen it coming.

Jesse smiled, then grinned, and finally let loose a rich, warm laugh that transformed his whole posture from distant and hard to downright huggable. "That's what you took from that conversation?"

His lips quirked in amusement, and she realized how hilariously God had undermined this stern, serious man by giving him dimples.

Talk about a divine sense of humor.

"Not the only thing. It's just—Yale is, like, famous."

"Do you know where it is?"

She wrinkled her nose. "Boston?"

"Not that famous, then."

"More famous than OU, which is where I figured you went."

He shook his head. "Mae and I both went East."

"Pricey. Bet your dad was hawking those bull semen straws like there was no tomorrow."

He laughed again. "Made them boys work overtime."

"I doubt they were complaining."

They smiled at each other, a moment so rare Kenzie wished she could drag it out. She didn't like Jesse, and she wasn't sure she ever would, but not hating him was a lot more fun than the alternative.

"I didn't know Custer was trash-posting about y'all."

"You're not an avid follower?"

"Can't say I am. He's talking about that vaccine company, right?"

Jesse waved a dismissive hand. "That's just one piece of a big, anti-Semitic conspiracy theory. He hasn't posted anything about it in months, and he wouldn't be trying to recruit me if he was committed to slandering my family."

"Still, that's nasty. Targeting y'all so specifically, and bringing religion into it, too."

He shrugged. "I've heard worse. We said next Thursday?"

"Afternoon is preferable."

"Fine." He nodded.

Kenzie groped for something else to say, some other excuse

to linger in his momentarily agreeable company just a few seconds longer.

She came up short, and settled on, "See you then."

He nodded farewell, then touched the brim of his hat like the gentleman cowboy his mother had raised. Exactly the sort of rodeo-adoring, cattle-assessing, principle-defending man Kenzie had hungered for on the few occasions she let herself dream at all.

Except he was also Jesse Singer, a man she trusted about as much as her own father—not at all.

She'd go along with whatever scheme he cooked up, she decided as she headed for her truck. She had to see what he was up to, for one thing. Keep an eye on him and make sure that diatribe to Custer wasn't just for her benefit, to throw her off the scent.

And on the off chance he was serious about putting a dent in Custer's plan, she'd come up with a few of her own ideas, too.

At worst she'd know he was aiming for Custer's prize and, as such, was far more treacherous and deceitful than she'd given him credit for.

At best he'd be her unlikely ally. A chance for the two top stock contractors to act in unity against this enemy of their sport.

An opportunity to protect the one thing they both loved before it vanished forever.

Chapter Seven

"How you?" Trixie dropped onto the end of the couch.

Jesse smiled, setting aside the contract he hadn't been reading anyway, and joined the game they'd been playing since he was ten and she was a chubby-cheeked three-year-old.

"Good. How you?"

She considered. "Bored. How you?"

"Tired. How you?"

"Also tired. *What* are you doing?" She broke their rhythm as she took in his makeshift office.

It was raining in Oklahoma, which merited celebration after a long, dry summer. Jesse had decamped in what his mom called the living room, one of the ranch house's many high-ceilinged spaces, with huge windows occupying an entire wall.

Hugo Singer had built the house in the early twentieth century, then Arnold Singer—Jesse's grandfather—had raised the roof and expanded it. Family legend held that he wanted to woo his future wife, Annie, away from her parents' grocery-store empire in Idaho, albeit less for her sake than to impress the exacting, Lithuanian woman who would become his mother-in-law.

Jesse never bought that. His grandmother enjoyed the finer things in life, but she'd also been a shrewd business partner, the analytical foil to his grandfather's gregariousness. Arnold was more likely the one who wanted light and air and lots of expensive glass. Annie would've been fine with a lick of paint.

He'd loved his grandparents. By the time he was born they'd

traded the ranch house for the single-story, two-bedroom property where his parents lived now, and Jesse had spent half his childhood riding out there to see them.

Annie and Arnold had moved there joyfully, excited to pass on the oversize family home to a growing gaggle of grandchildren, just as Hugo and Frida had done for them. Arnold gradually withdrew from the rodeo business, yet they kept busy, always on their way to somewhere. When they came to the ranch house for the holidays it was practically a red-carpet occasion. Jesse's fondest memories were of his grandmother murmuring the blessing over the candles, his grandfather straightening his kippah, the two of them whistling and hooting like they were rounding up horses as Jesse and his siblings raced to find the afikomen at Passover.

"Hey." Trixie kicked him, jerking his attention from the rain running down the glass and the low, gray sky beyond.

"Sorry, what did you say?"

"I asked what you were doing. You shouldn't be working today." She gestured to the stacks of papers and the laptop on the coffee table.

"I'm not working. I'm atoning."

He ignored Trixie's eye roll. Today was Yom Kippur, so his guilty ruminations were more structured than usual, but he'd been atoning every day for two years. Every email, every phone call, every dogged negotiation with a supplier or a creditor were his attempts to undo the harm he'd caused by not being here. To earn his brother's forgiveness, even if he was no longer around to offer it.

"Well, if you have anything you'd like to apologize to me for, I'm all ears." She stretched out on the enormous sofa, her ankles crossed and her toes brushing his thigh.

"There is something I've been meaning to do. I've been waiting for the right moment, and I think it's finally here."

Her head popped up from the cushion, her brows drawn together in concern. "What is it?"

"You know I love you, right?"

"Of course I do. I love you, too. What's wrong?"

"Then I hope you'll forgive me when I—" He moved fast, grabbing her ankles and mercilessly tickling the soles of her bare feet.

"Stop! Jesse, stop it!" Trixie squealed, laughing and wriggling, then hurled a cushion at his head, hitting him square in the temple.

He let her go, grinning as she scrambled to the end of the couch.

He loved Trixie. He loved all his sisters, and they brought out the best in him, in their own way. Billie steadied him. Mae encouraged him.

Trixie set him free.

Tzipporah on her birth certificate—though he couldn't remember anyone ever calling her that—the youngest Singer was flippant, fiery and foulmouthed. She was the antithesis of the polite humility and graciousness that rodeo expected from its female athletes, which, combined with her last name, divided opinion about her more than her record-setting barrel-racing times deserved. She was funny and foolish, and he'd do anything for her, had been wrapped around her finger since she was old enough to crook it. Hell, he'd cut off one of his own if it guaranteed her happiness.

His gaze drifted to the contract he'd been reviewing when she came in, an agreement Lee had signed with a pest-control company to do quarterly checks on the horse barn—the barn housing Billie's champion buckers and Trixie's high-octane racers. They were on the hook for another year of exorbitant monthly fees, and Jesse was combing the text for an exit. He hadn't mentioned it to Trixie or Billie. As soon as he'd squirmed out of the deal, he'd tell them it lapsed, then present them with a stack of hardware-store traps and his blessing to get another barn cat.

"You're evil," she informed him.

If only she knew how accurate that was.

"Then don't put your smelly feet on me."

"And you're rude. Be nice to me or I'll tell Mom."

The playful threat landed like a toddler smacking the keys in the middle of a piano sonata: loud, discordant, unintended, unignorable. They both sobered, the mood darkening as if the heavy, thick clouds outside had shuffled through a crack in the door and settled against the ceiling.

"Mae and I went out to see them this morning," he said.

Trixie winced. "I know. I'm sorry I didn't go with you. I know this is a me problem, and I need to work on it, it's just… I want to shake them sometimes, you know? Yes, Lee is gone, and it sucks, and they're sad. We're all sad. But sad can't be all we are. We have to live, and do stuff, and go places. Lee would hate to see them moping around, barely leaving the house, letting their world get smaller and smaller. It's disrespectful."

She slapped her hand over her mouth, then dropped it to reveal a sheepish expression. "I'm sorry. That's so unfair. I'm trying to be kinder about all of this, I swear."

Jesse lifted a shoulder. "I don't disagree with you. This isn't how I want them to spend their retirement. It's not what Lee would want, either. I just don't know how to reach them. They're so deep in this grief, they can barely hear us. Mae told them this morning they should go spend the weekend in Oklahoma City, and it was like she'd suggested they fly to the moon."

"People who spent forty years crisscrossing the country hauling roughstock."

Trixie sighed. "They both need therapy, but that'll never happen. What're we going to do, Jesse?"

"I don't know." He didn't: he'd shelved this problem. His parents were struggling, but they were safe. The same couldn't be said for Singer Pro Rodeo, or for the sport as a whole if Custer squashed the League.

Survival was his priority.

Thriving could happen later.

Which reminded him…

"Kenzie Wallace is coming over this afternoon."

Trixie's brows shot up. "Really? Will there be a duel? Can I watch?"

"We're meeting under a flag of truce to discuss Casey Custer and Supreme Rodeo." He caught her up on their discussion with Custer at Justin's production sale.

"Well, if anyone can take him down, it's you two. You've got the brawn and the brains, and she's got that wild-animal vibe. Like you're not sure she should be out in the daytime, and she might be diseased, and she's thinking about biting you in the face."

Jesse couldn't argue with any part of that description.

"Shout if you need backup. I'll be right outside the door, most likely with my ear pressed against it, listening for sounds of violence." Trixie stood.

"I'll be on my best behavior. But if she cuts my throat, promise you won't let her leave the ranch."

"She'll reside here for all eternity," Trixie assured him sweetly, then padded out of the room.

Jesse turned back to the windows. Gray mist obscured the horizon, concealing the vast stretch of Singer acreage. For a moment he could almost believe this was it, the sum of his concerns—a big house on a generous lot, and the lone barn he could just make out in the distance. No bulls, no horses, no sisters, no staff, no parents, no pressure.

Except he knew better than anyone what lay beyond this truncated view. The dreams. The ambitions. The triumphs and the defeats.

The past and the future of America's oldest and only Jewish rodeo dynasty.

Jesse sighed, already missing that momentary sense of smallness. Then he picked up his phone and dialed the pest-control company's number, ready to raise hell.

Kenzie hadn't expected it to be this hard.

As she drove beneath the metal letters spelling SINGER over the ranch gate, Kenzie rolled down the windows. The air was fresh and cool after the rain. The storm banished the last of the summer heat, the fields on either side of the gravel road dewy and verdant.

If she didn't know better, she might believe she recognized the smell of this place. That the land bounded by the Singer fence was somehow lusher and more dignified. Rich with the passion and commitment of the family that owned it.

Kenzie treasured every minute of the eight years she'd been part of the Singer story. She still had three copies of the trade magazine where her promotion to operations manager had been announced. That tiny box of text in a bottom corner was like a neon sign in Vegas, declaring her worth to the whole industry—including her father.

She imagined him reading it, like she imagined his reaction to almost everything she did. He probably grumbled at first, huffing about her mother's obnoxious lawsuit and mean-spirited attempt to destroy his life.

But then he'd soften. Read it a second time, and a third. Admit that Singer Pro Rodeo was the real deal, and she'd made a big move for someone her age, not to mention a woman.

You did good, kid. Then he'd smile, proud of who his daughter had become.

Until he heard she'd been fired.

Kenzie's mood darkened as the ranch house came into view. No matter how nice he was today, how constructive or helpful, she had to stay clear-eyed about Jesse Singer. He was incapable of love or care. A man who cruelly destroyed the lives of those with nothing and kept everything for himself.

Another version of her father. Another man who refused to recognize her worth. Who couldn't look beyond his own selfish interests to see the hardworking, sincere-hearted, amazing woman standing right in front of him.

Well, crap. Now she was going to cry.

"No, I'm not." She took a right at the fork.

The ranch office, a mid-century extension, had its own driveway and entrance, supposedly because the reigning Mrs. Singer at the time hadn't wanted ranch hands tromping through the house in muddy boots. Kenzie parked her truck on the grass and jumped down from the cab, crossed the gravel and rapped on the door.

She spent the minute it took Jesse to answer deciding this was a personal slight and an attempt to exert his power over the situation. Then he opened the door, and he was so goddamn handsome her ire melted away.

The dark hair normally tucked under a cowboy hat was mussed, as if he'd been running his hand through it. Jeans and a T-shirt wrapped his long frame, and although his eyes were shadowed and his face drawn, his smile seemed genuine.

"Hey. Thanks for coming." He stepped aside, letting her pass into the office.

"No problem. It's nice to see the place again. Been a while."

She'd meant it honestly, but as he shut the door behind her, she cringed at how barbed that sounded. She didn't want this meeting to be combative, not with the Custer clock ticking, so she plastered on a smile and spun to take in the room, poised to praise his decorative changes whether she liked them or not.

But he hadn't made any.

The office looked like Lee had just stepped into the kitchen to make coffee. His sunny personality and refusal to take life seriously were everywhere, from the brightly painted cow skull on the wall, to the jokey sign warning I Am the Boss of You on his desk.

The desk Jesse sat down behind.

Stern, severe Jesse Singer was so at odds with this environment, Kenzie winced.

Her sympathy weighed heavily as she dropped into a chair, understanding his reluctance to erase his brother's presence. She still had Lee's number in her phone, still replayed his voice mails, still scrolled through his texts when she needed to remember that someone had believed in her once.

What was it like for Jesse to come into this office every morning, and sit in his dead brother's seat to do his dead brother's job? No wonder he was always pissed off. He lurched through life in the footsteps of a ghost, following a path not made for his boots.

He watched her, one brow arched in challenge.

"It's just like Lee left it," she said.

"Hard to find time to redecorate when you've got an ex-employee with a vendetta," he snapped, then pressed his hand over his eyes. "Sorry. It's Yom Kippur. I'm starving."

"It's okay." She meant it—mostly.

"Congratulations on Saturday." He attempted a smile, referring to the Broken B outscoring Singer at last weekend's rodeo.

She wondered how much that cost him. "Thanks. So, Custer."

"Custer." Jesse scanned the desk for a notebook.

"His first event is on Saturday, in Chicago."

Jesse flipped to a clean page. "Perfectly timed against the Grundy County Rodeo."

"I assume Singer Pro Rodeo will be traveling to Grundy."

"We always do."

"The Broken B will be there, too."

"We're not bringing the top stock, though. Too far, too late in the season. Plus, I want to see the damage to the rider lineup now that we're competing with Custer."

"Same. We won't know the true impact until the cowboys draw their bulls."

Jesse frowned. "Are we playing into his strategy? It's easier to tempt the cowboys away if the alternative is a bunch of second-tier bulls."

Kenzie shrugged. "Maybe. But we have to risk it. The season's almost over, and the guys who've punched their tickets for the League finals will lay low, anyway. The only ones riding now will be on the bubble, trying to earn enough to make it into the top fifteen."

"And Supreme Rodeo earnings wouldn't count toward that total. You're right—the ones who need League rides will attempt them, and the ones who don't might not have shown up anyway."

She grinned. "See, I'm not as dense as you think."

"I've never thought that."

She had to look away from the blue eyes that suddenly made her want to fidget and hide. "Point is, there are still too many unknowns in this situation. That's why I'm planning to buy a ticket to Custer's event, and you should come with me."

"You'd skip Grundy County on Saturday?"

She nodded.

"Would we tell people we're going?"

"That sounds like you're in."

"It's a good idea, and probably the only way we'll know what we're dealing with. I'm just wondering whether both of us should be there. How that'll look, and what we'll say."

Kenzie stiffened. "Is this your way of sending me to Supreme Rodeo, then telling everyone I'm a traitor while you're back at Grundy?"

One side of his mouth quirked. "Didn't occur to me, but I like it. I was more suspicious that you wanted to check out Custer's event so you'd be better prepared to bid for his business."

"Then why would I ask you to go with me?"

"Hadn't gotten that far."

She rolled her eyes. “If we’re going to do this, we have to trust each other. Can we declare a ceasefire, at least as far as Custer is concerned?”

Jesse hesitated, his gaze tilting skyward before resettling on her with crisp determination.

“Yes. We can do that.”

He extended his hand over the desk. She leaned forward to shake it, and nearly reeled when the brief, dizzying tightening of his fingers around hers brought back their night on the bleachers.

The confident press of his lips. The slide of his tongue. The solidity of his shoulders, of his thighs, of his body pressing into hers, big and strong and unafraid.

Kenzie prided herself on her clear-eyed approach to sex. She was too shrewd, too skeptical, and too cautious to let her squishy feelings override her reason.

Yet when Jesse looked at her like he did now, so still, his eyes bright and blazing, she wanted to crawl into his lap and close her eyes against his neck. Let him wrap her up in his arms until her worries faded away. He’d protect her—he was that type. He stood in front of what he cherished and bore the worst the world could throw at it. He’d fight for her like he fought for his sisters. Like he fought for the dirt beneath the office’s hardwood floor.

He’d fight for someone, she corrected, withdrawing her hand from his tight grip. Not her. Never her.

“Why aren’t you married?” The question tumbled from her mouth before she had the good sense to stop it.

Jesse had that effect on her.

He sat back in the big leather chair, lacing his fingers over his stomach as amusement toyed with the edges of his lips.

“Because I’m a jerk. You know that.”

“Plenty of women out there who love jerks. Figured you would’ve found one, at your age.”

“I’m only two years older than you.”

“More than enough time.”

"I bet you didn't ask my brother these sorts of questions."

"I knew why your brother was single."

Jesse sat up straight, bristling. "What's that supposed to mean?"

She smiled. Yeah, he was the protective type all right.

"Dial it down, cowboy. I know Lee was gay. Yes, he told me himself, and no, I've never told another soul. And I never will, without him here to give me permission."

"He told you?"

"We were really close."

You'd know that if you ever came home to visit. She shoved that bitter, unfair thought aside. Lee never wanted help, especially not from the high-flying younger brother he bragged about every chance he got.

"I didn't think anyone outside the family knew."

"Maybe it was just me—I don't know. I do know he'd finally gotten serious with that guy in Austin, but he broke it off because he was afraid of the damage it would do to the business if anyone found out."

Jesse dragged his hand over his face, his defensive posture wilting. "I told him not to worry. We all did, from the day he came out to my parents in high school. My dad swore that Lee's happiness was his priority, and if rodeo could find its way around Jewish stock contractors, it could handle a gay man. Lee never felt ready, though. At least that's what he said."

"Maybe he didn't feel ready, or maybe he didn't feel safe. Either way, it sucks. He deserved better, and I hate that he never found his space in our community."

"I hate it, too. But I'm glad he could talk to you about it. He must've really trusted you."

"I've never felt so honored to be let in on a secret. And we had way too much fun with his dating app." She grinned.

Jesse straightened. "Chicago. I'll buy a ticket."

"I'll book a hotel room near the venue. It finishes late."

"I'll do the same. Any excuse not to sleep in an RV with my sisters."

"Great. We've got a plan."

Jesse nodded.

Kenzie glanced around the office, oddly reluctant to leave. The initial sting of loss had worn off, and she liked being back here. The Singer ranch had always welcomed her, made her feel at home, and this afternoon was no exception, even though she no longer had any claim on this place and never would again.

Jesse wasn't in a hurry to get rid of her, either. He watched her, his silence relaxed and patient.

Her gaze traveled over his shoulder to the window. The sun had dropped in that startlingly swift way of early fall. Streaks of gold reached across the land, and the clumped shape of a herd huddled past the fence.

"Are those the two-year-olds?" She moved past his desk to the window.

Jesse's chair squeaked as he rose. Then he was beside her, so close their arms would brush if she shifted her weight.

"No, those are the pairs."

Kenzie studied the multicolored array of mother cows with their long-legged calves. Their white or red or black or brown or speckled hides added up to a rich, earthy mix, like a Thanksgiving centerpiece. The moms stood at ease, their instinctive vigilance diluted by the comforting proximity of their babies, while the calves drank or ambled or sniffed the ground, their young worlds free from stress or danger.

A fat, sluggish June bug dropped onto a black calf's flanks. His hind legs shot up, his back bowing in the perfect shape to dislodge a determined cowboy. Kenzie gasped and grabbed Jesse's arm, too exhilarated by the raw skill on display to second-guess herself. Normal beef or dairy cows couldn't do what this calf was doing. He came from more than a hundred years of careful breeding, transforming dull, slow-moving livestock into talented, clever animal athletes whose desire to perform matched their strength and vigor.

Ninety-nine percent of people would see a baby cow kicking off an insect. For Kenzie, this was breathtaking.

The calf bucked twice more, his movements powerful and elegant as he tossed his head, as if he'd shown that bug who was boss.

"Did you see that?" She squeezed Jesse's arm harder, then let go, hoping the expanding shadows concealed the flush in her cheeks.

But Jesse wasn't looking at her. He watched the herd, his smile dreamy, his voice barely more than a murmur. "I saw it."

And she saw him like she never had before. In that moment he wasn't the heartless corporate outsider who'd fired her, who'd swept into the business he'd always ignored and taken control without a hint of humility or compassion. He wasn't the cold, hard-nosed aggressor who only cared about money, and he wasn't the unbidden interloper inserting himself into a community he'd abandoned.

Right now, Kenzie saw more. Affection and admiration she understood deeply.

Jesse was a stock contractor. A born and bred Oklahoman. A rodeo scion who lived and breathed and loved this sport, even if he hadn't always been here to show it.

He turned to her, as if he could hear the metallic scrape of her defenses slipping. In the gathering dusk his eyes practically glowed with intent, and she knew what he was thinking, because she was thinking it, too.

Kiss me.

She could start—she could make the first move. She could slide her arm around his narrow waist and press into his hard chest. She could shove her hand into his dark hair, lose her fingers in its softness. She could push up on her toes, tilt her chin, and bring her lips to his.

Nothing stopped her, and her heart raced at the idea. He wanted her—it was written in every taut line of his body. He wouldn't object. No one had to know. This could exist outside the rest of their lives, just like that night on the bleachers.

Her fingers twitched at her side. He swallowed. She wet her lips.

Do it.

Their phones pinged simultaneously, cheery electronic chimes instantly discordant in their unison.

Jesse cleared his throat as he reached for the phone on his desk. Kenzie pivoted away from the window, taking hers out of her pocket.

Submission Confirmation. Kenzie read the short email acknowledging the list of bulls she'd nominated for consideration for the League finals. Jesse lowered his phone at the same time, having received the same form reply.

"There goes my hope that you might miss the submission deadline," she joked.

"My list was in a day early."

Of course it was. She'd never underestimated Jesse's competitiveness, but she'd misjudged his passion. The way he'd watched that bucking calf gave her new respect for him as a cattleman—and new wariness for him as an opponent.

But she'd agreed to the truce, so she'd set that aside for now. Their nominations were in, and the bulls selected for the big show in December would be announced next month. Then it was down to each of them to ensure their animals won Bull of the Year.

For now, they were allies. And if they didn't stop Custer from steamrolling the sport, there'd be no more Bull of the Year plaques for anyone.

"I should go," she said. "The sun's almost down. I don't want to stand between you and your dinner."

"You couldn't if you tried, but I appreciate the thought."

She scanned the office once more. Her gaze snagged on the peeling corners of a two-year-old Singer production-sale flyer, and a sun-bleached Western lifestyle magazine with a now-retired steer wrestler on the cover.

"This office needs a facelift." She knew with every ounce of her heart it was what Lee would want her to say. She could almost hear him teasing Jesse about finally getting the shrine he deserved. Lee would've hated to see him so sad—and so stuck.

Kenzie expected Jesse to rear at her comment. Instead, he looked surprised, blinking at their surroundings as if he'd only just realized where he was.

She charged ahead. "This isn't your style. I don't know what your style is, but it's not funny desk signs and bobbleheads."

"No, but…"

But.

She understood perfectly. That short word held a lot, all of it awful. Grief. Sorrow. Regret. Aching for what used to be. Mourning what never would.

She picked up the magazine. "I wouldn't mind having this."

He studied the cover, then the rectangle it left in the thin layer of dust on the coffee table. "Go ahead."

"Thank you kindly." She tucked the magazine under her arm. "Let me know when you've got your ticket for Chicago. We'll figure out who we're telling and what we're saying."

Jesse dragged his attention to her before it drifted back to the table. "I'll be in touch."

"See you soon." Kenzie let herself out of the office. She threw her truck into gear as soon as her seat belt clicked.

Their meeting had gone better than she imagined, yet she was leaving more discomfited than ever. She wanted to hate Jesse—she *needed* to hate Jesse—and now here she was, all sympathetic and gooey-hearted for a man who'd nearly ruined her whole damn life.

For Lee, she told herself as she left the way she came. For the hole he'd left in the world, and the tomorrows he'd never enjoy.

"Liar." The word trembled in the quiet cab. She missed Lee, but she'd mourned him. This jagged ache was new because it was for Jesse. For the years with his brother he'd missed, for his desperate attempt to reverse into a space where he didn't fit, and for his impulse to show her, of all people, his pain, because protecting his family meant protecting them from his sadness, too.

She'd kept Lee's most closely held secret, and she'd keep this one for Jesse. Not because they were friends, and not because she liked him. Because she was a decent, loyal person, and everyone deserved one of those in their lives.

Even Jesse Singer.

Instead of driving back to the Broken B, Kenzie diverted to the Sinclair station in Caddo City, the thousand-person town halfway between the two properties. She put gas in the tank, bought a Diet Dr Pepper and sat in the driver's seat, methodically ripping the magazine to shreds. Page after page reduced to fragments the size of puzzle pieces and just as inscrutable. When she finished, she gathered up the glossy remains and shoved them into the gas-station trash can.

Kenzie stepped back and tilted her head toward the rapidly darkening sky. Jews didn't believe in the same heaven Christians did, so she wasn't sure where Lee's soul had ended up, but she thought of him as being somewhere overhead. Bright and free alongside the stars he'd always outshone.

"I'm going to beat his ass in the arena, but I promise I'll be nicer to him on the sidelines," she told Lee, her face tipped up. "Don't fret, boss. I got you covered."

"He says thank you."

Kenzie's gaze shot to the burly man standing outside the gas station, his black hair in two braids over his shoulders, his wrists nearly as thick as the foam cup in his hand.

"You reckon he heard me, huh?"

The man nodded. “He always does.”

“I wasn’t talking to God.”

“I know.” The man winked, then climbed into one of the oldest pickups Kenzie had seen in a while and pulled out of the lot.

Kenzie glanced skyward one more time, her eyes narrowed in thought. Then she climbed back into her own truck and headed home, her head quiet, her heart content.

Chapter Eight

The cowboy adjusted his grip on the rigging one more time, lay all the way back so his neck was just above the horse's flanks, and raised his free hand. He nodded. The gate sprang open, and the Grundy County Rodeo was underway.

Matilda, the chestnut bucking horse hand-raised by Billie Singer, leaped out and kicked like there was no tomorrow, her powerful build unrecognizable from the sickly foal she'd once been. The bareback rider's hat flew off, but he clung on, the padded neck roll strapped around his throat protecting his spine from the worst of the impacts. The crowd packing the fairground bleachers cheered and whistled, loud enough to compete with the heavy rock music pouring from the speakers as the seconds ticked up. Five seconds, six, six and a half…

The chestnut twisted mid-jump, putting blue sky between her and the rider. He landed off-center and Jesse knew that was the end. Once a cowboy lost his lower-body grip, recovery was nearly impossible. Sure enough, the next kick sent him flying less than half a second before the buzzer.

For a stock contractor this was triumphant; for the audience it was sympathetic. A collective "oh" warmed the arena as the cowboy hobbled to retrieve his hat, while Billie and Wyatt rode up to the chestnut and ushered her out.

"Let's give this cowboy some love, because that's all he's going home with tonight," the announcer urged, and applause filled the late-afternoon air.

"Matilda's in good form," Jesse remarked to Trixie.

Trixie stood beside him along the pipe fence beside the chutes, taking notes on Billie's horses. "She just bought us dinner, that's for sure."

Jesse hummed his agreement, surveying the arena while the next cowboy mounted up in the chute.

Apart from its proximity to Chicago, the annual Grundy County Fair and Rodeo was nondescript. From the prizewinning pies and quilts displayed in the Parks and Rec building, to the traveling carnival adjacent to the outdoor arena, this event matched hundreds of others around the country. The accents varied, as did the weather and the price tags of the cars in the lots, but their souls were the same. A once-a-year community gathering to set aside the pressures of modernity and cheer on the age-old contest of man versus beast.

Rodeo was straightforward and simple: hang on for eight seconds and get paid. For a couple of hours, everyone could pretend that life was fair, and full of equal chances. That the American dream persisted, and with enough grit and determination and refusal to give up, anyone could win.

Jesse knew better than most that was a myth. He'd moved among both the inconceivably wealthy and the down-and-out cowboys skipping meals to buy gas. He knew neither fate was necessarily deserved, and certainly not always earned.

Still, he loved the rodeo, loved this way of life, and would choose it every time. He loved the barrel man's corny jokes and the announcer's theatrical play-by-plays. He loved the tiny towns and the long drives. He loved the beaten-up pipe fences and the thick-thighed rodeo queens galloping around the arena with flags advertising local car dealerships. He loved the mediocre renditions of the national anthem and the awkwardness of army reservists as they stood through overlong military salutes. He loved the competitors who refused to be disheartened, who showed up week after unsuccessful week to try again, unshakable in the belief that this would be their turn for glory.

Rodeo could be brutal and hard and defeating, and it sure as hell wasn't inclusive, but it was honest. If enough people like him stuck around and supported it, they could keep dragging it forward, opening it up little by little until these arenas were safe, welcoming places for everyone.

For you, Lee.

"Ready to go?" Kenzie Wallace appeared at his elbow, her bleached hair tucked under a trucker hat.

Jessie's gaze meandered to her breasts before he could stop it, catching a thrilling impression of a sleeveless shirt pulled taut in all the right places before he yanked his eyes to the time on the scoreboard. He reminded himself for the millionth time to think with his brain, not his dick. He wasn't accustomed to this problem, but Kenzie pushed his limits where he never thought they'd go.

After she left his office on Yom Kippur, he'd felt more at peace than he had since he got the call that Lee was dead. Plenty of other, more important people in his life had given him tacit permission to depart from his brother's systems and make this job his own, but no one had ever plucked up a relic of Lee's presence and walked it out the door.

He'd stared at that gap in the dust for a good long while, waiting for the guilt, the regret, the anger at letting Kenzie interfere. Instead, he was unencumbered, and after breaking his fast with his sisters, he'd returned to the office. He'd wiped the table clean, then placed a statue of a saddle bronc mid-buck in its center. The bronze ornament had belonged to his great-grandfather, and Jesse liked the rider's classic pose—his arm flung out, his body stretched to counter the horse's nose-down movement. An iconic image of the rodeo. He thought Lee would approve.

Of course, the technique and finesse of saddle bronc riding—one of rodeo's founding events—were lost on Casey Custer, because buck-offs were rare and injuries rarer. Which was why that event was left out of the Supreme Rodeo Series altogether.

Jesse turned to Kenzie with fresh resolve. He was a man on a mission, and his libido would have to toe the line.

"Ready," he confirmed.

"I'll drive," she offered.

He didn't argue. Let her put the wear and tear on the Broken B's vehicle. He wasn't in the market for a mechanic's bill.

Trixie looked up from her notebook. "Y'all have a name for your little spy mission? Project Sooner? Sooner Strike Force?"

"Sooners Strike Back," Kenzie suggested.

Jesse shook his head. "This is serious. We need a serious name. Operation Death Knell."

Both women drew back.

He glanced between them. "What?"

Trixie wrinkled her nose. "You really took it there."

"It was the delivery. Sounded legit homicidal." Kenzie nodded toward the parking lot. "Come on, we'll be late."

"Be home by curfew." Trixie winked.

"Death Knell's not a bad name for a bull," Kenzie mused once they'd traded the buzzing arena for the grassy area where the contractors and competitors parked.

"Shouldn't put words like *dead* or *death* or *kill* in a bull's name. Bad luck."

"What about Buck Knell? Buzzer Knell. Bucky Knell. Buck-off Knell. Bad Knell? Or maybe I need to leave knell enough alone."

Jesse burst out laughing at her cringeworthy pun, surprising himself.

Kenzie grinned. "I've got a million more where that came from."

"I'll take your word for it."

"Not a chance. Brace yourself for wall-to-wall dad jokes from here to Chicago."

Jesse groaned as he climbed into the cab of the Broken B–branded truck. The newer vehicle was more spacious than his own, and the interior smelled like irises.

Like her.

At the gate Kenzie stopped to let one of the bullfighters, Rob Astley, pass in front of the truck. Recognizing them through the windshield, he stepped to the cab window. Kenzie rolled it down, and he leaned on the frame, grinning beneath the white crucifixes painted on his gaunt cheeks.

"How about that! Two sworn enemies going for a drive. They finally kick y'all off the grounds for fighting?" Rob asked.

"We got tickets to Supreme Rodeo in Chicago. Want to know what we're up against." Kenzie adhered to her and Jesse's texted agreement that in a whisper-happy community like theirs, honesty would be the best policy.

Concern cut through Rob's cheery expression. He had three kids, two bad knees, and was one of the older bullfighters on the circuit. Not a likely candidate for Custer's glamorous outfit.

"Be interested to hear what you find out." He brightened. "Hey, Singer, nice to see you back out. We missed you and your sisters these last couple of weekends."

"We had the Jewish holidays," Jesse explained.

"Gotcha. Well, I'll tell you what I always do. When you're ready to talk about Jesus, I'm here for you, buddy. I serve a mighty Lord and I'd love for you to know him."

Jesse sketched a salute and Rob pushed off the truck.

Kenzie pulled past Rob to the road, then gaped at Jesse over the gearshift. "Did he really just say that to you?"

"He usually does."

"I knew we had some hardcore evangelicals in our midst, but I thought they'd be polite enough to leave the Jews alone."

Jesse shrugged. "I'm used to it. I won't change his mind, and he won't change mine. No point getting het up about it."

She tossed him a sideways glance. "Never thought I'd say this, but you're being too nice. You should've told him where to stuff his Bible."

"And let word get around that I'm persecuting Christians? Not a chance. Some people in this industry accept us, but lots more only tolerate us. If we want to keep the door open for other Jews—for anyone on the margins—we have to be pragmatic, careful, and beyond reproach."

"Sounds exhausting."

"It's what I've chosen, and what my sisters have chosen."

Kenzie drummed her fingers on the steering wheel. "I get it, sort of. Not a lot of women stock contractors out there. Feels like I've spent my whole life trying to prove myself. Like there's always someone I need to impress, who'll laugh at me if I fail."

"On the upside, I bet no one tries to convert you to become a man."

Kenzie laughed. "Not yet, anyway."

"Never say never with this crowd."

"Ain't that the dang truth."

The hour-long drive into Chicago passed comfortably. Their conversation stayed within professional boundaries, sticking to high-level topics well away from their rivalry, before devolving into a team effort to navigate the urban traffic. Kenzie punctuated each sentence with at least three profanities, Jesse winced as other drivers flew past her stalwart dedication to the speed limit, and eventually they found a spot in a multistory parking garage near the lakeside arena.

"Maybe you should drive back." Kenzie slid down from the cab.

"Might not need to. Look at the hourly rate for this place. I don't think we can afford to leave."

She peered at the sign and groaned. "For real? This is on top of Custer's stupid ticket prices. I could go to ten small-town rodeos for what I paid. Probably more, if they're doing the discount for a donation to the food bank."

"We're not Custer's target demographic. Let's go see who is."

Their bootheels echoed through the quiet parking garage, but as they neared the arena, the sound blended in with hundreds of other pairs just like theirs.

Sort of.

Jesse's parents and grandparents had drummed into him and his siblings that rodeo was for everyone, and anyone was entitled to call themselves a fan whether it was their first time or their thirtieth. There was no right way to dress, no right way to watch, no requirement to be from a farm, or a small town, or have ever seen a horse in person before you rooted for one to buck off a cowboy. Rodeo was starved for audiences, and the sport had no business turning anyone away.

Jesse clung to that as they moved through a crowd of people wearing fake-leather boots and novelty hats. They were here, and they were enthusiastic, and that was good for rodeo. He'd be a hell of a lot happier if they were an hour south in Grundy County, but this was a start.

And if he didn't look down, he wouldn't see all those hems squeezing the ankles of boots like Noah's ark was ready to board.

Kenzie stuck close to his side as they joined the line to get in, her eyes wide, her head on a swivel. He fought an itchy impulse to put his arm around her shoulders and pull her close, which worsened when a trio of men in expensive button-down shirts and cheap bolo ties approached them.

"Bro, that buckle is awesome. Where'd you get it?"

Jesse looked down at the intricately carved, silver buckle on his belt from last year's League finals. "Vegas."

"No way, I'm going there next month for my bachelor party. What store?"

"I won it." He'd known guys like these in New York, early-career bankers or lawyers or whatever looking for fun ways to spend their hefty paychecks. They didn't need a lecture on pro rodeo's highest honors, nor would they ever travel out to a Pro Rodeo League event.

But they were here.

Vegas Bachelor Party raised his fist for a bump. "Yo, that's badass."

"Just got lucky." Jesse tapped the guy's fist with his own.

"I like your buckle, too." One of Bachelor Party's henchmen dropped his gaze to the smaller, older, cinched version Kenzie wore.

Jesse's magnanimous mood popped like a balloon. He slung his arm around Kenzie, glared at Sleazy Sidekick, and put every ounce of unhinged Oklahoman he had in him—which was a lot, it turned out—into a terse, silent shake of his head.

All three men stepped back. Sidekick raised his hands in apology.

"We're cool, dog. You two enjoy the show." Bachelor Party rounded up his bros and hightailed it to the back of the line.

Jesse watched them go, eyes narrowed.

Kenzie elbowed him in the ribs and shrugged out of his grip. "The hell was that?"

"I'm sorry, did you want to go on a date with a man wearing a plastic bolo tie and so much cologne it practically left a puddle? Because I can go get him."

"Obviously not. Doesn't mean I need you to fend him off. I can take care of my damn self."

"I'll remember that next time." He decided to ignore the little wound she'd opened.

Once inside they bypassed the eye-wateringly expensive concessions and grimaced at the merchandise booth, where images of American flags, cow skulls and pistols were screen printed on everything from sweatshirts to scented candles.

"The pistols are so you can shoot yourself when you realize you remortgaged your house to buy popcorn and a T-shirt," Kenzie muttered.

But the merch line was long, the concessions line even longer. At the door to the arena, Kenzie leaned over and plucked a program from a stack on a table, only to be informed by the staff member standing next to it that each one cost twenty dollars.

They finally made it to their nosebleed seats, which had the virtue of being in the middle of a mostly empty row—meaning people were willing to pay even more to pack the sections below.

"Should've brought binoculars." Jesse wedged his bootheel against the empty seat in front of him.

"Should've brought a sniper rifle. Settle this thing Wild West–style."

"Doc Holliday never—"

The lights in the arena lowered, and the crowd hushed. Red, white and blue lasers sliced through the darkness as a bass-heavy, sped-up remix of Johnny Cash's "Folsom Prison Blues" poured through the speakers. An announcer's voice boomed over the top.

"We've got the toughest, nastiest, deadliest bulls for you here tonight," he promised.

Jesse and Kenzie exchanged a look of distaste.

"And now, ladies and gentlemen, let me introduce your ringmaster for these lethal showdowns—Casey Custer!"

"He's gonna get in the barrel?" Kenzie called over the music.

Casey Custer would not, in fact, be painting his face and climbing into one of the reinforced barrels used by rodeo clowns, because at that moment he appeared in the bed of a six-wheeled pickup, waving his hat at the thunderous crowd.

The truck stopped well away from the chutes—too far to be of any help distracting an agitated bull. Custer took the microphone and reiterated the announcer's spiel, his voice low, his accent ridiculous.

Then the pyrotechnics started.

Fireworks exploded around the edge of the arena and flames shot up from the dirt-covered floor. They didn't stop, minute after minute of earsplitting detonations and hissing flames, while Custer stood in the truck bed grinning like a fool. Jesse had never seen anything so over-the-top, and the audience's initial cheering died down as thick, white smoke and the acrid scent of lit matches filled the arena.

By the time the last firework popped, Jesse's eyes stung and Kenzie was having a coughing fit. He took off his hat and waved it in front of them, trying to dispel the smoke.

"Who's ready for some bulls?" Custer asked from the arena floor, dragging out the last word. The crowd's reply was muted—probably because they were choking on firework fumes.

The announcer explained the unusual Supreme Rodeo structure. A round of bulls, a round of bareback riding, and then a second round of bulls, with the bull riders' winnings determined by an aggregate score.

Bull riding was so hard on the body that cowboys usually preferred not to ride more than once in a night, though they did when they had to. Jesse figured the bareback riding in the middle was intended to give them time to recover. Still, the setup demanded a lot from the riders, and meant Custer needed double the number of bulls, since no contractor worth their salt would ask their animal to perform twice.

Bobbing cowboy hats swarmed the chutes, signaling riders, contractors and staff getting ready. The one-on-one duel between a man and a bull required a surprising number of people. One person had to open the gate, another had to keep an eye on the bull, yet another had to help the rider pull his rope tight, and someone else had to hold the rider's protective vest in case the bull bucked in the chute. And that didn't include the cameraperson, the chute boss, the flankman, the judges or the general event staff.

Somehow Custer had found them all, though Jesse wondered exactly what quality of expertise was back there.

Jesse assumed the fireworks were the opening ceremony, but what came next in no way resembled the humble, earnest sequence of flag, prayer and anthem that was a staple of even the glossiest rodeos on the circuit. Custer's fifteen-minute spectacle involved lifted pickups growling around the arena, a horseback sharpshooter and an athletic dance performance by the Supreme Rodeo cheerleaders.

"The hell is this?" Kenzie gaped at the women in short shorts waving crimson pom-poms.

"A damn circus," Jesse muttered as the rest of the audience clapped in time with the music.

Kenzie shook her head as the cheerleaders lined up on either side of the arena, well within reach of a fired-up bull. "They can't stand there. That's so unsafe. They can't even climb up that siding to get away. Has Custer trained his animals with this many people around?"

"Has he trained them with people holding shiny pom-poms?"

"Let's hope so. I didn't pay all this money to see someone get trampled."

The announcer hyped the bull riding again, then spotlights illuminated the chutes. The first bull's name and picture flashed up on the Jumbotron, followed by the same information for the cowboy.

"Oh, no," he and Kenzie said in unison.

The first rider of the night was Redd Clarence, currently ranked fifth in the League and guaranteed a spot at the finals. Charming, impulsive and incredibly young, Redd had probably already spent the money he was sure he could earn tonight.

And if Redd was here, he wasn't at a Pro Rodeo League event.

Riders needed to win on the best bulls, and bulls needed to buck off the best riders, otherwise the competition fell flat. No one wanted to watch rank bulls tossing amateurs after half a second, nor was it fun to see skilled cowboys stuck to low-velocity animals like they were on a merry-go-round. The excitement was in the tension, the square matchup, the genuine unpredictability of who would come out on top.

If all the best riders jumped ship for Supreme Rodeo, it'd kill the Pro Rodeo League.

Kenzie hunched forward, craning her neck. "I should've sold a kidney and bought a better seat. Do you recognize those bullfighters?"

Jesse squinted at the two men who'd stepped out onto the floor, wearing the bullfighter's characteristically baggy, layered clothing that could be safely torn off by a stray horn.

"I don't think so. Are there no pickup riders?"

They scanned the floor for any sign of the two horseback riders who occasionally needed to rope wayward bulls and escort them through the gate, but they were conspicuously absent.

"Twelve cheerleaders and no pickup riders." Kenzie clucked her tongue in disgust.

"Spent all his money on the pyro, I guess."

Suddenly the music kicked up a notch and Redd appeared on the screen—wearing a cowboy hat instead of a helmet.

In fact, Jesse couldn't see any helmets gleaming behind the chutes. Technically the Pro Rodeo League didn't require them, but nine out of ten cowboys wore them—and the ones who didn't usually changed their minds after their first concussion.

The bull scrabbled against the metal wall of the chute with its front hooves, snorting and tossing its head, making it difficult for Redd to find his seat. Animals who misbehaved in the chute were far deadlier than the ones that bucked hard in the arena. Cowboys could be caught and crushed, their legs broken, their ribs smashed.

Jesse had spent countless childhood hours watching his father chute-train their bulls, offering them treats, scratching their ears, playing music and recorded crowd noise similar to what they'd hear in the arena. Singer bulls' patience and docility before and after they bucked was a long-standing point of pride for the family. As Custer's bull jerked around, Jesse felt like a disapproving dad watching badly behaved children on the playground.

"Redd, you stupid kid," Jesse murmured, full of very real fear for the nineteen-year-old scooting up on his rope.

Up on the Jumbotron Redd looked nervous but determined. He slid up on the bull's back, so his fist on his rope was tight between his legs. He raised his free hand and nodded.

The gate banged open; the bull shot out. The animal had a lot of emotion but little technique, bucking furiously yet without much height, turning in a steady, predictable circle. Redd nailed the eight seconds easily, barely shifting off his rope. The buzzer toned and the bullfighters moved in, waving their hands in front of the bull to slow it down so Redd could dismount.

Then the smooth ride got bumpy.

Redd half rolled, half jumped and landed on his knees in the dirt. He'd gotten one foot under him when the bull spun to face him, lowered his head and charged.

A collective gasp rose from the crowd as Redd staggered out of the way, barely missing the thrust of the bull's sawed-off horns. The bullfighters sprinted after him, but one of them slipped in the tire tracks left over from the preshow, and the other hesitated, meekly flapping his hand at the pissed-off animal instead of shoving himself in front of the cowboy like a true professional.

Redd managed to climb the chute gate, at which point the bull turned toward the nearest row of cheerleaders. He dropped his head and pawed the ground, standing between the women and their nearest exit. Their neat line dissolved into a clump as those closest to the animal backed away.

Jesse was halfway out of his seat when Kenzie clamped her hand on his wrist and pulled him back down.

"You can't do anything. We're too far."

"But those women—the bull—these bullfighters—where the *hell* are the pickup riders?" he spluttered, incoherent with outrage.

The bullfighter who'd fallen regained his feet, darted forward and tapped the bull on his side. That got the animal's attention, and after the bull took a leisurely lap around the arena—exactly the sort of dangerous, time-wasting stunt pickup riders would never permit—he decided he'd had enough attention and made his way through the gate.

Custer had been silent throughout the incident, but as Redd hopped down and unsteadily collected his rope, the son of a billionaire led the audience in a round of applause. As if nothing had happened. As if they hadn't been a bovine whim away from catastrophe.

As if his arrogant incompetence hadn't just endangered every life in the arena.

Jesse shot to his feet. "I need a drink, and I don't care if I have to put up Trixie's horse as collateral to pay for it. You want something?"

"Whatever you're having. If I'm not here when you get back, it's because I've been arrested for wringing Casey Custer's neck."

"Don't worry. I'll sell her other horse to bail you out."

He sidled down the row and jogged down the concrete steps, his legs as shaky as if he'd ridden that bull himself.

Chapter Nine

A jazz trio played at low volume in the back corner of the bar, although none of the suited men and gussied-up women clustered on demurely upholstered chairs seemed to notice. At almost midnight on a Saturday, the atmosphere was refined and sophisticated, with nary an overserved drunk to be found. The lighting was discreet, the colors muted, the furnishings polished and high-end. Even the bartenders wore crisp uniforms and polite smiles. Everything about this place added up to an ideal watering hole for well-heeled professionals to escape the urban rabble.

Well, everything except the two booted and buckled Okies propping up the bar.

"Thank you kindly." Kenzie smiled at the bartender as he set down another round of the cheapest beers they stocked, having apologetically explained they didn't serve pitchers.

Jesse and Kenzie had lasted through the middle of the second slate of bull riding, when watching the exhausted animals stumble and the saddle-sore riders limp became too much. They'd emptied their wallets to get out of the parking garage, checked into the hotel, then headed across the street to this bar.

Now Jesse was in eerily familiar surroundings, acutely aware of how much he'd changed by comparison. For all he knew he'd been here before, another of the immaculately manicured, olive-and-copper, deeply forgettable venues in the blur of business trips to cities he barely saw. That could've been him over there, in a chalk-stripe suit and burgundy tie, nursing a vodka martini, making all the right noises at his client or colleague while simultaneously calculating how best to position himself. How to make money. How to win.

The two years in between felt like a lifetime. That man who went to an expensive gym and rode the subway and sat in meetings was a stranger, someone he wasn't sure he'd ever really known.

"Cheers." Kenzie raised her glass.

Jesse clinked. "Cheers."

She took a long sip before continuing, "As I was saying, we can see all that's wrong with Custer's rodeo, but the audience can't. I don't know how we compete with that."

"I'm not sure we can. That crowd was urban. They were there because it was new and different and close."

"There are urban rodeos. Houston, Austin, Fort Worth, San Antonio." She ticked them off on her fingers.

"All in Texas, where rodeo is part of the culture."

"Puyallup is like an hour from Seattle. Salinas is sort of near San Francisco. There's that one in New Jersey…"

He shook his head. "Stealing his audience is a challenge we can't tackle. We need to focus on keeping our cowboys and our contractors. If he wants to run these things with a bunch of no-name roughstock riders, that's fine, as long as the best are on our bulls."

"Not easy when money talks, and it's pretty much the only language most cowboys speak."

Jesse trailed his thumb through the condensation on his glass. He didn't have a solution to this thorny problem—not yet. He was too deep in the middle to see a way out, too preoccupied with the scale and expense of the circus they'd just watched.

He was also too sober, he decided, and drained half his glass.

Kenzie propped her chin on her hand. "It's the magic, you know? That's what's hard to get across to people. What you only understand if you've experienced it. When I was a kid, the rodeo was the best night of the year—better than Christmas. I got to stay up late, eat popcorn, sit outside in the dark. For a couple of hours everyone is in a good mood, not worrying about bills, or family drama, or dead-end jobs."

He smiled. "You're from Perry, right? Did you go to the rodeo in Guthrie?"

"Too far, too pricey. I went to the Cherokee Strip Rodeo. It's real tiny, not sanctioned by the League. I loved it, though. Wanted to be a barrel racer, but I grew up in town. Didn't learn to ride a horse 'til your dad hired me and I had to."

"Seriously? You didn't grow up on a ranch?"

She shook her head. "Single-wide trailer."

He studied her over the rim of his glass, recalculating a whole load of assumptions. "You're a hell of a cattlewoman for a townie."

"I know." She winked. "Funny part is that my father is a rancher, but he had nothing to do with me until I was a teen-ager. Not even then, really."

"Who is he?"

She waved her hand dismissively. "A big shot in Perry terms. My mom waited tables at his favorite watering hole. He got her pregnant, then wrote her a check to keep her quiet. That ran out pretty fast, so my mom worked two jobs to support us. When I was in middle school, she met Ned, who's now my stepdad. He's basically the nicest man in the world. Ned convinced her to finally take my real father to court, because it was the only way I'd be able to go to college. My father fought hard, but she won, and I got my degree. Still, sometimes I think about the irony that neither of his kids went into agriculture, and here I am, breeding bulls, having never set foot on my own dad's ranch."

She shrugged and sipped her beer as if it was all just an odd twist of fate. A well-worn anecdote she'd repeated hundreds of times.

Jesse didn't buy it.

He also didn't know why she trusted him with this story, but he was inclined to encourage her.

Not because he was interested. He was accumulating knowledge to leverage later, he assured himself.

"No cozy, father-daughter reunion, huh?"

She snorted. "He won't even speak to me."

"That's harsh, Kenzie. I'm sorry."

"Whatever. Gives me incentive to show him what he's missing."

"His loss."

She smiled in a way he'd never seen before. Less brash, less bold. Quiet and small and a thousand times louder.

"I'll drink to that," she said.

They both did, emptying their glasses.

The bartender instantly reappeared, as if he had a sixth sense for refill opportunities. He poured them another round and lingered, his smile friendly and curious as he wiped down imaginary droplets on the bar.

"Where are you two from?"

"Oklahoma," Kenzie supplied.

"Wow, I've never been anywhere near there. Nice place?"

Kenzie shrugged. "It's like Kansas, but fun."

"Never been anywhere near Kansas, either," the bartender admitted. "Is it like Texas?"

"Yes, if Texas had no laws and no money," Jesse answered.

"Sounds awesome. I've lived in Chicago my whole life. I'd love to move somewhere like that."

"Do it. You can always come back," Kenzie urged.

"Nah. I wouldn't fit in. I might visit, though," he said in a way that confirmed he'd already talked himself out of it. He inclined his head in thanks as he moved along the bar to serve someone else.

"Not everyone can take the leap," Jesse said in answer to Kenzie's quizzical expression.

"Guess not. You did, though. Stillwater boy in New York City. I'd ask if it was hard, but I'm sure it was no big deal for a cool customer like you."

"It was a little hard." He relaxed into his slight beer buzz and Kenzie's easy nature. "College was harder, when I was fresh off the ranch. My clothes were wrong, no one understood my accent, and even my name was a joke. By the time I started working, I'd learned to blend in, but my coworkers still poked fun at how slowly I talked."

"I think you talk fancy."

He laughed. "Story of my life. Too country when I was in the city, too city now I'm back in the country."

"You're not *too* city—just a little city. Few more years, lots of Braum's ice cream, and you'll be sucked all the way back in."

"Maybe." He wished that could be true.

"Must've been nice having other Jewish people around though, right? Do you miss that about New York?"

He drummed his fingers on the side of his glass. "I had trouble fitting in with that community, too. Sometimes it made me feel even lonelier."

Jesse had no idea why he'd shared that with her—until he saw the sincerity in her pinched brows and the concern in her thinned lips. He couldn't remember the last time anyone who wasn't his sister had looked at him like that. Like she wanted to know more. Like his happiness mattered.

Like she cared.

"I didn't grow up going to synagogue. There wasn't one to go to," he found himself saying. "Everything we did, we did at home, as a family. But I felt Jewish—very Jewish. How could I not, when it set me apart from everyone I knew? Then I moved East, and I met all these people who were, like, *really* Jewish. Who read Hebrew fluently and observed our religion in ways

I never knew existed. Suddenly I didn't feel Jewish at all—or not Jewish enough, at least."

"Then you come back to Oklahoma and you're so Jewish that Rob the bullfighter is trying to convert you."

"Exactly. But that's how it's always been for me. Too much of one thing or not enough of another."

"That sucks."

He lifted a shoulder. "It bothered me when I was younger, but not now. I have no desire to be who I'm not. Doesn't make me popular, but that's a small price to pay to be myself."

"That's where you and Lee are completely different. He wanted so badly to make everyone around him happy, to be well-liked and trusted. He used to twist himself into a thousand dang knots so he could get to a yes, but not you. You're never afraid to say no."

That hit him like a sucker punch, hard and fast and totally out of nowhere.

She was right, but the way she was right had him reeling. Her words were underpinned by admiration, not distaste. She understood the flaws in Lee's affable approach, and the strength in Jesse's own detachment.

She saw him and who he was, despite everything he'd done.

"Let's get out of here." He signaled the bartender for the check. He needed to move. Needed to see the stars. Needed to get away from this world in which he'd only ever been a tenant, paying his dues to occupy his corner, living and working but never calling it home.

He needed to feel like himself. The man who'd gone back. Who'd stepped in. Who'd save it all.

Jesse paid the bill and led Kenzie out of the bar, into the late-night stillness. The downtown streets were half dead but they wandered them anyway, displaced country folk crossing wide avenues and weaving around skyscrapers. The city was so quiet, the vast spaces so empty, he felt like they'd stepped out of their real lives and into a dream. As if whatever happened next didn't matter, because it wasn't really happening at all.

"Holy crap, is that the river?"

He followed her to the concrete barrier in front of the drop down to the Chicago River. Constellations of man-made lights reflected on its surface, rippling lazily in the breeze.

"They do boat tours along here. Not this late at night, but earlier," he told her.

"That'd be so cool. Do people live in there, you think?" She pointed to a glass-and-steel building on the opposite bank, its smooth, indifferent facade interrupted by illuminated windows scattered across the surface.

"Probably."

"Imagine that."

He didn't want to. He wanted to remain rooted exactly where he was, in between worlds. With Kenzie at his side, the forgiving smudge of nighttime gave him a momentary sense of convergence. Like his old self and his new one had crossed paths, and exchanged a silent, approving nod.

Like all his disparate pieces and parts added up to something worthwhile.

Because of her, he realized as they left the riverside and returned to the labyrinth of tall buildings. Because she'd seen through to who he was, and what he had to offer. She'd acknowledged him. Understood him.

Liked him.

He let that fill him up as they wandered. Gave himself permission to set aside his daylight burdens. For now, he could be only what he saw reflected in Kenzie's eyes as she beamed up at him, without guilt. Without regret, or weariness, or impotent anger at his inability to change what had already happened. Instead, he was confident and lighthearted and finally, momentarily happy.

They stepped into a crosswalk at the end of the countdown

and had barely reached the double yellow line in the middle of the road when the orange hand flashed solid. Kenzie peered up and up, oblivious to the traffic, but Jesse spotted the car accelerating off the newly green light. They weren't in danger, not really, but he grabbed her hand anyway and tugged her to the curb.

When they got there, he didn't let go.

Kenzie held on to him, too, her fingers laced through his.

Distantly he knew this whole situation was a bad idea, but he just…didn't care. He'd slipped into a state of utterly not giving a damn, a disembodiment he hadn't experienced since a poorly judged encounter with tequila in college.

And it was such a relief. Such a weight off his shoulders not to be worrying about every comment she made or every word he said. That loosened him up more than the beer. He got so few opportunities to have fun, he couldn't bring himself to fuss over what this one might cost him.

Kenzie stopped short, her gaze traveling up one of the tall buildings, its windows lit up in random, square clumps of light.

"How many floors do you reckon that is?"

"A lot."

Without warning she turned and fell against him, flattening her hands on his chest. Automatically his arms went around her waist, the impulse natural and unstoppable. The big-city lights shone in her emerald eyes, the scent of irises fuzzed his thoughts, and he marveled anew that a woman this vibrant and beautiful was giving him the time of day.

"What floor did you work on?"

"Twenty-eighth."

"Real high for a flatlander."

"View's better on the ground."

He trailed his thumb over her cheek, let his hand rest at her nape. Her lips curled, playful and flirtatious. He wanted her, but that wasn't enough. That wasn't what he needed.

Want me, he pleaded silently. *Accept me just as I am. Show me I deserve this, because I'm not sure I do.*

"Jesse Singer," she breathed, pressing against him, her nipples stiff points in the soft flesh of her breasts.

He kept his mouth shut, figuring the hard-on dug into her pelvis got his point across well enough. He didn't trust himself not to say something embarrassing—not to beg her to promise that she didn't hate him, because her opinion had just rocketed to the top of his priority list.

She ran her hand down his chest and over his stomach, her pinkie toying with his belt buckle in a way that made him swallow hard. Then she slid it back up, slow and sensual. She stopped at his heart, which pounded against her palm.

Then she looked up at him and smiled, the tenderness in her eyes turning that bottle green into sun-warmed grass.

"Kiss me, cowboy."

Jesse obliged.

Custer's pyrotechnics had nothing on that sweet meeting of mouths, that first taste of Kenzie's petal-soft lips. Jesse snatched off his hat and Kenzie's quickly followed, leaving nothing in the way as he sank into her, cradling her head with one hand, pulling her close with the other.

Jesse wouldn't have been surprised to look down and find his boots hovering six inches off the ground. Everything weighing him down fell away as soon as his lips touched hers. Every analysis, every warning, every misbegotten belief that he could guard himself against Kenzie's irresistible pull—or that he ever should've tried. Nothing was as good as this, as good as her, or as worth an ounce of his attention as the faint taste of beer on her tongue, the whisper of her fingertips through his hair, or the way her sleek, supple body molded against his.

And her response, the way she flung herself into their kiss… Each mewling sound she made nearly brought him to his knees. She sought him harder, deeper, tilting her face to give him more, demanding the same with her tongue, her grip, the grind of her abdomen against his straining fly.

His pulse pounded louder and louder in his ears, overruling his reason, drowning out everything but Kenzie beneath his hands and against his body.

He'd take her back to the hotel, he decided frantically, his thumb circling her nipple, her hand sliding tantalizingly low on his stomach. They'd set everything aside, just for tonight. They wouldn't have to talk, didn't need to say anything except *yes*, and *more*, and *now*. He'd enjoy her, sure, but the real prize would be if she enjoyed him, too. He'd show her he wasn't all bad. That he could be good. Kind. Worthy. Maybe she'd grow to like him, because he sure as hell liked her.

Hypocrite.

The sneered accusation sent him staggering backward, out of her reach, putting inches between them as his bootheel crushed the crown of his hat.

Lee's hat.

Jesse barely registered the shock on Kenzie's face—he was too busy searching for the source of the voice that had been so clear, so near, he couldn't believe it was inside his head.

But as his heart rate slowed, he accepted that it must have been. And that although the tenor and tone were unfamiliar, the word had to come from his brother.

Lee would be disgusted. He'd been a man of integrity and loyalty, traits Jesse desperately admired yet never quite managed to emulate, not when he was paid so generously to be cunning and ruthless. His brother had warned him more than once not to let his boardroom persona bleed into the bedroom, and Jesse had listened. He'd never cheated, never lied, was never less than his best self when it came to the women he dated.

Until now.

You fired her, Lee would've said, revulsion plain on his face. *You threw her out on her ass and now you're coming on to her.*

Screwing up her career wasn't enough, huh? You have to toy with her heart, too? This is a new low, Jesse. Even for you.

Humiliation blazed in Jesse's cheeks as he stooped to pick up his hat. He was too mortified to do the decent thing and look Kenzie in the eye—to face up to what he'd started. He focused on reshaping the ruined crown, leaving her hanging in the awkward aftermath of a kiss for the history books.

Because that voice was right—he was a hypocrite. He'd fired her. He blamed her for the ranch's financial distress. He intended to defeat her in the arena, and do whatever it took to keep Singer at the top and the Broken B somewhere well below.

Yet he'd kissed her like he cared about her. Like he wanted to make her happy. Like he cherished her so much that for the briefest of moments, he'd permitted himself to find forgiveness in her eyes.

He was a hypocrite, and he was a liar, too.

"Sorry." He finally dragged his gaze to hers.

"It's fine."

He cringed at her false smile. "I mean it. I crossed the line."

"You didn't do anything I didn't want you to. Otherwise, you'd be on the ground, mourning the loss of that giant dick of yours."

His chest tightened as the traitorous length in question throbbed without mercy. "It's not giant."

"Could've fooled me."

"It's late. We should get back to the hotel."

She nodded stiffly, plucking her own hat off the ground. Jesse almost reached for her hand, then pressed his palm against his thigh.

Who was he kidding? He didn't deserve this. He hadn't earned a second of the bliss of Kenzie's touch. He was the scumbag who'd shut her out. Who'd snatched back the responsibility Lee had given her. Who'd parachuted in and changed everything.

He wouldn't apologize for it. His family came first. Didn't

matter whether Kenzie or anyone else thought he was a nice person. He didn't care.

This whole stupid interlude had been a desperate, pathetic fantasy. They wouldn't be friends. They definitely wouldn't be lovers. He was the bad guy for good reasons, but the bad guy nonetheless.

The sooner he accepted that, the better.

They didn't look at each other as they turned toward the hotel, their footfalls muted and sheepish beneath the watchful, disapproving gazes of skyscrapers looming over them. They walked back in silence, retracing the steps that had brought them here.

Chapter Ten

Kenzie hunched forward, her nose dangerously close to her laptop screen. She moved the progress bar beneath the video back, then forward, then back, then forward again.

Six minutes, thirty-four seconds. The exact time stamp at which she got her best view of him, arms folded, chin high, overseeing the chutes with the commanding authority of an army general.

Kenzie paused the video and leaned back in her chair. This was a phenomenal waste of time. Truly inexcusable. She had a literal pile of problems on her desk, yet she'd spent a huge chunk of the morning reviewing footage of a rodeo she hadn't attended, perving over each tiny glimpse of Jesse Singer.

Considering she didn't know the last names of most of the men she'd slept with, the way she'd snagged on Jesse after just a kiss disconcerted her, especially since he'd put up a wall thicker than Oklahoma sandstone. He'd stuck to impersonal industry gossip over breakfast in the hotel, and barely said a word on the drive back to Grundy County. When they parted, he was polite, personable and professional—and as distant from the man who'd held her as the stars that had cheered on their kiss.

Fine with her. Sleeping together would've been a huge mistake, complicating the uneasy truce guarding their livelihoods against Custer's encroachment. He hadn't rejected her, he'd just come to his senses first. If anything, it was a compliment. She was hot enough to melt the biggest iceberg in American rodeo.

That was what she told herself whenever she thought of him. Whenever she typed J-E-S-S-E into a search bar. Whenever she rolled onto her back in bed, withdrawing her hand from between her legs, sweaty and panting from another orgasm brought on fast and hard by the memory of his touch.

She'd believe it. Eventually.

Kenzie exhaled, gazing around the modular building that served as her office at the Broken B. She wasn't tidy at the best of times, but after the last rodeo trip of the regular season, her space was more chaotic than usual.

Singer Pro Rodeo and the Broken B had been at opposite ends of Texas this weekend. September brought cowboys' last chances to earn enough to qualify for Vegas—and the bulls' final opportunities to hike their scores before the judges made their choices for Bull of the Year. Not Nice had a ninety-point ride, near to perfect. His job now was to stay healthy and fit for December.

Hers was to clean up this damn mess and sort out everything she'd been ignoring during this busy end-of-season run.

She would. First, she'd rewind this video one more time.

At the soft rap on her door, Kenzie closed out of her browser like she'd been caught watching porn.

"Come in," she called.

Ramon eased through the doorway.

Her foreman had recently turned fifty, an achievement he credited to his unsuccessful bull-riding career, and realizing he was better at working cattle than staying on them. He had old-fashioned manners, forward-looking ideas, and just enough intractability to make him an ideal intermediary between her and the ranch hands, who still occasionally struggled with taking orders from a woman. As he removed his hat and settled into the folding chair in front of her desk, Kenzie once again thanked the rodeo gods for dropping him in her lap.

"Got a second to chat?"

"Of course. I was just looking at the footage from Comal County." She slammed the laptop shut.

"We were five guys short at head count this morning."

She frowned. "Is something going around? I gave them all time off to get their flu shots."

"That's what I was hoping, which is why I wanted to speak to each one before I came to you. It's bad news, Kenzie. They all quit. They got jobs at Supreme Rodeo."

Anxiety swelled in Kenzie's stomach. "What kinds of jobs? They're ranch hands, not arena staff."

"Custer hired them into the roughstock operations at his ranch, doing the same stuff they're doing here for fifty percent more money."

"Fifty percent?" Kenzie squeaked. She hated the shrill powerlessness in her voice. "They were already earning more than the industry average at the Broken B, plus all the benefits. I can't compete with a fifty percent uplift. No one can."

"Which is why they wanted to wait until the regular season was over before they jumped ship," he explained. "They all told me they respected you, and were proud of what they'd accomplished here. But we've all got bills to pay."

A chill ran through her. "We?"

Ramon looked down at the cowboy hat in his lap, his thumbs moving restlessly along the brim. "Custer made me an offer."

Panic seared through her mind, and she fought to keep her mouth under control. She wanted to argue, to insist, to spell out the hundreds of reasons why he was better off here.

But Ramon was a thoughtful man. He had a wife, two grown kids, and his daughter's wedding to pay for. Kenzie had never questioned his loyalty; however, his personal investment in the Broken B was nothing like her own. He wasn't trying to prove anything to anyone. This was his job, plain and simple.

And everyone had their price.

"How much?"

"Not the same hike as the other guys, but enough. About twenty percent more. With bonuses it could be closer to thirty, maybe thirty-five."

She took a steadying breath, careful not to let her terror hasten her words. She could never beat Custer on money. The only places she could outrun him were heart and soul.

"I told you about that Supreme Rodeo event I went to in Chicago. I think you should go to one, too, before you decide. It's not like what we do. He calls it rodeo, and I guess technically it is. A cowboy climbs on a bull or a bronc and he may or may not fall off, but that's where the similarity ends."

She shifted in her seat, facing him squarely. "Custer doesn't love rodeo. He loves money and attention, and as long as he has both, he doesn't care who gets hurt. I didn't see a single helmet in that competition. He has amateur bullfighters, no pickup riders, and bulls that were so unruly and aggressive. I think he must be doing something to make them that way. It wasn't rodeo. It was the prelude to a funeral."

Ramon lifted a shoulder, not meeting her eyes. "Maybe he's still ironing out the kinks."

"He wants the kinks. Remember why he got kicked out of the League in the first place? Too many injuries caused by his bulls. Bad ones. Career-enders. Life-threateners."

"It's a dangerous sport. We all accept that."

"And we all do what we can to make it safer, because we love our animals and our riders, and we don't want to see any of them get hurt."

He chewed his lower lip.

Kenzie leaned forward. "Someone's going to die in Custer's arena, Ramon. It's only a matter of time. No amount of money in the world will wipe that off your conscience."

Ramon shuffled his feet, still studying the hat in his lap.

She saw the conflict in his expression, and knew this respected, morally upright man was torn between providing for his family and the hypothetical tragedies that might bloody his hands.

Kenzie couldn't bear his fraught silence for another second. She threw her last card on the table. "Let me talk to Bob, at least. See what we can do about your salary."

His chin jerked up, his posture easing at this stay of execution. He had a reason not to give Custer a yes, or to delay his decision altogether, and for now that seemed to be enough.

Whether she could come up with the cash for him to tell Custer no was another matter entirely.

"That's fair. When can you ask him? Custer's putting me under a lot of pressure."

Kenzie hated that she hadn't known. Hated that he'd been silently wrestling with this for God knew how long.

"As soon as I can."

"Today?"

Kenzie grimaced. Asking Bob to top up Ramon's already industry-leading salary would be difficult. She needed time to prepare. To figure out her angle and get him in the right mood to say yes.

Time Ramon's strained expression told her she didn't have.

"Today," she promised.

"I really appreciate it. This has been hell on my nerves. I know we're doing great things here at the Broken B, but with Mariela's wedding, and Jorge applying to law school—"

"I know. I'll do everything I can. I don't want to lose you."

"I hope you won't." He flashed her a rueful, helpless smile.

Kenzie's heart ached. Ramon was a grounding presence in the Broken B's meteoric rise, and she wasn't sure she could function without him. He was a good man, honest and hardworking, and he deserved better than that trash at Supreme Rodeo.

She hoped she could keep him—and that she could convince Bob it was worth it.

* * *

From the outside, the family's recent wealth hadn't changed the Boyd farmhouse, though Kenzie knew the innocuous-looking seventies build now housed a series of enormous televisions, top-of-the-line appliances and kitchen gadgets, and more pairs of bespoke boots than Stillwater had places to wear them. Mrs. Boyd also had a penchant for Swarovski figurines, and Kenzie always held her breath as she walked past the glass case where they lived, terrified she'd put a foot wrong and send a year's salary of crystal creatures crashing to the floor.

She didn't have to worry about that today, because when she rang the doorbell, Bob's twenty-two-year-old daughter muttered something about the garage without ever looking up from her phone. Kenzie rounded the house to the oversize shed where the Boyds stored their vehicular fleet, and found her boss under his wife's fancy-pants SUV.

"Hey, boss. Need a hand?"

"Nope. All done." He emerged from beneath the undercarriage, wiping his hands on his overalls.

Like lots of men who spend their lives atop tractors in the Oklahoma sun, Bob looked older than he was. His hair was white, his skin ruddy and creased, and his stubborn disinterest in buying clothes meant everything he wore was full of holes.

He was also clever, calculating, and shrewd to an extent most people underestimated, given his humble appearance and slightly bumbling demeanor.

"You know how much they wanted for an oil change at the dealership in town?" He scooped up his tools and hefted to his feet. "Eighty dollars. *Eighty* dollars! Highway robbery. I turned right back around, told 'em I'd do it myself. Anyway, what'd you want to see me for?"

Kenzie glanced around, looking for somewhere to sit—it felt unceremonious to have this conversation standing in the middle of the garage. But the only option was to perch on the hood of a car, so she planted her feet. This would have to do.

"We've got a problem. Casey Custer poached five of our ranch hands for Supreme Rodeo." She crossed her arms, ready to share in her boss's outrage.

Instead, he lifted a shoulder, arranging his tools on a plank of wood propped on a sawhorse. "We're heading into the offseason. Not a terrible time to be light on labor. We've got plenty of people for Vegas. Don't rush to rehire. Let's take the temporary savings while we can."

Kenzie opened her mouth and then closed it, swallowing a rush of indignation.

Bob was not Lee, and she'd learned to strategize and self-edit rather than collapse into a chair and pour out her heart. Gone were the funny, friendly, meandering conversations at the end of the workday. Bob wanted the bottom line and the cheapest way to get there.

"That's not the end of it. Custer made Ramon an offer, too."

Now she had Bob's attention. He was fond of Ramon, whose no-nonsense approach aligned well with his own. And although he'd never admit it, Kenzie thought Bob liked having a middle-aged man around as a counter to the young woman he'd trusted with his costly rodeo venture.

"What kind of offer?" Bob propped his hip against the nose of his truck.

"Twenty percent extra, guaranteed. With bonuses he could end up thirty-five percent better off."

"That's a lot of money."

"It's an attack on our business, is what it is. Custer's deliberately picking off our staff, trying to hamstring us. We can't let him get away with it."

She suppressed a wince at the owlish gaze Bob turned on her. She'd put a foot wrong. She'd sounded too passionate, taken it too personally. Been too honest.

Bob didn't like emotive decisions, and he was inclined to paint hers as such, no matter how black-and-white they were. She knew it was because she was a woman, and she fought daily to muffle her hotheaded personality so he'd only see the confident, capable professional Lee had helped her become.

"Let's keep calm." Bob flashed the paternal smile she despised. "We can't increase the dollars going out unless we increase the dollars coming in. Money doesn't grow on trees, you know."

"Of course not, but—"

"As it happens, Casey Custer gave me a call, too."

Kenzie's whole body went cold. "He did?"

"Last night. Said he'd already approached you about potentially contracting to Supreme Rodeo, and wanted to make sure the message got through. Only it didn't, did it?"

She froze, feeling like she'd been caught with her hand in Mrs. Boyd's case of crystalline animals. Any wrong move—even the twitch of a finger—could send this situation toppling toward disaster, and she'd be blinking at the shards of her career scattered at her feet.

Bob tilted his head. "I know you don't like him, Kenzie. I don't particularly like him, either. What I don't understand is why you're so dead set against this new format."

Kenzie literally bit her tongue, visualizing herself extracting her hand from Mrs. Boyd's collection. She couldn't move too fast. She had to be careful, cautious, easing around Swarovski fawns and elephants and a disproportionately large bee.

"For a start, the safety precautions—"

"Rodeo is dangerous." Bob cut her off with a wave of his hand. "Like it or not, that's what gets people into the stands. Sure, you and I can appreciate the skills and the matchups, but your average viewer just wants to see a cowboy eat a dirt sandwich. That's why Custer's making so much money already. Did you know half of his events are sold out?"

She shifted her weight. Bob's immediate rejection of her most compelling argument put her on uneasy footing.

"The rodeo tradition is more than bulls and bareback. He's cherry-picked the two riskiest events and left out the rest."

"Tell me honestly, Kenzie. Does team roping give you a rush? Are you on the edge of your seat watching a man throw a rope at a calf's legs?"

"I like roping," she insisted.

"But you don't love it."

"I love barrel racing."

Bob smiled. "Interesting, because Custer told me he's thinking of introducing it to Supreme Rodeo next season. I can see why—it's fast, it's fun, and it gets him out of hot water about not having any female athletes."

There went her next objection. She rooted around for anything else she could throw at him, but it all boiled down to intangible passion for an enduring, time-honored way of life—and Bob had none.

"Now, I don't have firsthand experience of this thing," Bob continued. "You're the one who's been there and seen it, so you tell me. Did you find a good reason not to at least consider entering some of our bulls in Custer's events?"

Kenzie recalled the animal lineup in Chicago. The bulls' unruliness and aggression. Their middling athleticism and unpredictable temperaments. How the total lack of safeguards made them infinitely more dangerous.

She'd seen poor training, poor planning and a shocking lack of interest in the well-being of the humans involved. But she couldn't in good faith give a concrete reason why their bulls would be at any more risk than in a Pro Rodeo League performance.

Yet.

"I'll take that as a no." Bob smirked.

"I was in the audience. I didn't get a look behind the scenes. Who's to say—"

Bob raised a silencing palm.

"I'm not saying we need to quit the League and dedicate all our time and effort to Supreme Rodeo. But the landscape is changing. I don't want the Broken B to be left behind. Let's keep our minds open. I'll talk to Ramon, and I'd like you to talk to Custer. See what he's really about, and remember that higher fees will help our whole operation, regardless of where they come from."

Kenzie nodded. She'd trodden so warily, yet she could still hear the crunch of broken glass beneath her boots as she turned and left the garage. Only it wasn't a load of crystal figurines shattered on the ground—she was picking her way over the ruins of her dreams.

Drama queen.

Lee's voice rang in her head, his teasing wink glinting behind her eyes.

Buck up, cowgirl, he'd tell her if he was here. *He told you to dig deeper into Supreme Rodeo, so do it. Dig until you find where the bodies are buried, because we both know Custer's hands ain't clean.*

Kenzie stopped beside the ATV she'd driven over from her office and looked up at the sky, blue and cloudless on this late-September afternoon.

Lee felt close enough to touch. So real she was half convinced she'd glance over her shoulder and lay eyes on him.

If he'd left earlier or later that day, if he'd swapped the order of his errands, if that other driver had put down his damn phone and looked up at the stoplight, her life would be so different right now. They'd be facing this together, a united front. Lee would launch an atomic-grade charm offensive, and before long every stock contractor south of the Canadian border would give Custer a wide berth.

Without Lee, though…

Without Lee, she had Jesse.

Kenzie's blood pumped a little faster as the kernel of an idea formed.

Jesse didn't have Lee's influence, but he was smart as a serpent and twice as conniving. If they stuck together—if they didn't let that mistake in Chicago push them apart—they could do this. They could get what she needed to convince Bob—and convince the rest of the contractors, while they were at it.

She dropped behind the steering wheel and pulled out her phone, then tapped the text thread with Jesse that had been inactive for over a week.

She didn't bother with pleasantries, or small talk, or *hey, how are you.* She typed quickly, briefly, and hit Send before she could second-guess herself.

We need to talk.

Chapter Eleven

"Dang, did you see that airtime? That'll put a cowboy on his ass, first jump."

Jesse pumped excessive, artificial enthusiasm into his grin as he nudged his father. They stood outside the practice arena, elbows propped on the pipe fence, watching the latest crop of two-year-old bulls buck off weighted dummies.

Fred Singer grunted something resembling agreement, but his gaze was distant and glassy. Same as when Jesse had arrived at the house earlier that afternoon, holding the reins of two saddled horses and good-naturedly insisting his dad come out for a ride.

"I might start hauling this one, get him used to the noise and the travel. What do you reckon?" Jesse asked his father. It was a bad idea, a step too soon for an animal too young, and he hoped his dad would tell him so.

But Fred shrugged. "Whatever you think, Jess."

Jesse turned back to the arena and caught Billie's eye, sitting astride her bay dun horse. He shook his head. Her mouth pulled tight.

Jesse was at a loss. He and his sisters were sure his dad would enjoy this afternoon's itinerary. A leisurely ride across the pastures on a beautiful fall day, an unhurried sweep of the bull barn, a visit to Trixie and her horses, followed by front-row seats for the buck-off training that used to be Fred's favorite stage of the process.

Fred tried. Jesse felt it. He'd grabbed at the glimpses of his father occasionally breaking through Fred's flat, still surface, but they always sank back too quickly, disappearing into the depthless lake of his grief.

Maybe the impromptu nature of their outing was too much. Maybe Jesse should've planned ahead. His dad used to be the spontaneous half of his parents' marriage, but since Lee died he'd become anxious, and liked to know what he'd be doing and when he'd be doing it.

Of course, that usually translated to protracted worrying, hence Jesse's decision to catch him off guard. Next time he'd offer a little notice, but not too much. An hour or so. Enough time for Fred to feel ready without tying himself in knots.

"We should head back." Fred squinted up at the sun, bright and cheerful in its midafternoon position.

"Got somewhere to be?"

"Getting on for four o'clock," Fred replied, as if that explained everything.

"We're only crossing pastures. The rush-hour traffic should be fine, unless the squirrels decide to surround us."

"Mom's got the dentist tomorrow," Fred reminded him for the fiftieth time that day.

Jesse sucked in his cheeks, all out of good-natured responses to his dad's irrational preoccupation with a routine appointment nearly twenty-four hours from now.

What else was Jesse supposed to do—shake him? Shout at him? Stomp his feet and scream bloody murder until the powerful patriarch Fred Singer used to be reemerged?

"Okay," he said instead.

They mounted up and reined toward the gentle, grassy hills. Bounder shook his head as if he was disappointed their adventure was already over, but Stoney, Fred's horse, plodded straight ahead, perhaps having known this outing would be short-lived.

Familiar irritation prickled in Jesse's chest, only to be snuffed out by even more familiar guilt. He went through this cycle at least several times a day: dismayed at his parents' withdrawal, frustrated by their refusal to do anything about it, and then remorseful at his own impatience with their mourning. The weeks mounted and their world got smaller, and neither he nor his sisters had the first idea how to help.

Well, he had one idea. Might as well dredge up the same topic he always did.

"You know they can do counseling completely virtually these days, right? The girls and I did those sessions after the funeral. It helped a lot."

"I'm aware. You've told me a million times. When I decide to discuss personal matters with a total stranger on a screen, you'll be the first to hear about it."

"What if it was a rabbi instead of a therapist? That guy in Tulsa—"

"Drop it, Jess." The stern command was as close to normal as his dad had sounded in months.

Jesse wondered whether he could annoy his dad out of his grief.

"Circuit's wrapped up for the year. How're things looking ahead of the finals?" his dad said after a few minutes of silence, his tone conciliatory.

"Fine." Jesse lied easily, by now accustomed to hiding the business's gaping financial wounds beneath strategically arranged Band-Aids.

"All set for the winter?"

Inwardly Jesse let loose a wild, unhinged laugh. Sure, he was all set—all set to spend the next few months playing monetary Tetris. The end of the rodeo season meant no income and rising expenses as they kept their animals warm and fed through the bad weather—and that was before he heated the ranch house or bought human groceries.

Not to mention all his projections relied on Repeat Offender winning Bull of the Year, and bringing home the purse the prize carried. He wasn't sure what he could do if by some twisted turn of fate Kenzie pipped him to the post, other than turn off the furnace in the house and spend the winter sleeping in the barn. He'd have to convince his sisters it was a new training methodology. They still didn't—and would never—know how close to the wire the business came every day.

"Feed bill will go up, after the drought this summer. But I'll figure it out," he told his dad.

"You always do."

Jesse tried to hold on to the note of pride in his father's voice. So what if he didn't sleep, barely ate, and had waking nightmares about unpaid invoices? His parents and sisters were safe and well, their memories of Lee affectionate and untainted. Jesse owed that to his brother—to his whole family.

"What's happening with this Custer nonsense?"

"Nothing good. He made job offers to a bunch of the hands. Thankfully all but one of them came to me first, and the outlier wasn't a loss. Not thrilled to be pumping up the payroll right at the end of the circuit, though."

"Not ideal," Fred agreed. "But it's a good sign they spoke to you."

Jesse recalled the four dusty-booted men who'd fidgeted in his office, their hats in their hands, their gazes swinging everywhere but in his direction.

They were loyal, all right—loyal to his family. To his last name. To the historic outfit they'd always wanted to be part of.

But not to him.

So he'd bought them, acutely aware as he'd assembled the paperwork that Lee wouldn't have been in his position. Lee was persuasive, ingratiating and kind. People wanted to please him. Have that sunny smile shining down approval.

In moments like that, Jesse questioned how he'd do this long-term. Stressful as it was, fixing the financials was in his wheelhouse, and called upon his specific skills. But once he'd righted the wagon, how would he get everyone to follow? And which was worse, going down in financial flames not of his making or inspiring a long, slow, agonizing attrition until there was nothing and no one left?

"People won't really go for this Supreme Rodeo thing, will they?" his dad asked.

Jesse blinked back to the present. "Custer will fill his seats. We can't compete with what he does. We can't get fireworks and cheerleaders and turf out our ropers. It's the cowboys we need to worry about. We need them to keep riding with the League, and we need them alive and uninjured to do it."

Fred shook his head. "I tell you what, Jess, I've seen a lot of bad stuff in rodeo. Cheating, doping, racism, you name it. But we always came out the other side, and we were always better for it. Safer, fairer, more open-minded. This thing with Custer, though—this is new. This is outside of us. We can't control it, and we can't stop it. He's attacking our whole way of life, and I don't know that we can win."

"We can. We will," Jesse insisted.

Fred dropped his gaze to his saddle.

Jesse left his dad at his front door. His mom didn't come out to greet him—probably napping, his dad said. Jesse dallied Stoney's reins to his saddle horn, then waved to his dad as he set off, Stoney ponying at Bounder's side.

Jesse had plenty to think about on the ride home, yet his mind pulled back to the fear and defeat in his father's voice as he'd talked about Custer and the threat he posed. He supposed he hadn't thought about it in those terms. He'd focused on revenue and costs and dwindling audiences.

He'd never considered that Custer wanted to kill the culture altogether.

Not that he could—not technically, anyway. Plenty of small-scale rodeos in far-flung places persisted with no-name athletes and local stock contractors. They weren't in danger from

Supreme Rodeo, not when they barely covered their costs to begin with.

But the spirit of the sport, its dizzy highs and heart-stopping lows—that was what Custer was gunning for. That century-old American tradition, the display of skills born in the Wild West, the frontier legacy that had adapted to technology and urbanization and refused to be extinguished.

For now.

Why else would everything be so targeted? The dates, the locations, his blatant attempts to poach staff. Selling out his arenas and raking in profits wouldn't be enough for Custer. He wouldn't be happy until the Pro Rodeo League and the sport it had promoted for decades was unrecognizable.

He couldn't be that bitter about the investigation into his animals—could he? Bitter enough to destroy the League as a whole? He could've come back from that. He could've cleaned up whatever he was doing and tried again. Regained trust, regained contracts.

Whatever the reason, Jesse needed to step back and look at the larger picture. Custer had a big plan. If Jesse had any shot at shutting him down, he'd need one, too.

The muffled chime of his phone sounded from within the leather pouch hanging off his saddle. He hadn't looked at it all day, trying to give his dad his undivided attention, and he cringed at the slew of troubles that probably awaited him.

"Well, Bounder, this is one way to ruin a fine ride on a nice afternoon." He leaned forward and retrieved his phone.

His stomach tightened at the sight of Kenzie's name on the screen, like it did every time she crossed his mind—which was far too often. The only way he'd stopped himself from revisiting their night in Chicago in every spare moment was to make sure he didn't have any. He worked, and worked, and worked a bit more, yet she still managed to wriggle into the slivers of space between his worries and his stress. The taste of her mouth, the scent of her skin, and the lust he'd misread as her acceptance.

Jesse touched the brim of his hat, a felt one in dark gray he'd taken from the guest room closet that held the material remnants of Lee's too-short life. The straw hat he'd worn in Chicago was beyond repair, the crown crushed and torn by his bootheel.

There was a lesson in there somewhere, he thought unhappily, tapping Kenzie's message to reveal a single sentence.

We need to talk.

"Damn right we do," he muttered.

Supreme Rodeo was far more pressing than his wayward libido. Jesse might be drowning in overdue notices, but he'd never run from a challenge in his life. He'd destroyed supranational companies, made rich people inconceivably richer, and put billionaires on hold when they called.

"Guess the O.K. Corral moved to Wall Street," Lee had once remarked over the seder table, after Jesse regaled everyone with tales of his most colorful activist-shareholder clients.

His brother was right—he'd been a modern-day gunslinger, merciless and determined, wielding numbers instead of pistols. He could do it again. He could reach back into his corporate-raiding tool kit, find Custer's weaknesses and exploit them to the hilt.

Someone had to take down Casey Custer, and Jesse was the man for the job.

But he couldn't do it alone.

"No sale today, Singer."

The sale barn door fell shut behind Jesse, bells clattering against the glass. "Still serving lunch, though, right?"

The old man grunted an assent, returning his attention to whatever he was doing at the plexiglass-fronted cashier's desk.

Jesse crossed the tiny lobby to the door leading into the café, pleased their exchange had been less hostile than usual. Twenty years ago, the sale barn owner had accused Jesse's father of "Jewing out" of an agreed commission percentage. Not one Singer animal had crossed the threshold since. People used to fly in specifically to buy Singer stock, and the owner had never forgiven them.

Which was why Jesse liked holding meetings here. Petty, antagonistic and needlessly vengeful—just like him.

Plus the roast-beef sandwich was next level.

Stepping into the café was like riding a time machine to the seventies: wood-paneled walls, scalloped light fixtures, Formica tables and the greasy-grill scent of sizzling hamburgers. Two white-haired ranchers nodded as Jesse took a seat against the wall, and a minute later a new server—they were always new here; the owner wasn't any nicer to his staff—approached him with her pad.

"I'm waiting for someone." He waved off the menu.

She lingered beside the table, looking at him from beneath long lashes. Absently he realized she was strikingly beautiful, black-haired and blue-eyed. Yes, she was pretty. No, he wasn't interested.

Then Kenzie walked through the door and if he hadn't been sitting down, he would've fallen to his knees.

Her bleached hair stuck out like straw from her dirty trucker hat. Everything about her was a mess, from her mud-caked boots to her ripped jeans, to the dust streaked across her chambray shirt. With her heart-shaped face and luminous green eyes, she looked like a pissed-off pixie as she stomped toward him, and he gave in to the smile tugging at the corners of his mouth.

Jesse had tried to wall off his lapse in Chicago. Blamed it on beer, stress, two years of unspent sexual energy. He'd told himself a story about her seeing the real him—whoever that was—and he'd kissed her.

As soon as he saw her, though, something stirred in his chest. Something he hadn't felt in so long, he took a few seconds to name it.

Glad. He was *glad* to see her. Almost as if they were…*friends*.

"Don't even ask what kind of morning I've had." She dropped into the opposite chair.

"I won't."

Kenzie smiled at the server. "Hey, hon. Can I get the cheeseburger and a Dr Pepper? Thank you kindly."

Jesse placed his order for coffee and a roast-beef sandwich, then steepled his fingers as he turned to his temporary ally.

Who snorted and rolled her eyes. "Can you not do that with your hands? We're not in a James Bond movie, cowboy."

"Speak for yourself." He flattened his palms on the Formica. "How've you been?"

"Terrible. Custer stole five of my hands and he's pulling hard on my ops manager. Bob thinks Supreme Rodeo might become a good source of revenue for the Broken B. He's actually considering putting our animals in that circus, can you believe it?" Panic flickered in her eyes.

He snatched his hand into his lap to stop from reaching for hers. He hated seeing her so rattled—ironic, since he'd spent the last two years trying to rattle her.

"Custer came for my staff, too. I only lost one, but it was an expensive day. He's squeezing us. Making it harder to resist his offer."

"Well, it's working. I persuaded Bob to hold off for now, but unless I bring him a solid reason why Supreme Rodeo is bad for the Broken B, I'll be down there with those stupid cheerleaders."

She sounded miserable. Stressed. Desperate.

Screw it. He reached over and took her hand, squeezing gently. "That won't happen. We'll get this figured out."

Her fingers tightened around his as a disconcerting sheen crept over her eyes. Now it was Jesse's turn to panic—crying women were his kryptonite. Female tears melted him like the Wicked Witch of the West, and he'd say anything, do *anything* to make them stop—a weakness his sisters exploited way too often.

Today, for whatever reason, his survival instinct defaulted to being a jerk.

"Don't you dare cry on me," he commanded.

Kenzie yanked her hand back with a glare. "I ain't crying."

"Good."

Her eyes brightened with mischief. "Would it bother you if I did?"

"No." He spoke too quickly, and he bet she tucked that weapon away for future use.

The server brought their food. He added creamer to his coffee, Kenzie sipped from her pebbled plastic cup, and when they faced each other again they were back on practical, unemotional footing.

"I've been thinking about the way forward." He poured ketchup on his fries. "We haven't been focused. We went to Chicago in reconnaissance mode, thinking we were still at the sizing-up phase. But Custer's beyond that. He's stealing our staff, seducing our competitors and targeting our events. He won't stop until he's gutted the whole League, not just cherry-picked the best riders. He's moving fast, and we need to catch up."

She nodded, swallowing a bite of her cheeseburger. "So what do we do?"

"We kill it."

"What, his events?"

"The whole mishegoss. No compromises, no coexistence. No more Supreme Rodeo, no more Casey Custer, no more problems."

"Sounds great, but I have one minor question. How on earth do we do that?"

He leaned back in his chair. "Skeletons."

She blinked. "Beg pardon?"

"First piece of advice I always gave my clients when they were interested in a takeover—dig up the skeletons. They'll either put you off the deal, or they'll be leverage."

"Skeletons." Kenzie nodded.

"Custer doesn't have financial reports I can comb through, or disgruntled employees I can turn against him—not yet, anyway. We'll have to do the investigating ourselves. Go to another event, but let Custer know we're coming. Get him to take us behind the scenes, so we can get a good look at what he's up to."

"I like that. And here on the home front, we need numbers. If we can get a stock-contractor cartel going, at least for a little while, that should put everyone in a better position, and make it harder for him to pick us off individually."

Jesse grinned, delighted by the thought of Custer beating his head against a wall of the saltiest, most curmudgeonly group of businesspeople imaginable.

"Outstanding. Let's make lists of who we can pull in."

They both took out their phones and set them beside their plates.

"I can get to Justin Pitland and Bill Jessup." Jesse typed the names into his notes app—then his train of thought came to an abrupt halt.

He looked up at Kenzie, the one person he didn't want to admit this to—and the only one he could ask for help.

"This'll have to be on you. I don't have sway in this community. Not like Lee did."

There it was, her big chance to smirk and sneer and shove his failure in his face. He'd held the power when he'd fired her, but it was in her hands now.

"That's because you're a jerk." Her smile promised he wasn't all bad, her tone as light and sweet as pink lemonade.

He'd seen that look before, in Chicago—or thought he had. Not teshuvah, not forgiveness, not exactly—but the possibility might exist for him. He could become a better, nicer, more deserving version of himself.

He shook that off, hunching over his phone. He'd been beer-sozzled then; he was stress-addled now. He was imagining acceptance from the person who owed it to him least.

He'd wronged Kenzie. Only a fool would think she'd ever forgive him.

They added names to call—for *her* to call—until they reached the end of both their contacts lists.

Kenzie shoved aside her empty plate. "Good work, Singer. Here I thought it'd be awkward between us after Chicago."

He should've seen that open-palmed slap coming. Jesse fought for his composure, not sure what to say. He didn't disagree. He should be happy she'd already put their slipup so squarely behind her.

Yet he bought himself time, positioning his coffee mug in the center of its drip-stained saucer, willing his lungs to refill and his ears to stop ringing.

"Can you even imagine? The two of us?" Her laughter prickled through him like static. "I enjoy a good hate-bang as much as anyone, but we'd probably awaken some unholy, undead evil spirit that feeds on dislike."

His gaze snapped to hers and he couldn't dislodge it, hypnotized by that bottle-green gleam.

"There'd be natural disasters," he agreed. "Tornadoes. Hurricanes. A landslide."

"Icebergs would melt. Oceans would rise."

"Oceans would boil." He inched forward, drawn by an instinct he refused to name even as it thrummed insistently, suffusing his body with heat and hunger.

They stared at each other, their connection so electric it almost crackled. This all-consuming, all-powerful, reason-defying lust was new for Jesse, but he wasn't scared. He would've happily stepped outside his daily slog for a few hours of pure, carnal pleasure—with anyone but her.

"Anyway." She glanced toward the door, shattering the moment like a rock through a windshield. "We won't need to worry about any of that, because as soon as we've put Custer on his ass, I'm going to put you on yours."

"Never thought I'd say this, but I look forward to the day when you're my biggest problem, Kenzie."

Her smile was all they could've been—all that was lost to them now. They regarded each other for a minute more, the air between them rueful and a little sad. Then Kenzie slapped her hands on the table and stood up.

"I better hit the phone. Lots of people to speak to."

"I'll call Custer. Get us into his next event."

"What do I owe you for lunch?"

He shook his head. "It's on me."

"Much appreciated. I'll be in touch."

She turned on the heel of her muddy boot and walked out the door, leaving Jesse to his deflated fantasies, his ebbing pulse and the grim suspicion that he'd missed a chance he hadn't known was in front of him.

Chapter Twelve

"Hey. *Hey!* I asked for a room *near* the elevator, not right across from it."

If looks could kill, the man who'd just butted in front of Kenzie and slapped his key card on the check-in desk would be in neatly sliced pieces on the floor. The hotel clerk's deadpan expression convinced her to hold her tongue, which she would've otherwise unleashed on that jerk.

The lobby teemed with people wearing plastic belt buckles and cheap straw cowboy hats, the jostling and bumps from suitcases so bad that Jesse had positioned himself behind her, a taller, wider line of defense against the Supreme Rodeo fans constantly squeezing past. Kenzie couldn't decide what depressed her more, that these people had bought expensive tickets for Supreme Rodeo when one of the nation's oldest weekly rodeos was only an hour away, or that so many of them had traveled so far to Philadelphia that they needed to stay overnight.

Nothing about any of this appealed to her. She hated big cities, hated crowded sidewalks, and she hated flying—although she had to admit, traveling with Jesse improved that part.

Just as well, because it took a long time to get places when you lived in the middle of nowhere. They'd sipped coffee in silence before their crack-of-dawn flight from Will Rogers Airport, but when the bumpy takeoff triggered her anxiety and she white-knuckled the armrest, Jesse suddenly had plenty to say. He distracted her with funny stories and engaged her in a robust debate about which bulls would make the League finals when the list was announced that evening, and before she knew it, they were back in smooth skies.

The man's hidden talents didn't end there. During their layover in Chicago, they'd wandered into a bookstore. Jesse picked up a thick hardback, flipping straight to the index.

"'*The End of Oil's Colossus*,'" she'd read aloud from the spine.

"Wanted to see if I got a mention." He'd snapped the book shut and put it back on the shelf.

Kenzie glanced at him over her shoulder as that memory resurfaced. For so long she'd thought of him only as an invader, the heartless stranger who'd appeared out of nowhere to take what belonged to her. But he'd had a whole other life, full of other dreams and other places.

She wouldn't ask if he missed it—he'd never say yes, true or not. That impassive expression hid a heart of steel.

Imagine being fought for the way he fought for this sport…

But that was reserved for his family and the rodeo. Might be warm on the right end of his trust, but the wrong end was freezing cold.

"Sorry for the wait. Can I have the last name on the booking, please?"

Kenzie smiled brightly, motioning Jesse beside her. "The reservation is under Singer, but it's for two rooms."

Clackety clack clack. The clerk typed, frowned, pursed her lips, typed some more. *Clack clack clack.*

"Looks like I only have the one room for Singer. What's the other name?"

"Wallace."

Clackety clackety clack clack clack. "I see the reservation for Singer, but it only shows one room."

"Here's the confirmation." Jesse slid his phone across the desk, an email open on the screen.

More frowning, more squinting. The clerk looked up at them with a grimace.

"I do apologize for this. There's been an error with the booking. I see you paid for two rooms, but were only allocated one. Unfortunately we're fully booked tonight."

Her eyes widened in alarm.

"Is there somewhere else you can recommend?" Jesse asked.

"I can try, but most of the hotels in the area are sold out for this horse fair." She gestured to the packed lobby.

"It's a rodeo," Kenzie corrected.

"Sort of," Jesse added.

"The rodeo," the clerk repeated. "What I can do is offer a twenty percent discount on top of the refund for the second room, as well as two drink vouchers for the bar and two free breakfasts tomorrow. I really am sorry for the mix-up."

Kenzie pressed her fingers over her eyes. Jesse was a jackass, but he was also a ranch-raised gentleman with good country manners. If she wanted this room, he'd give it to her. She could take off her boots, rest after a long day, and not give a damn about how far he'd have to taxi to and from the event that night.

But she'd been raised right, too, even if it was in a leaky trailer a fraction of the size of the Singers' house.

"We'll share." She turned her finger on Jesse. "But if you start snoring, you're sleeping in the hallway, you hear?"

He turned to the clerk, his tone urgent. "It's a twin room, right? Two beds?"

The clerk bit her lower lip.

"There's only one bed."

"What? Wait," Kenzie protested, but it was too late—the clerk was typing again, glancing past them at the snaking line of waiting customers.

She produced key cards and vouchers. Jesse signed a slip of paper, and the couple behind them shoved them out of the way, the woman's high-heeled cowgirl boots nearly costing Kenzie a toe.

Jesse glared at the couple, the crowd, and the key cards in his hand. Then he hefted his duffel and started toward the elevators, moving so fast she had to jog to catch him.

When they made it upstairs, she and Jesse stood just inside the door, surveying their fate.

The room was small.

So was the bed.

Being this close to Jesse for the next fifteen hours was unnerving—and tempting. Kenzie second-guessed herself, almost suggested they search for somewhere else when Jesse heaved his duffel onto the desk and unzipped it.

"I'm taking a shower," he announced.

Before she could so much as nod, he'd grabbed an armload of stuff from his bag and shut himself in the bathroom.

She pried off her boots and sat on the end of the bed, then flopped onto her back and stared at the tiny red light on the smoke detector. She heard the water start in the shower.

Jesse was naked on the other side of that thin wall.

Kenzie imagined his long torso and longer legs, ducking his chin under the showerhead, the water flattening the hair on his chest into dark trails. He probably washed with the swift efficiency of a man reared on well water, who'd had three sisters banging impatiently on the door. No fussing, no fancy products, just bar soap and shampoo. Lather, rinse, done.

But if he'd been in this room alone, if he had an abundance of hot water and no one waiting on him, what would he do then? He'd linger, maybe. Close his eyes under the spray. Let it trickle all the way down his stomach to his erection, which would thicken and rise as he gripped its base.

Keeping her eyes trained on the bathroom door, Kenzie slid her own fingers over her nipple, then beneath the waist of her jeans.

He'd start with an experimental, considering tug. He wasn't in a hurry. The water would feel good on his shoulders, dripping down his back, dampening his palm. He'd pull a little harder. More firmly. The fingers on his free hand would twitch.

Slowly she rubbed her core. She strained her ears, feeling thirteen years old again as her whole body tensed, ready to pretend this hadn't been happening.

The water kept running, and so did her imagination. Jesse would pick up the pace, gradually at first, then with more urgency, his erection flushed and swollen in his hand. He'd shift his weight. Drop his head. Brace his free hand on the tiles, his shoulders hunching, bowed by the intensity of his desire. He'd think of her, touching her breasts, kissing her stomach, slipping his tongue between her legs, and then he'd gasp and shudder and—

Kenzie squeezed her eyes closed, slamming her forearm against her mouth to stifle her cry. Her body jerked and she pressed her thighs together, trapping her fingers against her core, prolonging her ecstasy as long as she could, despite being vulnerable and exposed. If Jesse walked in right now, he'd know exactly what she'd been doing.

He didn't. The water shut off as Kenzie gingerly retrieved her hand and sat up, shaky and disheveled. She fanned her face, finger-combed her hair, and walked unsteadily to her bag, barely able to see past her receding fantasy to the clothes she dug through.

A minute later the bathroom door swung open, unleashing a cloud of shampoo-scented steam, and Jesse emerged fully dressed. His hair was wet, his cheeks pink, and he looked everywhere but at her. She stepped aside so he could pad past in his bare feet, and as their arms brushed, she could've sworn there was heat pouring off him, their mere proximity making her flush in a way she hadn't during this whole day of traveling with him.

He rooted through his bag like it was his job, and the pieces clicked together. His stiff gait. His avoidant posture. The high color in his face…

No. He wouldn't. Not with her right there, a wall away. She had, of course, but he hadn't.

Or had he?

Kenzie snatched up her stuff and fled into the bathroom. She shut the door and leaned back against it, drawing thick lungfuls of the eucalyptus scent Jesse left behind.

"Down, girl." She turned on the water and stripped off her clothes, praying this temptation would run right down the drain—and that she'd survive the night if it didn't.

"Since Mr. Custer will be busy during the performance, he asked me to make sure you have whatever you need. Everything in the VIP room is complimentary, so please help yourselves to drinks and snacks. Then I'd love to tell you more about our roughstock incentives."

Kenzie glanced up at Jesse, who regarded their improbably upbeat, headset-wearing, tablet-toting liaison like a diamondback might size up an overconfident mouse.

The wariness that had wedged between them in their cramped hotel room vanished when they arrived at the arena, drawn together by their palpable difference from the thousands of people surging through the doors.

Kenzie was glad. Although she hated to admit it, she'd grown awfully fond of the dimple-cheeked man buried deep within those layers of ice.

"Can I show you to the bar?" asked their hostess, who'd introduced herself as Darcey-with-an-e.

"We'll find it." Jesse motioned for Kenzie to follow him to the glass-fronted room behind the VIP seats.

They weren't the only special guests that evening, but they appeared to be the only ones with a chaperone. Kenzie took stock of the other VIPs, white men and women in expensive yet discordant Western attire.

Kenzie hated the word *authentic* when it came to rodeo, believing there was no wrong way to participate. But as she scanned the other VIPs' heavy turquoise jewelry, snakeskin boots with out-of-fashion toes, and embellished designer jeans that wouldn't last a minute on a saddle, she made an exception.

Jesse nudged her, pretending to examine the charcuterie board. "Guy in the suede jacket used to be the CEO of a mining company. Three people died at one of their sites. Turned out he was short-changing the equipment maintenance, so the board ousted him."

"What's he doing here?"

"Spending his golden handshake, I guess."

They ordered two beers, and Kenzie watched closely as the bartender popped the caps. She wouldn't put it past Custer to slip something in their drinks and shove contracts in front of their cross-eyed faces. She avoided the spread of food for the same reason, although she snagged one of the fancy chocolate bars for later.

"All set?" Darcey greeted them with a smile when they returned to their cushioned seats. The noise of the excited crowd swelled in the rapidly filling arena. Ten minutes 'til showtime.

Darcey tapped her tablet. "I'll let you two get settled, and then I'd love to take you through just a couple of slides about our approach to stock contracting here at the Supreme Rodeo Series."

"We'd like to see the pens, if we can." Jesse remained on his feet.

Darcey blinked.

"Where you keep the animals in the back," Kenzie clarified.

"Oh. I suppose that might be possible. Let me make a quick call."

Kenzie watched her hurry up the aisle, her index finger pressed to her earpiece.

"Something tells me she ain't from our side of the fence."

"Probably came from PR, or investor relations. She's Custer's mouthpiece. Pretty, friendly, unthreatening."

She frowned. "You think she's pretty?"

"Objectively. Not my type, though."

"What's your type?"

Oh, crap—the fire was back. Flames licking behind his blue eyes, invisible to everyone except her, where they ignited matching heat in the center of her chest.

Darcey jogged back, her fake smile a welcome fire hose.

"Fabulous news—I got the go-ahead to take you behind the scenes. I thought we might wait until intermission. The opening ceremony is really something, and I'd hate for you both to miss it."

"We've seen it. Is this the way down?" Jesse thumbed toward an exit.

"Follow me," Darcey instructed, and the three of them began the descent from their Very Important heights.

By the time they reached the austerely functional, cinder-block-and-steel space where the arena's operations were staged away from public view, the pyrotechnics had started. Stamping hooves and the tense lowing of anxious bulls followed each muffled boom.

Kenzie recognized the maze of metal gates designed to channel the right animals into the arena in the right order, but the similarities ended there. The enclosures were too small, likely to encourage hierarchical jostling. The entrances and exits were badly laid out, requiring too many gates, with too many junctions where a bull could decide to camp out. Most importantly, the area was woefully understaffed, leaving the animals to fend for themselves while they waited for their turn, and putting dangerous pressure on the one person working should any of them misbehave.

Darcey waved down the lone employee left in charge of a million dollars' worth of roughstock.

Jesse leaned in. "Get a good look at the animals and the infrastructure. You'll know better than I will what's wrong. I'll keep our babysitter busy."

She shouldn't have swelled with pride at his simple comment, but she did. This man with rodeo in his blood relied on her judgment.

As well he should, she reminded herself.

She searched him, hunting for any sign of duplicity or an ulterior motive. He met her eyes squarely, that cool, blue gaze as wide-open as she'd ever seen it.

Kenzie should look away. Hell, she should turn and run, yet Jesse's attention rooted her to the spot.

Because when he looked at her like that, like he recognized how rare and good and *necessary* she was, the version of herself reflected in his pupils was the one she'd always wanted to be.

The one she wished her father saw.

"Let me introduce you to Richie, who oversees our backstage operations." Darcey led the man over.

"Wow, Jesse Singer and Kenzie Wallace. It's an honor." Richie couldn't have been more than twenty-two, his eyes round as he pumped their hands.

"Thought we'd have a look at your setup. Kenzie, why don't you let Richie give you a tour? I'd like to talk numbers with Darcey."

Darcey's smile became genuine for the first time since they'd met her, and as Jesse bent over her tablet, Kenzie set off with Richie.

"Gosh, I been watching your bulls for years. I'd love any pointers you got. Mr. Custer basically told me to put this all together back here, but I only have a year's experience behind the chutes, so some of it I had to fudge."

"You never ran an event before and Custer left you in charge of the whole system?"

"Yes, ma'am."

Kenzie nearly bit her tongue in half as she approached the first pen. Typical Custer. Pour out the prize money where everyone could see it, then take shortcuts behind the scenes.

She moved slowly through the pipe fences, assessing every detail as Richie worried aloud about the time targets Custer had set him, and his boss's dissatisfaction at the expense and complexity of rebuilding the framework at each new venue. Whenever he stepped away or turned his back she covertly took some photos on her phone, although she wasn't sure what she intended to capture.

"He wants me to find a lighter material that can snap together more easily, but it's all designed for construction sites and factories, not live animals."

Kenzie nodded, studying the bulls crammed into the pens. She wouldn't expect Custer's animals to be as friendly and even-keeled as her own, but these seemed particularly agitated. They snorted and bellowed, pawed the dirt, and those that had enough room to do so lowered their heads and shuffled sideways to display their size—classic signs of aggression.

She'd met some mean-ass bucking bulls in her career, but even the grouchiest were safe to handle due to generations of breeding for disposition. Could Custer be doing the opposite, and breeding for unpredictability and danger? Or was there something else going on?

By the time they reunited with Jesse and Darcey, Kenzie had more questions than answers. She was about to ask to speak to the veterinary staff when Darcey tilted her head, listening to something on her headset.

"Got it." She flipped on her fluorescent smile. "Mr. Custer would like our little backstage tour to move to the chutes, so you can both have a front-row seat for the competition. Right this way."

Kenzie waved goodbye to a bereft-looking Richie and hurried to keep pace with Darcey's brisk path through the fences. Darcey shoved open a heavy metal door, and the effect was like switching a phone call to top-volume speaker. Music, cheering and the announcer's voice reverberated through the arena, nearly drowning out the comforting, familiar clank of the metal gates. They stood in a no-man's-land between the end of the chutes and the arena wall, their view almost totally obscured by the sponsored banner hung over the fence in front of them.

Darcey cupped her hand over her mouth, shouting over the din. "As you can see, our athletes—"

"Can we go up there?" Kenzie nodded to the platform.

Darcey frowned. "What?"

"Come on." Jesse grabbed Kenzie's hand and tugged her to the edge of the plywood platform.

He hunched down and cupped his hands together. She put her boot on his palms, braced her hand on his shoulder, and he boosted her up before Darcey could argue. He hauled himself up after her, and they stood looking down at their flummoxed chaperone, whose pencil skirt and high heels meant the platform might as well as be wrapped in barbed wire.

"Excuse me, you can't be—hey, will you look who's here. Didn't know we had celebrity bulls running tonight." Farley Pollmeyer, a grizzled old chute boss who'd retired years ago, shook both their hands.

Kenzie shook her head. "We're just spectators."

"With all-access passes," Jesse fibbed.

"Glad to have you. Bet our riders will be, too, especially if this means they might get to climb aboard your bulls one of these days."

They can already do that at League rodeos. But Kenzie kept her friendly smile in place and turned her attention to the chutes. She easily recognized the cowboy tightening his rope—because he wasn't wearing a helmet.

She elbowed Jesse. "That's Chris Steeple."

They joined the clump of people gathered behind the chute. Chris ran his gloved hand up and down his rope, activating the sticky resin that would help keep his fist closed tight. The once promising Canadian had been plagued by injuries, and with two kids at home, Kenzie understood what brought him here, especially since he hadn't qualified for the League finals.

Why someone who'd already suffered multiple, severe concussions would climb aboard a fifteen-hundred-pound missile wearing just a cowboy hat, on the other hand, was beyond her.

Her heart twisted as Chris took his wrap. She didn't begrudge him stepping outside the League to earn some extra money. But why couldn't Custer take basic precautions? Helmets. Competent bullfighters. Pickup riders. None of that would make the event any less exciting—just safer.

While the announcer boomed Chris's accolades, the bull leaped in the chute, dislodging Chris's rope and forcing him to start over. Then it happened again, and a third time. Kenzie realized there was no referee timing the cowboy in the chute, and no chance to swap animals if the one he'd drawn refused to cooperate. There was, however, a man in a headset identical to Darcey's leaning over Chris, making a hurry-up gesture.

Chris secured his wrap on the fourth try, scooted up on his rope, and leaned off his pockets.

The gate swung open.

"He didn't nod! He should get a re-ride." She grabbed a handful of Jesse's sleeve. The cowboy's nod was sacred—the ride couldn't start without it.

Jesse's gaze was on the arena floor.

Bull riding was a sport measured in fractions of seconds, and it was amazing how much could happen so fast—and how quickly a situation could go from bad to worse.

Chris started unsteadily and stayed that way. The bull wasn't much of a jump-kicker, but it spun, and Kenzie saw Chris sliding sideways on his rope, getting pulled into the well. His feet were loose, he collapsed forward. Then the bull threw back its head, colliding with Chris's skull.

Chris's whole body went slack. His shoulders slumped and he fell to the ground. The disturbing vacancy in his rag doll limbs nearly stopped her heart. The crowd gasped, while halfway up the arena Custer lowered his microphone and stared open-mouthed at the unconscious cowboy.

The bullfighters were badly positioned, unable to get between the animal and Chris's motionless body. They inched forward and back, pathetic imitations of the real professionals who'd take a horn to the gut before they'd let a rider get trampled.

The cheerleaders edged along the siding as two men in EMT uniforms sprinted across the arena. But when the bull swung to face them, they hesitated, glancing desperately between the fallen rider and the bewildered animal.

Anyone who worked with cattle learned to read them, and Kenzie knew this bull wasn't about to charge—yet. He was confused, his head up, his ears flicking, unsure what to do or where to go. His lack of training showed clear as day, but he wasn't aggressive. He needed simple, calm direction before his bafflement became fear and he chose fight instead of flight.

The EMTs stepped closer, but stopped when the bull turned their way. One of the bullfighters tapped the animal's rump; the other danced from foot to foot off to the side. Farley was at Kenzie's elbow, his jaw as slack as Custer's over on the back of his pickup, while the announcer assured the crowd the medical team were the best in the business.

All these men getting paid to be here, and no one was doing a damn thing.

Kenzie crouched down and dropped her leg over the platform. Unlike the rest of these fools, she wouldn't just stand by while—

Jesse was already on the arena floor.

Farley finally emerged from his stupor and grabbed her arm

just as she swung her other leg over the edge. She tried to shake him off, swearing a blue streak, but he held her tight. She had no choice but to watch in mute terror as Jesse approached the bull.

He moved slowly, confidently, until he was perpendicular to the animal's side. He stopped, his bootheels beside Chris's arm. Positioned between the fallen rider and the bull.

A hundred outcomes raced through Kenzie's mind, all of them horrific. Jesse was alone, with no backup, nearly as vulnerable as the man lying prone behind him. Anxiety tightened her lungs and locked her joints. Her gaze ricocheted from Jesse's cautious posture to Custer in his pickup, to the EMTs, to Farley, and back, silently pleading for someone to help.

Jesse whistled to the bull, the same friendly, two-note sequence Lee used at feeding time. The bull spun to look at him, his posture defensive, but curious.

Jesse whipped off his hat and tossed it like a Frisbee. It landed beyond the bull's backside, and the animal did a hundred-and-eighty-degree turn toward it—then spotted the open exit gate behind it.

The bull loped gratefully toward the fence. The bullfighters flanked the animal, but there was no need—he was happy to trade this vast, disorienting space for the snug smells of the pens. As soon as the gate clanked shut behind him, Jesse dropped to one knee, put his hand on Chris's shoulder, and left it there until the EMTs reached him.

The whole catastrophe played out in less than three minutes, but Kenzie felt like she hadn't inhaled in an hour. The lights came up, signaling an impromptu intermission as a second team of medical staff hustled to join the first. The next rider in the lineup climbed out of his chute, the waiting bulls were unloaded back to the holding pens, and it seemed the building itself exhaled in relief.

The men who'd watched Chris nearly get trampled eased off the platform to the dirt-covered floor. They stood in anxious clumps, hovering near the unconscious man, assessing the medics' progress as the bull rider was loaded onto a backboard.

"Now everyone's a hero," Kenzie muttered.

The real hero stood a few feet from the medics, his face pale and drawn as he ran his hand through his dark hair. He nodded absently to the people who approached him, his eyes never leaving the bull rider.

You fake-ass idiot. Jerks don't throw themselves in front of pissed-off bulls. All that bad-guy swagger, when deep down you're as good as they get, you liar.

Kenzie sniffed hard, giving herself a shake. She couldn't let the adrenaline carry her away. Jesse was no saint, and one act of bravery didn't erase what he'd done to her.

Although it did push her a little closer to forgiving him.

The EMTs hefted the backboard and left the arena. The people gathered on the dirt floor formed a would-be receiving line for Jesse, who regarded his admirers with the enthusiasm of a kid being called in from recess.

He sought her gaze over the heads of the men—and cheerleaders—vying for his attention. She hopped down and cut through the group, not-so-subtly knocking a cheerleader out of the way.

"You okay?" she asked.

He shook his head.

Approaching movement caught her eye. A shiny suit and shinier boots.

"Custer's coming."

"Get me out of here before I break his neck."

She didn't need to be told twice. She took Jesse's hand and yanked him away from the clustered admirers, away from the cowboy headed for the ambulance, away from Darcey and her boss speedwalking to catch them. She pushed open the heavy door they'd entered through and closed it behind them, shutting out that whole miserable mess.

Chapter Thirteen

Kenzie turned her phone face down on the bar.

"Erica says Chris is awake and talking. Doesn't remember a thing. They're going to do an MRI, but the doctor's optimistic."

"Should've been wearing a damn helmet." Jesse swirled the untouched whiskey in his glass. The thought of throwing back two fingers of hard liquor had motivated each of his shaky steps on the walk back to the hotel, but now he was too queasy to drink it.

"Yes, he should have. He should've been protected by bull-fighters who've done more than watch *8 Seconds*, and a medical team stationed near the chutes instead of at the opposite end of the arena."

Kenzie's levelheaded, reassuring presence was the only thing tying him together. Jesse was rattled and angry, and although it looked like everything would turn out all right, the memory of Chris's blank, colorless face would stay with him for a long time.

He'd seen plenty of wrecks in his many years in rodeo, men getting stepped on and run over and tossed by a bull's horns. He knew audiences liked the danger. Hell, most of the competitors liked it, too.

But there was a fine line between knowing something bad might happen and watching it unfold for real. That was when excitement turned to horror, when cheers became prayers, and when people covered their mouths and closed their eyes and turned their children's heads.

Thanks to the layers of safety required at League-sanctioned events, those moments were few and far between. When the worst happened, he knew the cowboys were in the best possible hands.

He hadn't expected those hands to be his own.

"Goddamn Custer. That son of a bitch."

"I must have fifty missed calls from him." Kenzie sighed.

"Same. What does he think he can say to either of us, after that?"

"That it was an unfortunate accident, these things happen, he'll be learning from this to make improvements in the future."

Jesse rolled his eyes. "He needs to do better than that."

"No, literally, that's what he said in a voice mail. My phone transcribed it."

His frustration swelled enough for him to finally lift his hand, and he took a small swallow of whiskey. It burned when it hit bottom, but it helped.

For a few minutes they sat in contemplative silence—or as much silence as possible in the noisy room. People in Western wear filled the tables behind them, Supreme Rodeo attendees who'd gotten back early enough to grab space in the hotel's small bar. None had recognized him, thank God. He'd lost his hat in the arena, and except for the bartender, was the only bareheaded man in the place. Kenzie had her usual trucker hat on, so with their boots and buckles pointed toward the bar they probably looked like the outsiders in this rodeo-enthusiast crowd.

Just as well. He was fresh out of polite.

"You did the right thing, Jesse," Kenzie said.

He found her penetrating gaze, the lights behind the liquor shelves illuminating the facets in her bottle-green eyes.

"You really think so?"

"Calling me a liar?"

The question was playful, and he smiled for the first time since leaving the event.

"It was pretty stupid, in my opinion. Impulsive and reckless."

She shook her head. "You stepped in when no one else did. It's no exaggeration to say you might've saved Chris's life tonight."

"I don't know about that." Jesse hung his head. That should've made him feel good, but instead it brought on another wave of nauseous discomfort.

"Hey." Kenzie squeezed his wrist. "Would it help if I told you Lee would've done the same thing?"

He considered. On some level, that was exactly why he'd done it. He nodded.

"That's too bad, because it ain't true. He would've given everyone on that platform hell until they did something. Would've screamed blue murder at those bullfighters, and maybe tried to find a rope and snag the bull himself. But he never would've jumped in."

Jesse frowned, her description totally at odds with the rough, tough older brother he'd grown up with. "Of course he would've. He was fearless."

"No, he wasn't," she told him gently. "He wasn't nearly as confident or decisive as you. He just hid his wavering behind that big, Buffalo Bill personality."

"We'll have to agree to disagree." But he was uncertain. The version of his brother he'd discovered on paper certainly fell far from the one he thought he knew. Maybe moving away meant he'd missed even more.

"If looking up to him gets you out of bed in the morning, don't stop," she urged. "Lee was a great man, and I try to remember the best of him. I'm just saying, sometimes your best is better."

Jesse stared at her.

He wanted to kiss her so badly it hurt.

She saw it, too. Her eyes flashed, and her expression softened.

He braced himself for rejection. She'd been clear with him

back at the café—clear enough that the thought of their tiny hotel room sent fresh misery slicing through his gut. There was so much sewage-stinking water under their bridge, they'd never rise far enough above it.

Although from the way she looked at him now, her eyes wide, her chin up, her lower lip caught between her teeth, he could've sworn—

"Hi, can I get a mojito and another glass of the IPA?"

A man with a yoked shirt and a Sopranos-worthy accent leaned into the space beside Kenzie. He gave them a curious once-over, then a friendly smile.

"You guys in town for the SRS? Cool show, right? I love all that cowboy crap. John Wayne, Clint Eastwood. I had no idea it still happened in real life. You ever been to the rodeo before?"

"Couple times," Kenzie responded.

"That's awesome. This was my first one. Freaking wild stuff. Did you see that guy get knocked out at the beginning?"

Jesse nodded. "We saw it."

"Scary. He seemed okay, though, thank God. Then there was that other guy halfway through who got his hand caught in the rope. You think, he's got the eight seconds, he's good to go, but then there's this whole dismount they gotta do."

"The get-off," Kenzie offered.

The man frowned. "The git what?"

"The get-off," she repeated.

He still looked blank.

"The *get*-off." Jesse flattened the *e*.

"That's what I said," Kenzie told Jesse.

"Gotcha. The get-off. Sweet." The man beamed.

"If you're interested, there's a weekly rodeo about an hour from here. Real traditional, with all the events—plus the bull riding, of course. It's nice and small, too. Not a bad seat in the house," Jesse ventured.

"What other events are there?"

"Barrel racing, tie-down roping, steer wrestling—"

The man snorted a laugh as the bartender arrived with his drinks. "What, like wrestling an actual cow? No thanks, bro. I'm into the action, you know? Not the farmer crap. Anyway, I better get these back before my girlfriend files a missing person report. Have a good night."

Their new friend walked away, and with him went the brief improvements to Jesse's mood.

"There you have it—the future of our sport. All action, no farmer crap." He gulped his whiskey.

"He's just one guy—one who never would've seen a rodeo at all, otherwise."

"Six million people went to the rodeo last year, Kenzie. That's hundreds of rodeos held over multiple days, all across the country, twelve months of the year. So we're talking, what, hundreds of people per night? There were at least ten thousand people in that arena. We may not like it, but Custer's onto something. This country's changing, and our slice of it is dying. Has been for a long time. Maybe Custer's doing us a favor, ripping the heart out. At least it'll be over quick."

He stared unseeingly into his glass, gazing past the amber liquid to the bleak years ahead. Lower-ranked competitors. Underutilized bulls. Dwindling audiences. The gaping holes in the schedule from shuttered rodeos. Less money, less incentive, less point.

He'd have to go back to work. Mae would be fine, but every penny of Trixie's and Billie's incomes were earned on horseback. He wouldn't find another strategy-consulting job in Oklahoma, but if he moved to Dallas—

The toe of Kenzie's boot nearly took a chunk out of his calf.

"The hell?" He massaged his leg through his jeans.

"Keep sulking like your pa shot your puppy and you'll get another one. What happened to killing Supreme Rodeo? Thinking big enough to take down the whole mezuzah?"

"Mishegoss."

"Whatever. So we had to cut out a little early tonight, and we didn't get the hard evidence we need. Doesn't mean we're done."

"But that guy—"

"Screw that guy. We won't get him, but we'll get someone. We'll shut Custer down and use what he's done to grow our audience, not shrink it. He's doing something bad, and you know it. We just need more time to figure out exactly what."

Jesse shook his head. "I can't go to another one of these. Not after tonight."

"Then I'll do it, and you can stay home and do whatever it is you do on Saturday nights. I'm guessing it involves mint schnapps, golf highlights, and a five-step skincare routine."

He smirked. "Seven steps."

She laughed, sunny and infectious. "Dang, who knew our offseason Saturdays were identical?"

"Real talk, I've played on some of the fanciest courses in the country, and golf is the most boring waste of time in the world."

"Were you any good?"

"Awful. It got so embarrassing I had to start faking injuries so I didn't offend my clients when I begged off. And let me tell you, it's hard to come up with an injury that prevents you from sitting on your ass in a cart and swinging a club."

"No thanks. Give me a dirty rope, a bitchy horse and a muddy calf any day."

"Cheers to that." He clinked his glass against hers.

Their gazes snagged over the rims of their drinks. Kenzie didn't have pink hair anymore, but she sure had a way of running a bright streak through his dark thoughts.

He was halfway through swallowing when she slammed her pint on the bar and dug her elbow into his ribs, making him cough and splutter.

"Jesse, look at the time. They're announcing the qualifiers for the finals in five minutes."

The moment they'd been working toward for nine months, and they'd almost missed it. How had that happened?

He flagged down the bartender and pointed to the TV. "Excuse me, can you get the Cowboy Network on that?"

The bartender's eyes lit up. "I've been waiting for someone to ask. We just subscribed. Seems like rodeo's the hot ticket these days."

He consulted a laminated list of channels, then pressed buttons on the remote. Three old, white, cowboy-hatted men, one Black man—a former world-champion bulldogger—and one blonde woman appeared behind a table, representing the slowly diversifying senior leadership of the Pro Rodeo League. The League's logo hung in front of the cloth ruched beneath the tabletop, and was printed on the backdrop behind them, interspersed with the logos of the League's biggest sponsors. The camera was a little too far away and the backdrop a little too narrow. Jesse smiled at the imperfections typical of their media-unsavvy sport. What rodeo lacked in gloss, it made up for in passion. Heartened by Kenzie's belief, he swore to himself yet again that he wouldn't let it die without a fight.

They'd tuned in toward the end of the CEO's introduction, praising not only the competitors and stock contractors, but all the people who made rodeo successful, down to the administrators and volunteers at the smallest local levels. He previewed the sequence of announcements to come, but Jesse knew roughstock would be first. Human competitors always had more fans than the animals they rode, so there was more suspense around their lineups.

The CEO offered a stiff smile, and the screen cut to an ad for an equine hoof-care product.

"What's this low-rent crap?" a man in a pearl-snap shirt demanded as he approached the bar. "What happened to the sports?"

The bartender glanced their way. "It's the rodeo channel."

"We've had enough rodeo for one night. Switch it back."

"It's fine. Thanks anyway," Jesse told the bartender.

The bartender gave them an apologetic shrug and changed the channel. "Sorry about that. Anything else I can get you?"

Jesse shook his head, taking out his wallet. They had about three minutes to get upstairs and stream the announcement on their phones.

Three minutes until he found out whether he'd won the first round of this game he'd nearly forgotten he was playing.

Kenzie was extremely close to Jesse. Close enough to smell him. To feel the heat of his body. So close that every time he breathed, his arm moved against hers, leaving a sparkly trail of sensation penetrating all the way to her bones.

Not like they had much choice. They pressed together on the edge of the bed, hunched over the phone propped on his knee. They'd wasted a full minute trying to find the Cowboy Network on the hotel room TV before abandoning it for the app.

Three months ago Kenzie had tossed around the idea of a viewing party at the Broken B. Set up a projector in one of the barns, put out coolers full of beer cans, and she and her staff could lounge on hay bales, jeering the rest of the nominated bulls, then hooting and high-fiving when Not Nice's name filled the screen.

She felt like a lifetime had passed since then. That was before Custer, before he stole five people on her staff, before Bob Boyd insisted he needed a good reason not to be part of the dangerous spectacle that would stamp out their sport for good.

Back then Jesse was barely a real person, just a two-dimensional, cartoon villain. The evil corporate predator who hadn't blinked when he terminated her. The cold-eyed nemesis stalking the platforms at rodeos, so far up on his high horse he barely deigned to glare at her.

Now they were allies. She'd go so far as to describe them as friends. They'd kissed—more than once—and her breath caught at the memories of those fleeting connections. She was jammed up against his side on the bed they'd have to share tonight, near enough to count the threads in his jeans, her body thrumming with what she assured herself was excitement, *not* arousal.

Nice try. By the way, your pants are on fire.

They sure would be if these announcements dragged on any longer. She'd hardly heard a word of the droning speeches, so het up with pressure and anticipation and dread that her bare toes twitched on the thin carpet.

Finally John Webb, the legendary steer wrestler, took the microphone. His big smile lit up the screen, but when he said he'd be revealing the list of bulls selected for the League finals, Kenzie's back teeth ground together.

"Mother's Little Helper, High Rise Rodeo," he began.

Jesse was inhumanly still beside her as John read the names.

There's no reason to believe Not Nice won't make it. She snatched at her composure. *His average is right up there, he's a good performer, and he's as safe as they get. Unless there's something about me they don't like. Some bias against a woman, concern that I can't behave after that stupid fight with Jesse...*

And with that, her anxiety doubled. Good talk, Coach.

"Cherry Pie, M and J Cattle Company. Buccaneer, Singer Pro Rodeo. Hobgoblin, Singer Pro Rodeo. Lawn Gnome, Singer Pro Rodeo. Repeat Offender, Singer Pro Rodeo."

Jesse tossed the phone in her lap and stood, running his hands over his face and through his hair. She envied the relief etched in every line of his body, but it vanished almost instantly. When he sat down again, she felt the tension running through him, from his high shoulders to the stiff way he propped his palms on his thighs.

She frowned at him, her own uncertain fate momentarily forgotten. "You did it. You got all four bulls into the finals. That's a huge deal. Aren't you happy?"

“I’m happy,” he said in the unhappiest tone ever, resuming his intense focus on the screen.

Kenzie didn’t have the energy or the inclination to unravel the mysteries of Jesse Singer right now, not with her own career on the line. The top edge of his phone flashed with congratulatory notifications as John continued reading the qualifiers in what felt like a completely random order. Each time he opened his mouth she held her breath, bending toward that first syllable, and each time she slumped down again, the cycle of disappointment and optimism making her heart thump erratically.

She hadn’t kept track of how many bulls he’d announced, but they must be getting to the end of the list. A terrible knot of defeat formed in her throat, as she went from imagining how she’d celebrate to scripting how she’d justify herself to her boss. He’d hired her on the promise she’d get the Broken B to Vegas. If she didn’t deliver, and with Supreme Rodeo as a viable alternative—one he knew she disapproved of—she’d have an uphill battle clinging to her job.

She wished she could hold Jesse’s hand—and decided she would. There was so much more between them than their silly rivalry, now, and he was the only other person she knew who understood how she felt at this exact moment.

As John read out another name that wasn’t Not Nice, she reached over and laced her fingers through his. He squeezed her hand and held on tight.

“Southern Gothic, Occupy Rodeo. And our final selection for this year’s League finals in Las Vegas, Nevada, is Not Nice, from the Broken B Cattle Company.”

Kenzie was on her feet, then off them, because Jesse picked her up and swung her around the tiny hotel room. He whistled and whooped and she clung to him, wanting to cry, wanting to scream, wanting him to hold her like this forever and never put her down.

He didn't. She wrapped her legs around his waist and leaned back just enough to take in the full effect of his dimpled grin.

"Congratulations, Kenzie. You deserve it."

"Thank you," she told him. "Can't say I expected you to be this happy, though."

"Winning in Vegas won't count unless I beat the best. You're the best."

She stared at him, incredulity warring with hot-blooded yearning for this man whose honest, genuine admiration suddenly meant more than anything. More than her paycheck, more than the League finals, more than all the mistakes they'd made these last two years.

Jesse understood what this moment meant better than anyone, including her own boss. He was proud of her. He wanted her to succeed, even at his own expense, and that was more than she could say for almost anyone else in her life.

Her phone vibrated on the bedside table. This was her moment of glory, the first few minutes of the two months she'd spend basking in praise before she traveled to Vegas and the real games began. Her chance to preen, be victorious, and quietly gloat to her skeptics and detractors, finally deploying all the passive-aggressive thank-yous she'd mentally stockpiled.

Not to mention, with Custer's shadow creeping across the League's future, this could be her first and last trip to the finals. She should soak it all in while she could.

But Kenzie couldn't take her eyes off the man who still held her. His grip was strong, his blue-laser gaze steady.

None of that petty point-scoring mattered. She knew she deserved this. That was enough.

She tightened her arms around Jesse's neck, comforted by his solidity even as a shock of desire ripped through her.

This is what I want, she decided, brazen and free. *This is what I deserve.*

She breathed his name, an invitation and a plea. Instantly his mouth was on hers.

The buzzing of her phone became indistinguishable from the lust buzz clouding her brain. Jesse was big, and firm, and he smelled so damn good. She could get drunk on his scent, on the taste of his mouth, and on the delicious, anticipatory shivers that coursed through her body.

He was also impatient. He pinned her against the wall, palming her ass, his other hand teasing beneath her shirttails. She kneaded his shoulders and sought his tongue so urgently their teeth clicked together. Their movements were aggressive, hungry, raw, but this was no hate-bang.

They were finally claiming their dues.

In between kisses he gasped her name, tugging questioningly on the hem of her shirt. She managed a nod, then refocused on sucking his lower lip as he labored over her buttons.

He paused every few seconds, running his fingertips over the latest stretch of skin he'd revealed, jerking his head back to examine what he'd uncovered. Each time she appreciated his admiration for all of five seconds, then tightened her fingers in his dark hair and yanked his mouth back to hers.

Soon her shirt was open almost all the way to the bottom. Jesse scowled as he fought with the final button, leaned away from her to get a better look—and froze, his eyes leveled at her plain, cotton bra.

"Take that off." His voice was low and taut, his audible self-restraint making her tremble.

"As if I'd take orders from you. Put me down and strip, cowboy."

Jesse obeyed without question, easing her onto legs so weak she had to grab the edge of the dresser for support. He made quick work of his shirt, quicker work of the white T-shirt he wore beneath, hardly giving her more than a second to enjoy the play of his long, lean muscles as he pulled it over his head.

Then he unhooked his League finals belt buckle—good God, that was sexy—and stepped out of his jeans.

Kenzie took one look at the retro-style cowboys patterned on his boxers and busted up laughing.

"Is he lassoing a cactus? That's classic. Where did you get those?"

"The internet."

"I love it. Send me the link. That's freaking adorable."

"Not really the reaction I was hoping for."

"Then you should've worn something less distracting." She ditched her own shirt and moved against him.

He slipped her bra straps off her shoulders, then brushed his fingers over the tops of her breasts. While she reached behind her back to undo the clasp, he opened her belt and her jeans, then scooped his palms inside to squeeze her ass.

Kenzie sucked in a breath as her bra fell to the floor. She felt Jesse's gaze on her bare breasts, her tight nipples. She exhaled, acutely aware of how each tiny molecule of her flesh moved with that motion, as if he'd rewired her nerves simply by looking at her. His attention amped up her awareness, making her skin hum, her body delightfully hypersensitive.

He ducked his head and kissed her, then dropped his lips to her collarbone, to the space between her breasts, and to each nipple in turn. He sucked her stiff peaks until she had to bury her hand in his hair and clutch his upper arm just to stay upright.

He straightened long enough to tug her jeans down her hips, then he guided her onto the bed, trailing kisses along her stomach as he crawled up her body.

Even propped up on his elbows, he was a heavy, warm weight on top of her, and that first jut of his erection against her pelvis snatched the air out of her lungs.

"How am I doing?" His hand drifted down her side to her hip.

"Good. Real good."

"I'm surprisingly good at following directions in situations like this. Tell me if I'm going wrong and I'll fix it."

"You? Following directions? That is surprising."

"Only happens when I'm naked."

"You're not naked," she pointed out.

He shifted onto his side, yanked off his boxers, then eased over her again. With that thin, cotton barrier gone, the fullness of his heat and rigidity pressed into her thigh. She squirmed as desire pooled between her legs.

His fingers returned to her hip, daring under the waistband of her panties.

"Can I take these off?"

She nodded, too caught up in the hammering need swirling through her chest to find trivialities like words.

He slid off her panties, then replaced them with his warm, wide palm, cupping her sex so the heel of his hand put the faintest pressure on her core.

She couldn't help it—she rocked against his hand. She twisted within the welcome cage of his body, her nipples rasping against the soft hair on his pecs.

For a few minutes he toyed with her, flashing those evil dimples as he parted her and explored her, stroked her and teased her. Then he withdrew until she arched against him, silently begging for more.

"Please, Jesse," she whimpered, pulling his face down for a kiss.

"Please, what?"

"You know what."

He shook his head. "You have to say it."

"Please put that big cowboy dick of yours inside me."

His gaze clouded, and she felt the shudder that ran through him.

"But I haven't tasted you yet."

"Later," she promised, which she guessed meant this wasn't

a one-off. Whatever—at that point she would've handed over everything she owned to get him between her legs.

He plunged his finger inside her once more, tormenting her slippery heat. Then he moved across the room to his suitcase and produced a roll of condoms. He slid one over his thick, flushed erection, then returned to the bed, bracing his hands on either side of her.

She reached between them and rubbed the tip of him down into the slickness at her entrance and back again, relishing the way his eyelids sank and his jaw slackened.

Who's in charge now? She smiled.

He pushed inside, and whatever illusion she had that she could do anything but grit her teeth and hope she made the eight-second buzzer vanished, along with her last rational thought.

Their connection was wild and intense, throbbing and tight, and as messy and exhilarating as their whole dang story. Jesse's self-control faltered early, his fluid thrusts becoming uneven and desperate, but she didn't care. She was right there with him, moaning, squeezing, wrapping her legs around his waist and holding on for dear life.

Her arousal coiled at the apex of her thighs, pulsing and incandescent, and her toes curled in anticipation. This was like nothing else—Jesse was like no one else. The way he touched her, the way he gripped her, the way he kept pushing up to look at her made her feel like someone different, too.

No—not different. This was her, as bare and real as she got. Who was with her—that's what had changed. She'd found a man whose gaze was thick with worship, and not just when she took him to bed. He wanted her—all of her.

And when she was with him, tucked behind the protective shield of his respect, she had nothing to prove.

Her orgasm was a snapped limb, an unexpected, awesome rending that sent shock waves through her whole body. She dug her fingertips into Jesse's shoulders and pressed her face into his neck, her ragged groan coming from somewhere so uncharted it took her a second to realize it was hers. He wrapped her up tight, strong arms anchoring her trembling body, never letting go even as she whimpered and went limp and he throbbed inside her.

Kenzie sank back on the bed, finding space between the twitching aftershocks to register his searching, hesitant expression.

She smiled, lazy and feline. "If you think I'm done because I'm done, well, bless your sweet heart. I ain't heard the buzzer. Let me feel you finish, cowboy."

She clamped her hand on his ass and squeezed.

Turned out he really could follow directions.

Jesse groped for her in the predawn darkness, half awake and full of need.

He found her. Soft and warm, her breath feathering against his chest, her naked body the perfect combinations of plump and firm, downy and smooth.

And stiff, yes, two eager peaks insisting against his palm. He urged her onto her side and snuggled up behind her, pressing his insomniac erection into the cleft of her ass. He closed his eyes and drew a mental map of her breasts, filling his hands, gently pinching her nipples.

Kenzie squirmed against him as her breathing changed. He felt her heartbeat hasten, and he smiled into the pitch-black.

He didn't open his eyes—there was nothing to see. Her body told him everything he needed to know, from her subtle shiver when he circled his fingertip around her nipple to her shaky exhale when he slid his hand between her legs.

She was soaked, so wet that moisture streaked the insides of the thighs she parted for him. He'd made her that way, first with his erection, then with his tongue, and now he'd do it again. Coax another round of fresh, spring rain from her luscious, secretive slit.

He stroked her, toyed with her, until she got close. He couldn't help himself—he demanded another few seconds of her slick heat, even as she feebly tugged his wrist to pull his hand away.

Then she whispered magic words like *please* and *need you* and *inside*, and he plucked a condom from the box on the bedside table. He rolled on the latex, guided her hand so she could feel that he'd done it, and nearly choked on a flash of arousal when she hefted his balls and squeezed his base.

Kenzie planted her foot behind his legs, tenting her knee, opening herself wide. He nudged inside, slowly, slowly, then all the way, her answering moan nearly ending him.

He held himself still for a moment, cherishing this first second of connection. The stretch and the slide and the seamless joining. For once in his life, he was in the right place, at the right time, with the right woman.

She began to move, bucking against him, impatient and greedy. He touched her breasts, touched her core, kissed her shoulder, and in no time at all she was convulsing around him, gripping his forearm like he was the last thing tying her to earth.

Hang on as hard as you need, he told her silently, her climax accelerating his own until it was banging on the door behind his eyes. *You're safe with me. I've got you.*

Then she moaned his name, the rough sound part sob, all desire, and he shattered. One, two, three thrusts and he was gone, exploding into the amazing woman beneath his hands, finally a good man with the best intentions.

"Did you jerk off when we first got here?"

Jesse stopped short, the water he'd carried in from the bathroom sloshing over the edge of the glass.

"Beg pardon?"

"Right after we checked in. When you had a shower. Did you jerk off?"

Heat flamed in his cheeks as he set down the glass and slid

beneath the covers. They'd opened the curtains to admit the early-morning sun, but that was the extent of their progress toward actually leaving the bed.

"How did you know that?"

"You looked guilty when you came out. Don't worry, I indulged in a little self-relief around then, too." Kenzie patted his thigh consolingly.

His boner entered the chat.

"Imagine that, both of us having dates with our right hands on opposites sides of that wall. That's a missed opportunity if I ever saw one."

"I use my left hand, actually."

"That I would like to see."

"Play your cards right, maybe you will. But not this morning. We need to get organized, otherwise we'll never escape the nasty Northeast and return to God's favorite state. You know, the one with the panhandle."

Then she burrowed into his side as if she intended to be there a good long while.

Damn, this felt good. The physical satisfaction, sure, but also the easy comfort, the companionship, and the trust.

That was the kicker. For so long he'd been a threat to nearly everyone he encountered. The companies he was hired to dismantle, the colleagues he beat to promotions, and to her, the long-serving, keystone employee he'd yanked out and thrown away.

But last night she'd taken him into her body like he deserved to be there.

He pulled her in for a hug and planted a kiss on her forehead. She cuddled close with a contented sigh, and he put his arm around her shoulders, toying with the ends of her hair.

"Your hair used to be pink." He threaded his fingers through the bleached-blond strands.

"You remember that?"

"I liked it."

"So did I. Had to bleach it out when I went job hunting, though. Most ranchers aren't as open-minded as Lee was."

That landed between them like a chunk of plaster falling from the ceiling. Filthy, damp, and a harbinger of far bigger problems.

They eased apart. Kenzie drew the sheet up over her breasts and Jesse sat forward, propping his elbows on his thighs.

He blew out a breath, then turned to face her.

"I'm sorry. Sorry for what I put you through. I shouldn't have been so harsh, and I should've given you the benefit of the doubt when it came to the financials. I could've handled the whole thing a lot better."

"But you're not sorry for firing me."

"I can't afford you. I don't even pay myself. I would've had to let you go eventually."

She studied the hands knotted in her lap.

After a beat of silence she said, "That's good to know, I guess. That it wasn't personal. Not *all* personal, anyway."

"You're really good at your job, Kenzie. Look at Not Nice. Hell, look at Repeat Offender, who you worked with when he was a calf. I was grieving, I was angry, and I took it out on you. I'm sorry."

His heart clenched at the vulnerable smile she lifted to him. She was on the verge of offering him something rare and fragile, and he better steady his hands and keep it safe.

"That means a lot, you saying so. It's not something I hear too often."

He remembered their conversation in Chicago, the father who wouldn't speak to her. He pictured Bob Boyd, tightfisted and critical. He looped his arm around her waist and pulled this brilliant, sexy, hardworking woman back to him.

"I've never underestimated you," he murmured into her hair. "That's why I fought you so hard. You were the biggest threat

Singer Pro Rodeo's faced in a hundred years, until Custer came along."

Her breathing hitched. She surged up to kiss him, flattening her palms on his cheeks.

"Thank you," she whispered against his mouth, then eased back down, resting her head on his shoulder.

"Everybody'll be saying it soon. You're taking a bull to the finals, cowgirl."

"Dang, I nearly forgot all that."

"We got distracted."

She grinned. "Yeah, we did."

"We better not get distracted again if we want to make it to the airport on time," he cautioned—as he slid his hand over her thigh.

"I need to ask you something first."

"Shoot." His hand moved higher, promising himself they'd make it quick.

"Is this a what-happens-in-Philadelphia-stays-in-Philadelphia deal?"

He straightened, retrieving his hand. "What do you want it to be?"

"I'm not really looking to date."

"Neither am I," he said.

"But we could…hang out."

He nodded. "I like hanging out."

"We won't make a big thing out of it. We don't have to tell anyone."

"Definitely not."

She smiled. "I think we're finally on the same page, Singer."

"Same bed, at least."

She laughed at that, then clambered over to straddle him, her arms around his neck. He kissed her, she threaded her fingers into his hair, he cupped her ass.

They missed their flight.

Chapter Fourteen

Kenzie paused in the entrance of Singer Pro Rodeo's indoor arena and took a slow, deep breath.

She'd missed this place.

It wasn't better than what she had at the Broken B. Singer's arena was old, small, and—the punch line of a family story about Fred deciding to save money after a particularly mild winter, only for the next one to set subzero records—uninsulated.

No, the arena was no great shakes. Corrugated metal siding, ugly fluorescent lights, a dirt floor.

The animals that passed through here, though—that was its unspoken magic, what made the ground beneath her feet unlike any other in the sport. Decades of finals qualifiers, of finals winners, bulls and broncs and barrel horses. This arena produced the best roughstock in rodeo. There were plenty of challengers, but Singer would always be the best.

If it survived.

She walked inside, nodding to the other stock contractors already gathered on mismatched folding chairs set up in loose lines. Two chairs at the front faced the rest. She glanced around, spotting Jesse deep in conversation with another rancher.

The body on that man… She bit her lower lip. He wore a gray, felt hat with a cattleman crown, snug jeans and a long-sleeved Henley that clung indecently to the muscles in his upper arms.

She couldn't wait to get her hands on him again, and her optimistic underwear choices today reflected her hope they'd find time alone after the meeting.

This homebound period between the end of the competition circuit and the start of the finals in December was the slow season in rodeo. With just twenty-odd miles between them, Kenzie thought she and Jesse would have plenty of opportunities to fool around. But they'd both been so busy with the to-do lists they'd neglected during months of summer travel, they hadn't seen each other in person since they left Philadelphia two weeks ago.

They'd spoken plenty, though. Texted every day. Swapped a few photos.

And…had phone sex.

Kenzie dropped into one of the chairs at the front. They took a while to ramp up from emoji-laden flirtation to out-and-out dirty talk, but last night they got there. Her cheeks heated as she recalled Jesse's fiery expletives when she'd sent him a picture of her vibrator—and her back-arching climax when she let him listen to her use it.

He caught her eye, and his wolfish smile said he remembered, too.

"Howdy." He took the seat beside her, and the rest of the gathered ranchers sat as well.

"Howdy, yourself."

"Ready for this?"

She nodded. They'd been preparing for this meeting for two weeks—longer if they included the socializing beforehand, 90 percent of which had fallen to Kenzie. Assembled in the arena were all the rodeo stock contractors within driving distance, plus at least another twenty dialed into the videoconference open on Jesse's laptop.

"We good to start?" Jesse asked the room at large, receiving a chorus of nodded heads.

"Y'all hear us okay?" Kenzie waved at the computer propped on a card table. A sea of thumbs popped up on the screen.

"Thank you all for coming, for a start. I know we've got chore lists longer than our arms, so Kenzie and I appreciate your time. We'll keep it short. Over the last month or so, Singer Pro Rodeo and the Broken B have teamed up—"

"Did hell just freeze over?" one of the ranchers joked.

Jesse smiled. "No, but anyone with pigs might want to check whether they've flown off. Anyway, we've worked together to lift the hood on Casey Custer and Supreme Rodeo. See what it's all about and understand what it means for our sport."

Everyone leaned forward, anxiety tightening the atmosphere.

"It's bad, y'all," Kenzie said.

She and Jesse shared their experiences and their suspicions. Their industry peers listened intently, expressions flitting from concern to anger and back again.

"If Jesse hadn't jumped in, we might be at Chris's funeral right now," Kenzie insisted, ignoring the displeased look Jesse shot her. He hadn't wanted to include this anecdote at all, but already she could see its effect as their listeners recast him from inscrutable, big-city outsider to everyday hero worthy of his family name.

"He's pissed off with me for telling you this, but I'm not exaggerating. The bullfighters were nowhere, the EMTs didn't know what to do, and without any—"

Movement at the back of the arena caught her attention. The door slid open and closed, but the brief interval of light in between illuminated the newest arrival as he raised his hand apologetically and took the nearest seat.

Jay McCutcheon.

Her dad.

Her train of thought ran off the rails and fell over a cliff. What was he doing here? Was he trying to sabotage her? Was this some sick joke?

Or was he actually interested in what she had to say?

Jesse picked up where she left off, and from his questioning glance she could tell he didn't know who McCutcheon was. She wasn't sure how she felt about that—that the man whose attention she cared so much about wasn't even a blip on the radar of the Singer Pro Rodeo boss.

Kenzie made it through the rest of their spiel, but McCutcheon's presence dented her confidence, and she couldn't smooth it back out. She struggled to focus while Jesse outlined their plan for a stock-contracting coalition to boycott Supreme Rodeo, starving Custer of high-quality roughstock. Her mind drifted back to her father. Was he impressed that she sat at the head of this influential group? Did he know her bull qualified for the finals? Or had he written her off as riding on Singer's coattails, a pathetic hanger-on who couldn't let go even after she'd been fired?

"Kenzie." Jesse's tone implied it wasn't the first time he'd said her name. "Anything else?"

She shook her head.

"Then let's talk it over. Who's got something to say?"

They all did.

For the next forty-five minutes a roomful of work-roughened, obstinate ranchers—plus the ones hollering through the laptop—bitched and debated and argued. Everyone agreed that Supreme Rodeo was a problem, but the decision to turn their noses up at its lucrative contracts was trickier. The more successful the operator, the more willing they were to stand on principle, whereas the smaller-scale folks wondered aloud if there wasn't a way to take Custer's money without killing the League.

"I got mouths to feed," said one such rancher. "None of my animals made the finals, and just one of these events would take a big chunk out of the winter feed bill."

Nat Ware from Occupy Rodeo—a relatively young, Black stock contractor whom Kenzie had admired for years—raised his hand.

"We can all agree that boycotting Supreme Rodeo is asking more from some of us than it is from others. Maybe one of the benefits of joining the coalition, then, is being able to ask for help from other members. If your roof leaks, and the only way you can pay to repair it is to take money from Supreme Rodeo, you come to the membership instead. We all chip in with labor, or materials, or whatever it takes to get you fixed up without having to jump ship."

The crowd's reactions were mixed. Ranchers were notoriously thrifty, and although they all got along, at the end of the day they were competitors, too.

"Singer will commit to that, Nat. Happy to help others hold the line," Jesse said.

Instantly the power of the Singer name was palpable. Skeptical expressions turned thoughtful, and vocal confirmations popped up around the room like spring buds. Soon everyone was in agreement—except her father.

Who hadn't said a word since he'd walked in.

It took another twenty minutes to finalize the terms of the coalition, then Jesse stood to signal the end of the meeting.

Whether they'd all formally join remained to be seen, but Kenzie was happy. She'd expected a lot more reluctance and refusal but was pleasantly surprised by the willingness of these independent operators to join forces against a common enemy.

Either these salty stockmen were going soft in their old age, or they saw as clearly as she did that Supreme Rodeo could destroy their sport forever.

She mingled, keeping a close eye on McCutcheon at the edge of the group. The ranchers gravitated toward the big coffee carafes, fortifying themselves for the late-afternoon drive home, leaving him isolated. She wondered for the thousandth time what the hell he was up to.

Her suspense didn't last long. Jesse approached her father with his hand outstretched, with no idea they were connected.

Kenzie exhaled, squaring her shoulders. She could sidle away and let Jesse handle her dad, but this was her meeting. She'd treat McCutcheon like any other attendee.

Kenzie was twelve when her mom had told her Jay McCutcheon was her father, and she'd spent the next twenty-one years making peculiar orbits around him whenever they encountered each other in public. She'd slunk along walls, ducked behind pillars, pretended not to notice him while sneaking as many glances as she could. His presence intrigued and panicked her. Made her wonder what she'd missed—and whether he even cared.

Today she walked straight up to McCutcheon and looked him in the eye. She stuck out her hand, and he shook it—the first time in her life she'd touched her own father.

Hi, I'm the daughter you've never spoken to. Did you find the place okay?

They didn't introduce themselves. McCutcheon regarded her stiffly, then returned his attention to Jesse. "As I was saying, Custer approached me about supplying steers for the calf scramble."

"Calf scramble?" she repeated. "There was no calf scramble when we went."

"He's introducing afternoon performances, before the nighttime shows. They'll be shorter and more family-friendly, with mutton busting and the calf scramble."

"He's already bucking his animals twice. Is he planning on making them perform three times in one day?"

Her father shrugged, then rolled his eyes back to Jesse conspiratorially, as if he wasn't quite sure what this hothead expected him to say.

If he'd been anybody else on the planet—anyone but the dad some tiny, little-girl part of her still reached for—she would've chewed him out on the spot for that disrespectful, condescending gesture, unleashing her temper and not giving a damn whether he hated her for life.

Instead, she shrank. She ducked her head, barely noticing how Jesse angled himself in front of her, because she was too busy trying not to cry.

She shouldn't care about this man. He was vile, a creeper who'd impregnated a much younger woman, who had to be dragged through the courts before he'd cough up any money. He was immoral and unimportant, and already she'd flown far beyond him.

He was also her dad. Not the one she'd dreamed of, who'd roughhouse on the playground, and dance her mom around the kitchen, and read her a story at bedtime. But hers nonetheless. Half of her was him, and always would be.

She just wanted him to like her.

"I'm new to the stock-contracting game, myself. Finally able to have a little fun with my money now I'm done paying for college." McCutcheon gave Jesse an ingratiating smile.

Kenzie looked up. Was that a dig at the settlement that paid for her to go to school?

Jesse didn't respond, letting McCutcheon's attempt at humor fall flat on its face.

Her father cleared his throat, shrugging on a professional air. "Anyway, I'd love to get to know my neighbors over here at Singer. Maybe pick up some tips."

"The cattle I work with are slightly larger than the ones you're discussing with Mr. Custer." Jesse smiled, brutally patronizing.

Kenzie cringed on her father's behalf.

McCutcheon's wheedling expression collapsed into shock, but he recovered quickly.

"Steers are just the starting point, of course. Bulls are the big prize. Let me ask, do you golf? I'm a member of the country club over in Perry. It's only nine holes, but it's a sweet little course, and I'd be happy to—"

"I hate golf."

Jesse's posture became impatient. As he looked over McCutcheon's head at the ranchers filing out of the arena, Kenzie understood why he'd been so successful in the cutthroat corporate world.

He could be a real dick.

"Got it—no golf. Just a drink at the bar, maybe. Or I could come here?" McCutcheon suggested.

"I don't think so. If you'll excuse me."

Jesse walked away, already flagging down another stock contractor.

Then Kenzie and her dad were alone, facing each other in uneasy silence.

McCutcheon summoned a friendly smile—and she dared to hope that she read a dash of regret there, too.

"Saw the news about the League finals. Congratulations."

"Thanks," she said.

"Good bull you've got there."

She nodded, not sure where this was going—or where she wanted it to go.

He seemed to be waiting for her to say something, so she fumbled for a reply.

"So, uh, you're thinking of getting into stock contracting?"

His eyes lit up. "I am. It's something I've always wanted to try, and I have most of the infrastructure already. With the right modifications and a couple of leads on high-potential bulls, I could—"

"Kenzie. I need you," Jesse called from the other side of the arena, the sentence a command, not a question.

On one hand, she could've kissed him for springing her from the most uncomfortable conversation of her life—and she would.

Later.

On the other, she was oddly reluctant to step away. This was as close as she'd ever gotten to a civil conversation with her father. She wasn't sure when or if an occasion like this would arise again.

"He can wait." Could her dad see how much power she had? Not even Jesse Singer could tell her what to do.

But his attention had drifted. He looked over her shoulder, and Kenzie felt the door to this moment fall shut.

"Go ahead. There's someone I want to catch."

"Speak soon, maybe," she offered.

"Maybe," McCutcheon echoed.

But Kenzie knew it was over. He wouldn't follow up, and neither would she. They were exactly where they'd always been.

Nowhere.

She rejoined Jesse, and after another twenty minutes of the protracted, Great Plains approach to saying goodbye, they were alone. As soon as the final pickup disappeared into the dusk, Kenzie flung her arms around his neck, pushed the brim of his hat out of the way, and kissed him hard.

"Thank you," she told him when she let him up for air.

"For what?"

"That thing with McCutcheon."

"Who?"

"The guy trying to take you to the country club."

Jesse frowned, then recognition dawned. "I couldn't figure out why he was here. He wasn't on either of our lists. He must've heard about the meeting and decided to crash."

She could leave it there. Jesse didn't have to know that pompous gate-crasher had supplied 50 percent of her genetic makeup. She could simply savor the memory of Jesse's dismissal, and in moments of weakness, use it to remember how little Jesse had thought of her father, and how much less he mattered as a result.

But she wanted him to know. She wanted him to know everything, because it was the only way she'd trust whatever he said afterward.

"Jay McCutcheon is my father."

Jesse blinked. "That guy with the gray streaks in his hair? He's the rancher from Perry?"

"That's him."

Jesse planted his hands on his hips and exhaled, his gaze drifting out the propped-open door. When he dragged it back to her, he winced.

"I was pretty rude to him."

"It's fine."

"I didn't like how he spoke to you, and he wasn't even supposed to be here, so—"

"It's fine," she repeated. "We're not—we don't talk. He can barely look at me."

She pursed her lips before they could tremble, but Jesse used his thumb and forefinger to tilt up her chin. His gaze was soft and sympathetic, and she knew he'd seen it. He'd noticed how her father had cowed her. How she'd withered beneath his disdain.

"He doesn't deserve you."

She broke.

For years she'd told herself her father wasn't worth crying over, but now all those bottled-up tears came spilling out. She hated him, she loved him, she didn't want him, but she wanted him to want her, and soon she was a blubbering, sobbing mess.

Jesse snatched her into his arms, wrapping her up tight. "Please don't cry, Kenzie. He's a nobody. Not worth your heartache. Definitely not worth your tears."

"I know, it's just—it's so embarrassing. Why do I let him get to me like that? Why do I care so much about someone who couldn't care less about me? It's pathetic." She pressed her forehead against Jesse's chest.

"No, it's not." He urged her out to arm's length. "He's your dad—of course you care. It'd be weirder if you didn't. I'm just sorry he's disappointed you so badly."

"I guess he has." She framed it to herself in those terms for the first time. She thought about her father only in one dimension, as this omniscient perspective that refused to be impressed whenever she succeeded, poised to criticize if she failed.

But he had ownership here, too. Her perspective also mattered. And in that respect, he'd disappointed her constantly.

Jesse swept a lock of hair off her cheek and tucked it behind her ear. "You're a big freaking deal, Kenzie Wallace. Let him earn your attention if he wants to, because you've got plenty else to deal with."

She smiled. "I'll try. Thanks, Jesse."

"Anytime. One question, though."

"What's that?"

"Perry has a country club?"

Kenzie laughed. "It does. It's pretty nice, actually."

"Dang. Missed my chance."

"I'll take you sometime. I'm not a member, so we'll have to sneak in."

"Even better." He grabbed the belt loops on her jeans and tugged her against him. He dropped his head and kissed her, long and sweet and slow, exactly the balm her bruised soul needed.

"Want to sleep over?" he asked against her mouth.

Her eyes flew open. She'd been hoping for third base in a hayloft. A sleepover at the Singer ranch house was another prospect altogether.

"Are you sure?"

"Would I ask if I wasn't? No one will bother us. Mae's at her house in town. Trixie's at some girl-power conference in Miami, and Billie's helping Wyatt hide from his future mother-in-law. Even when they're all home they scatter at dinnertime. And my parents haven't been up to the house since… They won't come knocking. I promise."

Unexpected sadness streaked through her at the thought of Jesse all alone in that vast house every night, but she shook it off. Tonight, he'd have company—and she'd have him.

Kenzie beamed. "Got a spare toothbrush?"

"I'll rustle one up. Come with me."

He held out his hand, and she took it.

Jesse showed her parts of the ranch house she'd never seen with Lee. There hadn't been room for her then, not with Fred and Ruth still around, and various combinations of the Singer sisters camping out in their bedrooms during renovations on their own homes. She'd eaten countless meals with Billie and

Lee when they were on the road for rodeos, but her invitation expired at the ranch house's front door.

Not that she minded. She was Lee's friend and his employee, but she had her family, and he had his. She'd hosted plenty of Thanksgiving dinners for Ned and her mom in her single-wide on the Singer property. Now they came to her small house at the Broken B for Easter, enjoying the first breath of spring on the yawning acreage that constituted her front lawn.

Yet following Jesse through the unending, high-ceilinged spaces felt like watching a Labrador trotting down the length of an historic cathedral. He was oblivious to the tiny details that stopped her in her tracks. The enormous fireplace. The stately wooden beams overhead. Not to mention the one-of-a-kind pieces of rodeo history stashed on every spare surface.

"Holy crap. Can I touch this?" She pointed to a wood-mounted brass plaque propped at the end of a bookshelf.

"Sure."

"'Kansas State Fair, nineteen twenty-eight,'" she read aloud. "That's before the Dust Bowl."

Jesse lifted a shoulder. "Singers have been rodeoing a long time."

Eventually they made it to the oversize kitchen. It retained the rustic flooring and carved, wooden window frames from its earliest origins, despite being more up-to-date than much of the rest of the house.

"For an old house, everything sure is huge." Kenzie sat at the island while Jesse pulled ingredients from the fridge.

"It started big, then it got bigger. My great-grandfather built it, and he was a larger-than-life character. Then my grandfather took over and doubled down. He used to say, *What's the point of all this land if you're gonna plunk a tiny house in the middle?*"

Kenzie grinned at his hammed-up accent. "Is that how it works? The oldest son gets the house and the business, royal family style?"

Lee's presence shimmered in the corner, responding to Kenzie's inadvertent summons. Jesse's hand paused over the carrot he was chopping, but he resumed, and she felt the specter of his brother quietly dissolve.

She couldn't be sure, but she'd bet Lee was smiling.

"Not necessarily—just worked out that way, so far. Lee got involved early, but my parents would've handed over to any of us. Mae chose medical school, Billie's only interested in horses, and Trixie, well, her idea of money management is sweet-talking free drinks at the bar."

"So after Lee died, the business fell to you."

"I wanted it." He moved on to a zucchini. "No one asked me—I offered. I had the education, the experience, and nothing I couldn't leave behind."

She tilted her head. "Nothing—and no one?"

His expression darkened. Maybe she'd pushed their newfound openness too far.

Then he looked up at her with eyes as clear as a summer sky, and a smile bright enough to match. "I belong here."

Dinner was delicious, and so was the man who'd made it. They lingered over bowls of Braum's, she helped him wash up, and he led her up the wide staircase.

Jesse's room was even bigger than she expected, but it was boring. No art on the walls, only a few books on the desk, the linens plain, pale blue. She knew instantly this hadn't been his childhood bedroom, as definitively as she knew she didn't want to ask who used to sleep here. They were here, now, together. Dragging in the past wouldn't serve either of them.

She let it slip away, and take the future with it, freeing her mind to think only of the present. Of Jesse's light touch as he unbuttoned her shirt. The brush of his lips over her collarbone. The scent of his hair when she lowered her face to the crown of his head, leather and frost and secretive shadows.

The first time was quick, neither of them able to stall their mounting lust for a minute longer. The second time was playful, full of teasing smiles, laughter, and fun, flirty kisses.

The third time changed everything.

Kenzie was in a thick, dreamless sleep when Jesse reached for her, the kind that took a while to crawl all the way out of. She became aware of him in fragments—warm palms, hard leg, the press of the hot length that instantly flooded her core.

She rolled over to look at him, enjoying that strange, fleeting equality of perspective when two differently heighted people were face-to-face on the pillows. She stroked his stubble-roughened cheek and he stared at her, intent and unblinking.

Something brewed in his blue eyes—something she couldn't articulate. Radiant and enduring and terrifying, it shimmered inside her, too.

She couldn't look at it anymore. Couldn't bear to watch it flicker in this man's eyes, or to let him speak it aloud. That was a step too far, a step toward the edge of a cliff. She didn't know what might be at the bottom, but she had no intention of perching on the edge to look.

So she took him in her hand, teased the head of his erection over her entrance. His eyes closed, and he cupped her breast, and she was safe. She kept him busy with her mouth and her fingers. Then he was inside her, and they both had more urgent things to think about.

His strokes were long and unhurried, easing in and out. He flashed her a haughty smile when she bucked against him, her climax already breathing down her neck. He dropped to his elbows, and she clamped her thighs around his hips, silently begging for more, for him, for everything.

Her orgasm ripped through her, a scalding, throbbing pulse that made the world go white. She froze, digging her fingertips into his shoulders, every muscle immobilized—and that's when the ember she'd shut out found its way back in.

It glowed in her gut when Jesse shuddered on top of her. When he kissed her deeply after tossing the condom. When he fell asleep beside her, his arm heavy across her waist. She lay still for a while, willing it away, but it brightened every time he breathed. Finally, she slipped out of the bed and walked to the window.

Jesse hadn't closed the curtains—not unusual for a ranch-reared cattleman who rose with the sun. Stars were abundant in the inky sky, and the rolling swells of Singer land seemed endless.

Kenzie inhaled, giving herself over to a flash of reckless imagination. Dreaming for the briefest of seconds that she could be here. The man in the bed could be hers. She'd be part of this family, this legacy, in a way she'd never thought possible.

That Jesse might love her as much as she was beginning to love him.

She whipped back toward the bed as fear rose in her throat.

Don't be ridiculous. This wasn't love—it was neediness. Weak, pathetic desperation for a man's affection and approval.

Jesse had helped her loosen the grip of her father's opinion. Now she was replacing her dad's power with Jesse's, trading a disinterested parent for an unavailable rival.

Because that was what he was, at the end of all this. They'd always be on opposite sides of the scoreboard, their own success hinging on the other's failure. That was no basis for a relationship. They probably couldn't even be friends.

This was a short-lived self-indulgence, that was all. A way to vent the stress of Casey Custer that'd expire as soon as they arrived in Vegas. No need to make any more of it than that. Enjoy the sex and move on.

But when she eased back into the bed, when Jesse murmured in his sleep, when his hand found the small of her back and stayed there, she knew it was too late.

This would end.

And it would hurt.

Chapter Fifteen

Jesse stared at the rack of cowboy hats in the guest room closet, his gaze snagging on the two holes disrupting the rows of perfectly shaped, diligently maintained crowns.

The one he'd broken in Chicago, and the one he'd lost in Philadelphia.

Lee'd had a thing for hats. He bought too many, too often, ignoring their dad's grumbling that a man only needed three: summer, winter and wedding. Still, Lee accumulated more. Pricey ones, too. Fur felt and straw, black and pecan and charcoal, all types of creases, all manner of buckle sets, all perfectly shaped to fit his head.

Jesse brushed his fingertips over a sandy-colored brim. Lee had bought it in Wichita Falls. Jesse was home from college for the summer, hauling bulls around the country in dusty jeans, while his friends wore ties and interned at investment banks. His life at Yale felt so far removed from the stuffy cab of his brother's truck that sometimes he questioned whether he'd been there at all, or if the last year had been a dream.

"Detour," Lee had announced as he'd taken the exit toward Wichita Falls. Jesse bitched and moaned, called it a waste of fuel. Said Dad would hand them their asses if they weren't home in time to help unload.

Lee just smiled and turned up the radio.

When they got to the Western wear store, Lee browsed for ages. While his brother debated between sand-colored and beige,

Jesse sulked in an upholstered chair, feeling so much bigger than this life, this succession of tiny towns, empty diners, miles and miles of highways. One of the other customers made a tasteless political joke and Jesse stormed out to wait in the truck, leaving Lee to smooth things over. To excuse his hotheaded Ivy League brother and turn an offended stranger into a friend.

Not that Lee mentioned it. He'd simply emerged with his freshly shaped hat, patted Jesse's arm and pulled out of the lot.

Jesse raised his fingers to the hat in question, then dropped his hand. He couldn't wear that one. There'd be another, a hat that wasn't wrapped up in memories and heartbreak. Maybe that black felt, up top. Awful wintry for October, but—

"Here you are."

Mae stood in the doorway, eyes soft. Although he spent the least time with her, he had a special closeness with his fraternal twin. As toddlers, they'd even had their own language. She was the sister he wouldn't speak to for six weeks, then call in a moment of crisis, and she'd know exactly what to say.

"What're you doing out here?" he asked.

"Bringing Trixie a bunch of dresses. She's doing another one of those free gown closets at the high school, this time for the winter formal."

"She couldn't pick them up in town?"

Mae smiled. "Maybe I wanted to check on you, too."

"And drink my wine."

"And eat your food. What're we having?"

"You're in luck. It's taco night."

Mae raised her fist in triumph, then lowered it as her gaze slid to the hat rack.

Jesse said nothing. He sat on the edge of the bed, and Mae sank down beside him.

"I lost those two," he told her eventually, indicating the gaps. "Can't even keep his hat collection intact. Probably shouldn't borrow another one, but here I am, taking what isn't mine."

"It's not borrowing. Lee's gone, and this is what we have left. These are all yours, if you want them. Personally, I think Lee would've been over the moon to see one of his treasured hats on your head. He was so proud of you."

Jesse swallowed hard. "He always overestimated me."

"We're not talking about hats, are we?"

Jesse looked up at the rows of color-coordinated crowns, the gradient from crisp, off-white straw to rich black.

The beautifully curated collection of a well-heeled connoisseur.

A lie.

Lee spent money like he was landed gentry. As if the Singer name alone was enough to maintain their status as rodeo aristocracy. But this was America; this was Oklahoma. Seasons changed, fortunes rose and fell, and one's own labor was all that could be relied upon.

Jesse didn't hold it against his brother. Lee was a showman, at his best when he was pumping hands and slapping backs. He wasn't cut out for the financial intricacies of a tight-margin, high-cost business like theirs. Jesse should've realized that the day his brother emptied a tank of gas diverting to Wichita Falls to spend five hundred dollars on a hat. Jesse could've focused his studies on commodity futures instead of stock markets, learned the ins and outs of small businesses instead of global corporations. He could've come home and been Lee's second-in-command, locking down the finances and freeing Lee to do what he did best.

But he'd waited too long. And now it was too late.

Out of nowhere he thought of Kenzie. Her quiet forgiveness. He'd taken so much from her, yet she'd given him her body and her trust.

Maybe he owed it to her—and to himself—to offer a little of his trust, too.

"The business is in bad shape, Mae."

His sister frowned.

"I've stabilized it," he went on. "I've stopped the bleeding. But I can't breathe out until we've taken home a big chunk of the purse in Vegas. It'll be at least another year before we can think about growth, or upgrades, or new investments. That's if Supreme Rodeo doesn't shrink the whole industry—or kill it completely."

"Back up. When did this start?"

"The minute I opened Lee's ledgers."

"But that was two years ago," she exclaimed.

Jesse nodded.

"And you haven't told us? My God, Jesse, this is way too much for you, for anyone to..." She exhaled, briefly closing her eyes. "Say what you don't want to say."

He shook his head.

"You have to."

"There's no point."

"Say it."

Jesse blew out a breath, focusing on the rows of hats. The remnants of a life lived with foolhardy joy, irrepressible optimism and stalwart love.

I'm sorry, brother.

"Lee mismanaged the finances for years. He constantly overspent, and he made no effort to reduce expenses. Another six months, maybe a year, and we would've been bankrupt."

"Bankrupt." Mae pressed her hand against her stomach.

He knew the feeling. The same sinking nausea that'd robbed his appetite since he took over. The sickening horror that a hundred-year legacy was on its knees, and the gnawing guilt at being part of the generation that destroyed it.

"I'm turning it around, Mae, I swear. We won't lose this place. We'll be fine. All of us."

"Of course you are. I don't doubt that for a second. But why are you doing this by yourself? Why didn't you tell us?"

"Because y'all didn't need another reason to be sad. Billie

couldn't say his name without crying. Trixie was having panic attacks. Our parents still struggle to leave the house. I wasn't here when he needed me, so I owed him this, at least."

"Oh, Jesse. Please don't tell me you think this was your fault." She put her hand on his arm.

He'd knotted his fingers on his knees, and now he squeezed them so hard his knuckles went white. "I could've helped him. If I'd been home more often, he would've asked me. I could've prevented this."

Mae murmured his name, the two, faint syllables heavy with sorrow. She withdrew her hand into her lap and for a minute they sat in silence. Jesse felt his dead brother behind him, looking on from his place beside the window. Near enough Jesse expected to feel Lee's hand on his shoulder.

Please don't hate me. But Jesse had broken his last promise. He deserved Lee's disappointment.

"I wasn't at work that day," Mae blurted.

He turned to her, surprised. Her expression was closed, her gaze fixed on her hands.

"I was supposed to be, but I switched shifts. I worked the overnight, so I could go to the rodeo that weekend. The stupid rodeo," she spat, the words thick and bitter.

How self-centered could he be, thinking he was the only one with guilt? Walling himself off, wrapping up his catastrophic financial secret in brotherly joviality. Believing he was protecting his sisters when really he was protecting himself from their grief. He'd never once asked himself whether he might be the only one nursing regrets. He accepted his sisters' outward despair and moved on, doing his best not to add to it but never offering to lighten it, either.

Not anymore. He had to be more than the business-minded leader and the meticulous accountant. He had to step up and be the solid foundation on which his trembling sisters could lean. The reliable, unjudgmental haven he should've been for Lee.

He gentled his voice and reached for her hand. "Even if you'd been at the hospital that day, it wouldn't have changed anything. The doctor—"

"Has nothing on me," she interjected, tears spilling over her cheeks. "I'm one of the best emergency medicine physicians in the state, if not the country. I could work anywhere, any system, any city. But no, I climbed up on my high horse and preached about expanding access to health care in rural America. Then my own brother gets in a wreck, and where am I? Asleep in the middle of the day, so that weekend I can go splint the finger a bronc rider got caught in his rigging."

"Now you're talking nonsense, and you know it," he told her. "There are rodeo competitors alive today who might not be if you hadn't been there."

"And I'd trade every one of them for our big brother."

"I know, Mae. I know. But it doesn't work like that." He pulled her to his chest.

Jesse held her while she cried into his shirt, and he remembered his dad holding his grandmother after his grandfather died. He thought of the funeral, one of his first real encounters with a synagogue. The trip to Tulsa, the rabbi who welcomed them so warmly. His faith had been at the forefront in a way it never was otherwise, an early awakening to how different he truly was to the rest of his community. Those days had solidified his identity as a scion of America's greatest Jewish rodeo dynasty.

He reached for that now, past the gnarled mess of his feelings to the truths he'd known all his life, and the beliefs that steadied him when the earth shook violently beneath his feet.

"Hey." He eased his sister backward, finding her pleading expression. "You're a doctor, in a specialty that sees more death than most. What do you tell yourself when you lose a patient?"

She sniffed, wiping her eyes. "I did my best to sustain life, but death is God's decision."

"Then Lee's death can't be a mistake. If you were supposed to save him—if he was supposed to still be here—he'd be alive."

"Pretty arrogant to think otherwise, I guess."

"Not arrogant. Human. We're all trying to make sense of what happened."

"When we should be focusing on his memory, and how we'll affirm all the best parts of him in our own lives."

Jesse smiled. "Did you just trade guilt about his death for guilt about mitzvot?"

"No. It's a reminder, not a scolding. Not that you need it, sneakily keeping all the financial balls in the air."

"You literally save people. I just haggle."

She rolled her eyes in playful admonishment, but the smile she managed wasn't totally convincing.

"Should I tell you what you already know?"

"I need to let Trixie and Billie in on the state of the business? No. You don't have to say a word."

"Then I'll trust you to choose the right time, and to pull me in if I can help."

He nodded, an implied promise he had no idea how he'd keep.

Mae turned back to the hat rack. "Have you decided?"

Jesse took in the orderly rows one more time, his gaze lingering on the one from Wichita Falls. He stood up and shut the closet door.

Mae sprang to her feet and hugged him, catching him by surprise. She released him just as suddenly, the smile she tilted toward him packed with pride and relief.

"You said tacos, right?"

"And wine," he confirmed.

"Don't need to ask me twice."

"I didn't ask you once."

"Why yes, I'd be delighted to dine with you, dear brother. Shall we?" She extended her hand.

"Go open the bottle."

Mae flipped her hair as she walked out, tossing him a warm, grateful smile over her shoulder.

Jesse stood for a moment in the empty room, wondering if Lee could feel him.

Wondering what Lee thought.

He caught movement in his peripheral vision. Jesse spun, coming eye to eye with his reflection in the mirror on the closet door.

Lee was here. Jesse couldn't see him, couldn't touch him. But his soul was close enough, Jesse could've sworn the old floors creaked under his brother's weight.

He froze, unsure whether his virtue or his betrayal had summoned his brother. After a moment's uncertainty, though, Jesse exhaled. Air moved through lungs feeling wider and looser than they had in years. His shoulders dropped, his fingers uncurled at his sides.

Lee forgave him. He knew it without a doubt. Lee understood why he'd concealed this awful secret, and he gave Jesse permission to unwrap it. He wouldn't want his younger brother staggering beneath the burden of his poor decisions. Lee never hesitated to take whatever blame he deserved.

"Thank you," Jesse told the empty room, the indifferent space that may not have held any soul but his. He got no answer, no flickering light or chilly wind, but he decided to believe anyway.

Lee had forgiven him. His chosen truth.

Whether he could forgive himself was a question for another day.

"This one?" Jesse held the phone up to the potted clump of flowers.

"Does that look golden yellow to you?"

"Yes."

Ruth Singer's exasperated sigh was so loud, Jesse smiled

apologetically at the people down the aisle. He cut the video and took the phone off speaker.

"Those are yellow bells. You're looking for sneezeweed. They have dark green—"

"Dark green leaves and golden-yellow flowers. I know. So do fifty other plants in here."

"These have what might look like a big ball in the center, and the leaves..."

Jesse tuned out the same description his mother had given him five times in two different nurseries before this one, staring helplessly at the rows of plants. He could assess a cow's conformation from ten feet away, but these bunches of green and yellow all looked the same.

"It'd be a lot easier if you came out here and did this yourself." He bent to examine yet another yellow-flowered plant.

"I told you, Dad has a headache, and I don't want to drive that far on my own."

Jesse pinched the bridge of his nose, biting back the fed-up comment balancing dangerously on the tip of his tongue.

"Hold on, I need someone to help me."

His searching gaze must have broadcast his bewilderment, because within seconds a woman with a sunny smile and a blue streak in her gray hair walked over.

"Anything I can help you with?"

"Yes, ma'am, my mom is looking for—actually, I'll let her explain." He passed over his phone.

He studied the woman—Irlene, according to her name tag—as she listened to his mother's explanation. He'd never been here before, yet she looked familiar. Something about the shape of her eyes, that natural upward tilt of the corners of her mouth...

"Oh yes, we have sneezeweed. Just a minute."

She motioned Jesse over, then handed him his phone. "Can you make it so she can see?"

He switched back to video.

"That's it!" his mother exclaimed. "Thank you so much for giving my son a hand. All that money we spent sending him to Yale, and he can't tell yellow bells from sneezeweed. Jesse, grab five of those. Actually, make it six."

Jesse smiled at Irlene as he hung up, ready with a joke about his mother's name-dropping, but her friendly expression had turned openly hostile.

"Jesse Singer?"

"Yes, ma'am."

"Ned," she called in a tone that suggested Ned might be the security guard. Instead, a reedy, bespectacled man hustled over, his eyes wide with alarm.

"This is Jesse Singer," Irlene said.

Ned's face froze over with icy disdain.

Jesse raised his hands and glanced between the two of them, bewildered. "I'll pay for the plants. I wasn't going to steal them."

"Stay right where you are. Don't move an inch." Irlene turned to Ned. "Keep an eye on him."

"Oh, I will." Ned crossed his arms.

For a few minutes he and Ned remained in an uneasy standoff as Jesse tried to figure out what had brought them here. Was his mom a serial plant thief? Had Trixie broken their son's heart? He hadn't personally deflowered anyone he knew of, but he supposed—

"Here he is," Irlene announced, leading a woman in muddy rubber boots and overalls.

A woman who instantly brought a smile to his face, despite the circumstances.

"Afternoon, Miss Wallace." He touched the brim of his pewter-gray hat.

Kenzie's eyes sparkled with amusement. "You're awfully far from home today, Mr. Singer."

"He just waltzed on in here like it was nothing." Irlene propped her hands on her hips.

Suddenly it all made sense. His hunt for sneezeweed had taken him farther and farther from Stillwater—and closer to Perry. Kenzie had told him her mom worked in a nursery, and now the resemblance between the two of them was so obvious he couldn't believe he hadn't seen it.

"Should we take him out back?" asked Ned—who must be her stepfather.

"Y'all do what you want, but I ain't got bail money." Kenzie grinned. "Come on, you two. I told you, Jesse and I are friends now."

"He's no friend to me," Irlene humphed.

Kenzie briefly glanced skyward. "Jesse, let me introduce you to my charming mother, Irlene, and her kind and generous husband, Ned."

The couple exchanged a wary glance, then took turns shaking Jesse's outstretched hand.

"You made a big mistake, letting her go," Irlene informed him.

"I'm reminded of that every time she outscores me."

"Which is often." Kenzie beamed.

"Y'all got any more of these Supreme Rodeo excursions lined up?" Ned asked.

Jesse sensed Ned was grateful for the cessation of hostilities. He clearly wasn't the confrontational type, so Jesse respected him even more for standing up for his stepdaughter.

"Not yet." Kenzie turned to Jesse. "What are you buying, anyway?"

"Sneezeweed. For my mom."

"Ned, why don't you get that set up for him at the register, and I'll show him the pumpkin patch."

"Great idea." Ned put his arm around his still-glaring wife.

Kenzie took Jesse's elbow and steered him toward the back exit.

"Thought I was about to be a victim of frontier justice," he told her as soon as they were out of earshot.

"Insult my mom's daughter and due process goes out the window. You're lucky I'm here today." She led him outside, where rows of orange pumpkins brightened the overcast autumn day. She guided him to a tidy wooden shed, tugged him inside and shut the door.

Kenzie threw her arms around his neck, and that was all the invitation he needed. Within seconds he had her perched on the edge of a cluttered worktable, oblivious to the probably sharp, possibly dangerous objects thudding to the floor. He kissed her like it had been years since they'd seen each other, because that was how it felt. Like every minute he spent without her was three times as long and a hundred times emptier.

Too soon she pulled back, giving him a rueful smile.

"If I wasn't wearing overalls, I'd have you between my legs already."

"We could figure something out." He unclipped one of the straps and palmed her breast.

She hissed with pleasure, then leaned out of his reach and redid the buckle.

"Tempting, but if a kid wanders away from the pumpkin patch and discovers a full-on porno in progress, it'll be bad for business."

"All right. For the children."

He helped her down and she took him back outside, where he unzipped his jacket to the chilly air in the hopes it might cool the erection throbbing in his jeans. Kenzie pointed out the different features of the pumpkin patch, ending on the tractor.

"That's my job, today—hayrides. I can't normally help during the week, but they were short-staffed, so I'm filling in."

"Does Boyd know you're moonlighting as a tractor driver?"

She shrugged. "It's the offseason. Not much to do over at the Broken B where, ironically, stuff is a lot less broken compared to your place."

"Hundred-year-old name, hundred-year-old equipment. Don't

remind me. This is a hell of a setup." He scanned the various activities.

"Gets more complicated every year, but they love it, Ned and my mom. It's funny, she's so outgoing and he's so mild-mannered, but when the rubber hits the road, he's always the push my mom needs. For years and years she just went without, because she couldn't bring herself to stand up to my biological father. Ned did that—he convinced her to believe in herself. To be brave and ask for what she deserved, and not care what my father thought about her for doing it."

"And that was helpful? That push?"

"It was more of a repeated, gentle nudge, but yes, because it came wrapped up in love and support."

"Good for him. And her."

The door from the nursery swung open to admit a mother and two little boys, who eagerly claimed the first pumpkins they touched.

Kenzie nodded inside. "Let's get going while I can still squire you through your transaction. I don't think my mom's carrying, but you never know. I like your hat, by the way."

He reached up to square it on his head, still getting used to the fit. "I just bought it."

"It suits you," she said.

Kenzie dropped his hand as they rounded the corner to the till, but from the way Irlene's sharp gaze softened, Jesse knew they'd been caught.

He held his breath, waiting for the panic—but none came. In fact, he liked the idea of making their relationship public, at least to their families. They had two months until the finals—two months to figure out how to take this forward. Two months to be together with minimal complication and build a foundation that might withstand the inevitable conflict ahead.

He'd ask her, he decided on the spot. He'd tell her he was ready to drop the secrecy, if that was what she wanted, too.

"Here they are, the *friends*." Irlene dragged out the word as she looked between the two of them, her disapproving scowl undermined by a teasing smile.

"Yes, Mother. You taught me to open my heart to all comers, even douchebags like Jesse." Kenzie batted her eyelashes in mock sweetness.

"And you're her friend now, are you? You're sure about that?" Familiar green eyes turned on him.

"Yes, ma'am. We didn't know each other well before, but now that I've seen how smart, and strong, and resilient, and courageous she is, not to mention funny, and caring, and sincere, I realized that…"

I'm falling in love with her.

They were all staring at him, Ned and Irlene with endeared smiles, Kenzie with wide eyes.

He cleared his throat, shifting his boots on the ground that seemed to have tilted.

"I realized that she's great," he finished.

He couldn't look at her. He worried if he did, he'd see regret or withdrawal or, worst of all, pity. For months now he'd found belonging in her eyes—or thought he had. Finding something else at this moment, of all of them, might kill him.

He focused on his purchase, pulling out his wallet, nodding without hearing Ned's instructions about watering. Ned and Irlene arranged the pots in a cardboard tray, and Jesse pulled out his credit card—then held it back.

A repeated, gentle nudge, wrapped up in love and support. Like Kenzie said.

"On second thought, can we swap these for the yellow bells? If it's not too much trouble."

Irlene frowned. "It's not, but your mom wanted—"

"I know what she wanted. This might nudge her in a better direction."

He found the wherewithal to glance over at Kenzie, and her soft, knowing smile warmed him from his head to his toes.

This could be it. He held the thought at arm's length, terrified the idea might vanish if he reached for it too fast, treated it like anything other than a whisper of possibility. *We might have a chance.*

Kenzie left for her three-thirty hayride, shooting him a lingering glance over her shoulder. He helped Ned exchange his yellow-flowered plants for different yellow-flowered plants, relieved to find Irlene's not-at-all-homicidal smile when he returned to the register.

"I'm glad to see you two kissed and made up, such as it is." She handed over his receipt. "But if you mess with my daughter again, I'll cut off your dick myself."

"Irlene," Ned exclaimed.

Her sweet smile only deepened. "Rusty gardening shears, Mr. Singer. I have several pairs."

"Yes, ma'am," he croaked, then plucked up his box of plants and hightailed it out to his truck.

He hadn't even turned the key in the ignition when his phone buzzed with a new text.

Kenzie's name was at the top of the screen.

Come over tonight.

He smiled. As if wild horses could keep him away.

Her mother, on the other hand…

Chapter Sixteen

She clung to him in the predawn darkness, her face buried in his chest, her arms tucked inside his unzipped coat. The porch beneath her bare feet was cold, but she was bathed in his warmth. It soaked through the oversize T-shirt she'd slept in, and so did the feel of him, denim and cotton and muscle and bone. Yet when she shifted her weight, her bare leg brushed jeans made cool by the early-morning chill, and she knew the day ahead was tugging him away from her, its urging fingers unknotting their bed-warm closeness.

Kenzie was being greedy. She'd had him for four nights and the whole of Sunday, knowing full well he'd need to leave before sunrise on Monday to get back to the ranch and start the week. Still, she wanted just a minute more. Another few breaths of the only man she'd ever loved.

Because she did love Jesse, whether she wanted to or not. These last several days had confirmed what she hadn't been brave enough to admit.

He was a welcome, seamless presence in her bed, in her house, in her life. They'd talked shop over the dinners he'd made, adding more stock contractors to their informal alliance, mapping out which bull riders they could convince to join them. They drafted a letter to the League, asking for public condemnation of Supreme Rodeo as a perversion of the sport, and resolved to send it as soon as they had concrete evidence of Custer's wrongdoing. They tossed around the idea of sending in a mole, someone Custer wouldn't suspect, and got as far as jotting down a couple of names before the lure of the bedroom became too strong.

That was when she truly lost herself—when Jesse's touch, his body, his murmured adulation overwhelmed her deepest doubts. He made her feel powerful, gorgeous and extraordinary in a way that lingered after each climax, becoming increasingly permanent. Bedding into her self-perception whether he was there or not.

"I'd like to tell my sisters about you. About us," he'd said that first night.

She'd hesitated, concerned the unforgiving light of other people's opinions might shrivel their still budding connection. But last night she'd finally agreed, emboldened by the tunnel vision she'd found when she was with him. She'd barely thought about her father all week, never mind what he might think of all this.

Jesse didn't think he was important, and that gave her permission to forget about him, too.

"I have to go."

His soft words drew her back to this cold moment on the cold porch, and the cold demands poised to take him from her.

"When will I see you again?" Kenzie resented the entreaty in her question, but she couldn't help it. She was addicted to him, and she'd be counting the hours until she was in his arms again.

"Tonight. It'll have to be late—Billie will be at the house. Come over afterward. Spend the night."

She nodded. "I will."

"I'll tell them on Friday. We're having dinner with my parents. Then we won't need to sneak around anymore."

She nodded again, less convinced this time. "Okay."

He smiled. "It'll be fine. They'll love you. Just like—"

He caught himself, but it was too late—her reckless heart filled in the end of that sentence.

She wasn't ready to hear it, and she sure as hell wasn't ready to say it. She took the coward's way out and kissed him, silencing the words that would change everything.

He sighed when she finally released him, pressing his forehead against hers. Then he straightened, set his hat on his head, and let her go.

The cold was instant and penetrating. She wrapped her arms around herself, feeling oddly exposed as her nipples tightened against the thin fabric. He'd seen every part of her, pushed his tongue inside her most intimate flesh, yet she didn't want him to see her like she felt right now. Needy, scared and vulnerable.

Didn't want him to know he'd made her that way.

Thankfully, he walked to his truck in blithe ignorance, pausing by the driver's-side door to give her one last hot, heavy look. Then he was gone, and she hurried inside.

Her feet warmed, her hands lost their numbness, but the unease in the center of her chest remained.

Kenzie loved Jesse, a fact which exhilarated and alarmed her in equal measure. For so long she'd worked to become who she thought someone else wanted—the successful, ceiling-busting stock contractor her dad couldn't help but be proud of. The thought of entrusting her whole self to someone, her *real* self, the one that fretted, and failed, and got scared, and got sad… That was a lot.

And to place that soft, shivering self in the hands of Jesse Singer, of all people—that was even more.

She'd have to think this through. Decide if she was ready—or if she ever would be.

"Here you are." Bob Boyd stepped through the door of her office.

Kenzie smiled a greeting. "Here I am."

"What're you up to?"

"Reshuffling the rota. We'll be shorthanded this winter. I've explained to the guys they may need to work shifts outside their normal hours. They seem okay, but let's see how they feel once we get into the holiday season."

He shrugged. "If they don't want to work, we don't need them here."

Kenzie let that slide. Bob's interest in the business waxed and waned depending on what else he had going on. While the harvest was in full swing, he was content with weekly updates and screenshots of prize-money deposits.

Now the last soybean crop was finished and the fields were empty, turned over to the cattle to forage. From the way he shifted in his chair and glanced around the office, Kenzie knew she'd be seeing a lot more of him.

Fine. If he was in the mood to be involved, she'd involve him. "Where are we on Ramon's salary?"

To her astonishment, Bob grinned. "We're going to match Custer's offer. In fact, I'm planning to give everyone a raise, including you."

Kenzie brightened. "Really? Thanks, Bob. That's great news. The guys will be delighted, and this will be a weight off Ramon's mind. I know he didn't want to work for Custer, but the numbers made it a hard decision."

"Well, he might have to change his tune on that, since he'll be working with Custer after all."

She froze. "What?"

"The Broken B is going to Supreme Rodeo. Yeehaw!" He shaped his fingers into pistols and pretended to shoot in the air.

Panic took root in Kenzie's stomach and began to grow, a twisting, vining weed that wrapped around her lungs and her heart and squeezed.

"We can't. It's not safe."

"Safe!" Bob scoffed. "What does safe even mean in a sport like this one?"

"It means basic precautions to keep riders alive without compromising standards or intensity. Helmets, bullfighters—"

"He's got bullfighters."

"Might as well not. At the one I went to in Philadelphia, Jesse had to—"

"Jesse Singer?"

She paused. "Yes."

"You went on that trip with Jesse Singer?"

"We've been working on this together. Finding ways to protect the League from losing its best athletes and roughstock to Supreme Rodeo. We've got a whole group of stock contractors willing to boycott Custer's events, in the hope that keeping the best bulls means also keeping the best riders."

Bob's face changed while she spoke, shifting from interest to irritation. She folded her hands in her lap, reminded of that day in Lee's office, Jesse's hard expression as he'd spread pages of financial statements in front of her.

"Lee gave me a budget." Her gaze had darted nervously from one giant number to the next.

"Correct. This is your budget, here." He'd pointed to a figure. "And this is how much Singer Pro Rodeo lost last year." He'd dragged his finger to another, much bigger one, circled in red.

She hadn't been angry at Jesse that day—not yet. Her anger had taken a while to build, to elbow out the shame that dogged her steps off the Singer property.

He was right—she'd screwed up. She'd taken Lee and his numbers for granted. She hadn't been critical or careful. She'd done what she wanted, when she wanted.

And now she'd done it again.

"When were you planning to tell me all of this?" Bob asked.

"The stock contractors' group isn't finalized yet. Once I had the full terms, I would've brought them to you."

"How about this cozy new partnership with Singer?"

"It's not like that. We just happened to be the two people who decided to do something."

"So that was someone else in a Singer Pro Rodeo truck driving through the south gate this morning?"

Kenzie's cheeks were on fire, and she willed herself to be strong. Maybe she'd taken her autonomy a little too far, and she should've kept Bob better informed. Other than that, though, she'd done nothing wrong.

Bob leaned back in his chair. "Listen, Kenzie, I don't care what you do in your own time, or who you do it with. I don't care about the Singers at all—never have. You were the one who said they were our biggest competition, and we needed to pour money into developing the one bull we have who might beat them. Granted, Not Nice will go to the finals—but so will four of Singer's bulls. Even if we win Bull of the Year, they stand to make more money overall. And what if Not Nice doesn't win? What if he doesn't place at all?"

"He will. I know he will."

"Fine—then we cash the check. But this whole operation can't ride on Not Nice's back, especially not when you're asking me for higher wages. We've tried your way. Now it's time to try mine."

"Supreme Rodeo." Her weedy panic clinched tighter.

"Don't worry, I'm not sending Not Nice on a stadium tour." His tone verged on mocking. "We'll bring the younger crop. The up-and-comers."

"We can't." She bolted upright in her chair as memories of Custer's last event careened through her mind. The messed-up layout of the pens. The hesitant bullfighters. The animals' alarming, unprovoked agitation.

"They're still learning the basics—how to stand in the chute, what the crowd sounds like, where to go when they're finished. This is a delicate time for these animals, and we need to create positive experiences for them at the right pace, or we could cause permanent damage. If at any point they feel stressed or threatened, it could create a fear response we'll never train away."

Bob folded his arms, looking exasperated. "They're cows, Kenzie."

"And cows have really good memories."

"Yeah, well, so does my bank account, and right now the signing payment from Custer is making it mighty happy."

The vine clenched around her stomach, its thorns sharp and unrelenting. "You already signed the contract?"

"Deal's done." He slapped the edge of her desk. "We're heading to Atlanta in two weeks. Choose whichever buckers you think won't be traumatized by the horrific experience of raking in more money in one night than in a month of League rodeos."

Bob stood, and she did too, fumbling for a way to stop this, searching for the words that would make him understand Supreme Rodeo was an abomination.

"Bob, please, let's talk about this. I know Custer pays well, but what will Supreme Rodeo do to the League? What will it do to the sport as a whole? Killing traditional rodeo is Custer's intention, not a side effect."

"So?"

She blinked at her boss.

He threw up his hands. "So it dies. That's how the world works. Rodeo's had a good run, but times change, and nothing lasts forever."

She gaped at him. "But isn't that why you got into this in the first place? Because you love rodeo. Because you've always loved it."

"Sure, I love the rodeo. It's fun and exciting—and so is Supreme Rodeo."

"Custer's events aren't rodeo."

"Of course they are," Bob insisted. "The League is not the ultimate arbiter of who gets to hold a rodeo, Kenzie. You know that. Hell, you bitch about the League all the time. They don't pay well enough for women's sports, they're not welcoming to other faiths… You spent ten minutes ranting about how reducing their competitors to *cowgirls* and *cowboys* isn't inclusive for gays."

"For queer athletes," she clarified. "And it isn't."

"But now they're the be-all and end-all of the sport, huh?"

"The League has problems. I won't deny that. I just think Custer's are way worse."

"Then we'll change them." He took a step forward, his smile encouraging. "Come on, Kenzie. Think of this as a blank slate—one that's sitting on a whole heap of money. We'll still do League events, and we'll still focus on getting to Vegas. We'll let Custer bankroll our bulls, and we'll work from the inside to make Supreme Rodeo better."

She shook her head, at a loss. How could she explain that rodeo was more than the sum of its parts? It wasn't just about the prizes, and the winners, and the night spent under the stars.

Rodeo was a way of life, and to be part of it was to be part of a century-old American tradition, one in some ways nearly unchanged from its earliest origins. Yes, it was imperfect; yes, it needed to evolve. The Singers knew that, Nat Ware knew that, she knew that, and they were all doing what they could to push their sport forward. To keep what worked, shed what didn't, and nudge the door a little wider every year.

Casey Custer didn't care about any of that.

Neither, apparently, did Bob Boyd.

Kenzie stared at her boss, the man who'd plucked her out of the darkest period in her career and given her a second chance. He'd trusted her with so much—his money, his staff, his property. She'd be nowhere without him.

She'd never felt so helpless—or so defeated.

"I don't like this," she said.

"I know. We're doing it anyway."

What else could she say? She wasn't a Singer—she wasn't even a McCutcheon. She worked or she starved. If she lost this job, she'd never get another one in rodeo. No one wanted a two-time reject.

Three times, if you counted her father.

"Okay."

Bob grinned. "Sorry, couldn't quite hear you there."

"I said, okay."

"Glad to have you back on board, Kenzie. I don't care what you have to do to get yourself out of this stock contractors' alliance, but make sure it doesn't get back to Custer. I want us to start off on the right foot for what will hopefully be a long and prosperous journey." Bob winked at her as he let himself out of the office.

As soon as the door closed behind him, Kenzie collapsed into her chair and pressed her palms over her face.

She was so furious, so frustrated and dismayed and upset, she didn't know where to start. This was a disaster, the worst possible outcome, and a single sentence reiterated itself over and over at the core of her troubled thoughts. Behind it trailed a dreadful certainty, and an ending she knew she'd have to face when she saw him tonight.

Jesse's going to be so disappointed.

Kenzie stepped onto the ranch house's wide porch and squared her shoulders.

She felt sick. Her stomach was knotted, her breaths rasped, and she had a throbbing headache from hours of clenching her jaw. She longed to turn around and drive away. To block Jesse's number and pretend the last few months hadn't happened.

But he'd find her. Better to make sure he didn't start looking in the first place.

She raised her hand, then dropped it before she pressed the bell. This would be the last time she set foot on the Singer property. She paused, giving this moment the respect it deserved.

Only her mind didn't travel backward through the happy

years she'd worked here. It reached forward, snatching at fragments of a future she'd barely begun to imagine.

Waking up in Jesse's bed. Finding him in the office, placing a cup of coffee at his elbow. Swinging open the door to the bull barn, being greeted by eager snuffles and shiny, black eyes. Sitting down to dinner at a table full of Singers, his sisters, his parents. Feeling welcome and embraced and, whenever she looked at the man who subtly squeezed her hand under the table, loved beyond measure.

"Pathetic," she muttered.

She wasn't in love with him, and there was her proof. She was dreaming about a job, not a wedding. She missed working here, she liked having sex with Jesse, and she'd bundled those two into the misconception he was the solution to all her problems.

Jesse didn't love her, and he never would. He'd end up with someone pretty and put-together, who'd never disappointed anyone, never failed so much as a spelling quiz. He'd marry a woman his family would be proud of—the type of woman her own father wished she was—and that was fine.

That was why she was here.

She supposed she should be grateful to Bob Boyd, in a way. He'd given her the perfect excuse to shut this down before it ran even further off the rails. This would hurt, but not as much as it would have in another few weeks, or months, or however long it took for Jesse to decide he didn't want her.

This will hurt. She forced her chin up and set her back teeth.

Kenzie rang the doorbell.

She expected Jesse to take a minute or two to cross the big house. He must've been waiting for her, because in just a few heartbeats he flung open the door. His grin was big and broad, and before she could object, he tugged her into his arms, bundling her face into his chest.

Her resolve melted like ice cream in August. She leaned into him, let him take her weight. Closed her eyes and tried to memorize how he felt, how he smelled, and the perfect, impenetrable sense of safety that soothed her every time he held her.

"I missed you," he murmured.

Kenzie let those words break the spell. She stepped out of his reach, refusing to return his happy smile.

His expression deflated. "What's wrong?"

"Bad news. Boyd signed a contract with Supreme Rodeo." She hid her determination beneath a nonchalant tone, delivering the words exactly as she'd practiced.

"Damn." He glanced away.

Kenzie could tell those sophisticated mental gears of his were grinding at breakneck speed, and she braced herself for his scorn. For the accusations she wouldn't bother to deflect. He couldn't hurt her, because she didn't care. He couldn't reject her, because she didn't want him.

Instead he smiled, knocking her completely off her game.

"Don't worry. We'll figure this out. I guess you couldn't talk him out of it?"

"Obviously not," she retorted, blowing up her plan to stay cool and detached.

Jesse nodded, maddeningly sympathetic. "Maybe I should go over there and speak to him. If he hears from—"

"Hears from who—a Singer? You think that means your opinion would outweigh mine?"

He blinked. "No, just that—"

"News flash, Jesse—not everyone thinks your family are rodeo royalty. Bob doesn't give a crap about you or even the League. He wants the money, and he's made up his mind."

"There must be some way—"

"It's a done deal," she informed him, regaining her steely footing.

He stared at her, disbelief and anger warring behind his eyes. "So that's it? You're just going along with this?"

"What else am I supposed to do? Quit?"

He was on the verge of saying yes—she could see it. She let that wind her up. Let it reignite the indignant, resentful embers these last few weeks had extinguished.

"This may come as a shock to you, but most of us don't inherit our careers. I can't just walk into a new job on the strength of my name."

"Of course you can," he insisted. "You're Kenzie Wallace. You can go anywhere you want."

A dangerous wave of longing reared in her rib cage, threatening to wash away her fury. Did he really believe that? Would *he* want her?

No. That was her father's voice, disgusted and dismissive. Jesse could've had her two years ago, but he hadn't even given her a chance.

He wouldn't make a fool of her again. She didn't need him. She didn't need anyone.

She rolled her eyes. "Spoken like the entitled rich boy you've always been, insulated from the reality the rest of us have to deal with every day."

His eyes widened. She'd finally landed a punch.

"Rich?" he repeated with a bitter, incredulous laugh. "You know better than anyone my family's business is on its knees, because you pushed it there."

She ignored the sting of that old blame, focusing instead on the soft spot he'd just revealed. "What do you mean, better than anyone? What about your sisters? Your parents?"

He glowered at her, ducking behind well-worn hostility, but it was too late. She'd caught him, and she couldn't afford to let go.

"They don't know," she said slowly, watching for the telltale flash of guilt that would confirm her suspicion.

There it was—that momentary drop of his gaze, the tautness around his mouth. She'd found what she needed to hurt him—and make sure he couldn't hurt her.

I'm sorry, Jesse.

"You haven't told your family, have you? You've been keeping this nasty secret all to yourself, letting everyone else believe nothing has changed."

"I'm protecting my brother, and I'm protecting them. What's wrong with that?" he demanded.

"It's deceitful, it's manipulative, and it's goddamn arrogant, is what it is. Who put you in charge of the truth? Who appointed you savior?"

"You did," he shot back. "You put me in this position, Kenzie. You didn't stand up to Lee, and I bet you didn't stand up to Bob Boyd, either."

She took an unsteady step backward, rocked by a memory she'd kept hidden for years. Peeking around a corner, her mother sobbing on the couch, Ned holding a trifold piece of paper—a lawyer's letter denying that Jay McCutcheon was her father.

"Stand up to him," Ned had urged, his gentle voice turned forceful and stern. "Stop letting him run over you. You've been weak for ten years, but for her sake, it's time to be strong."

Kenzie had spent her whole life telling herself she was tough. Hard. Had a tunnel-vision focus on her professional goals and didn't give a damn about anything else. She was a woman in a man's world who could take on Singer Pro Rodeo and win.

That wasn't true, though, was it?

She'd ignored Lee's reckless spending because she didn't want to ruin their friendship. She'd accepted Bob's decision about Supreme Rodeo because she was scared to quit.

She'd lived for twenty years beneath her father's imagined scrutiny, yet never once walked up to him and said hello.

Jesse was right—she was weak.

Just like her mother.

She buried her pain under rage, shoving it deeper and deeper until it was no more than a faint gleam beneath the thick, dull anger she'd piled on top.

Then she picked up the heaviest weapon she could find and hit back.

"Just when I think you couldn't have known your brother any less, you say something like that."

He jerked like she'd struck him.

She swung again. "I knew you didn't come home a lot, but I had no idea you two were complete strangers. Do you really think I could've influenced Lee one way or the other? If that's what you truly believe, you have no idea who your brother was."

"I know," he shouted. She hardened herself against the bald sorrow in his voice, against the impulse to throw her arms around his neck and soothe his grief.

"You don't have to tell me it's my fault—I know. I should've intervened, somehow. I should've done better. I should've *been here*," he insisted, the words desperate and full of pain.

Kenzie fisted her hands at her sides. This was almost over.

"There you go again, proving my point. Lee didn't let *anyone* help him, Jesse. I knew more than anyone, and what he showed me of the financials barely scratched the surface. If you think he ever would've let his brilliant, high-flying younger brother know he was struggling, you're more deluded than I thought. On the other hand, if you want to be just like him, congratulations. You're succeeding. Lee isolated himself, thinking he could protect everyone from reality while he fixed it. I thought that obsessive secret-keeping was a Lee thing, but apparently it's genetic."

Jesse said nothing. He simply stared at her, helpless and wide-open. She'd cut him so deeply she could practically smell the blood, bright red and fresh, yet there was something in his expression that discomfited her.

Kenzie wanted to see hatred. Animosity. That cold determination to defeat her that had glittered from the opposite end of countless chute platforms.

Instead he looked…lost. Like she'd ripped away something precious. Something he wasn't sure he could live without.

She looked away first. "Anyway, I guess I'll see you in Vegas. Good luck."

She spun on her heel, then turned back when Jesse called her name.

"What's this about?" he asked.

She sighed impatiently, clamping down hard on the yearning that quickened her heartbeat. "What do you mean?"

"If you wanted to end this, you could've just said so."

No, I couldn't, because I'm weak and pathetic and I love you so much I need you to despise me, or I'll never get off this porch. Never stop wanting you until you've used me up and thrown me out—again.

"Did something happen? Did I do something wrong?" he pressed.

She took a step backward, panic rising in her chest.

"I care about you, Kenzie. If there's something I can fix, or something I can work on, I'll do it. I was going to tell you tonight that I'm—"

"I don't want you, okay?" She stumbled toward the top of the steps, tears blurring her vision as she fought to keep her voice steady. "*I'm* ending this. *I'm* saying no. Get it?"

He hesitated, and then he nodded. "I got it."

She whirled around and jogged down the steps, clinging to the handrail. She was crying before she reached her truck, but he wouldn't see—it was too dark, she was too far, and the Oklahoman weather had compassionately unrolled a thin, humid haze while they'd been talking. She was cloaked in it as she climbed into the driver's seat, wrapped in its forgiveness and understanding.

You're powerful, she heard it say. *You set the terms and you made the decision. You're not weak anymore—you just proved that. You walked away from the man you love, and that means you're strong. You can walk away from your father's rejection just like you walked away from Jesse.*

Then she turned on the headlights. The twin beams sliced through the darkness, lighting the way forward and banishing the whispered lies she knew were her own.

Maybe she'd made a mistake—and maybe she hadn't.

Didn't matter. She'd decided.

She put the truck into gear and started down the long, winding driveway. She didn't look over her shoulder. Didn't check the rearview mirror. Didn't so much as glance in the direction of the man she knew was still standing on the porch, watching her disappear.

Chapter Seventeen

Flickering candlelight sent long, amber-rimmed shadows dancing across the big oak table, which was full for the first time in nearly a year. The four remaining Singer siblings had taken turns gently prodding their parents to join them for Friday-night dinner at the ranch house. Now, after a week of nudges, they were here.

While his mother lit the Shabbat candles and his sisters toted the last of the plates from the kitchen, Jesse gestured for his father to take the seat at the head of the table.

Fred shook his head. "That's yours."

So he sat, with his sisters on his left and his parents on his right, and tried not to think too carefully about the empty chair beside his mother.

In fact, he tried not to think too carefully about anything, skimming the surface of their wide-ranging conversation. Get any deeper and he might think about *her*, and what he'd done, and all he'd lost.

Except not thinking about her was the same as thinking about her, and his mind kept snagging. He was like a cowboy being pulled into the center of the bull's spin—getting sucked into the well, they called it. Clinging on but hopelessly off-balance, slipping sideways, inching closer and closer to failure with no way to stop it.

Except when he finally lost his grip and hit the dirt, he didn't spring up and run for the fence. He sprawled on the floor, staring up at the stars, regret knocking the wind clean out of his lungs.

Never in his life had he so badly wanted a do-over. He should've been caring. Understanding. Worked with her to find a solution, not hurled accusations and dug up old resentments.

But that was his modus operandi, wasn't it? He was all stick, no carrot. He got what he wanted through heartlessness and hostility. Even when he tried to do the right thing, he used manipulation and dishonesty—just like Kenzie said.

He was the bad guy. Not even falling head over heels for his rival had changed that.

And what she'd said about Lee, that Jesse had turned into his brother in the worst way possible… He couldn't stomach that final betrayal of his brother's memory. Accepting Lee's financial ineptitude was bad enough. Believing he'd understood the extent of his mismanagement and willfully concealed it—no. Not his funny, generous, bighearted brother.

Even if on some level Jesse had the terrible suspicion it was true.

Trixie's elbow dug into his arm. For the hundredth time that night Jesse dragged himself back from his grim ruminations and reoriented in the present.

Billie was still talking about Wyatt's wedding, telling a funny story about his future mother-in-law's demands on the florist. Mae and his parents listened attentively. Trixie was the only one looking at him.

"How you?" she asked.

He found a smile. "Fine. How you?"

"Unconvinced. How you?"

"Distracted," he admitted. "How you?"

"Worried. How you?"

"Fine." He deliberately redirected his gaze to Billie.

"So the florist says, well, I guess I could try to have some flown in, but it'll be expensive. And Lynne goes—and this is an exact quote—*you of all people should know that correctly balanced floral decor is priceless*."

Everyone busted up laughing, and Jesse managed a chuckle, too.

"How a woman sweet as Bettina sprang forth from that uptight witch, I'll never know," his dad mused.

"No need to insult witches like that," Mae countered, and laughter rang again.

Jesse leaned back in his chair, acutely aware this moment was precious and significant and should be making him immensely happy. His parents were here, they were engaged, they were having a good time. This wasn't just a step forward—it was an epic leap.

But his heart couldn't get on board with his head. He felt detached. Numb. Empty of everything except his preoccupation with Kenzie, and his desire to be left alone so he could repeat their argument word for word and come up with a thousand new ways he could've handled it better.

He should've kept his temper in check. He should've assured her he didn't blame her for Bob's decision. Insisted he didn't blame her for what happened with Lee, either. He should've made her feel safe, shown her how he'd changed, told her their petty past paled in comparison to the enormity of his feelings for her.

He'd let those tired transgressions rear their ugly heads instead, and he'd paid for it.

"Speaking of flowers, did y'all know your fool brother went all the way to Perry to get me some sneezeweed and came back with yellow bells?" His mom turned a playfully chiding frown his way.

He shrugged. "They're both yellow."

Ruth rolled her eyes. "Well, I wasn't about to drive all the way out to Perry, but I went back to the local nursery. They still didn't have sneezeweed, so it looks like we're having yellow bells this year. Anyway, I ran into Michelle Carlisle, remember her?"

Jesse and his sisters exchanged subtle, victorious smiles. They knew all about his mom's trip to the nursery, the one she hadn't been nearly so casual about a few days ago. They'd banded together then, too, coming up with excuses why they couldn't go for her, and lightly mentioning all the reasons it should be a quick, easy errand.

Now she was gossiping about the goings-on in town like she drove off the ranch every day. For the first time in years Jesse believed his parents would emerge from the black cloud of Lee's death.

They all would. He glanced again at the empty chair next to his mom's. Grief may have chased them into their separate, isolated corners of this ranch, but they wouldn't stay there forever. There'd be more nights like these, more time together. They wouldn't be the same, but they'd be strong.

They were Singers. Their family had survived worse. They'd survive this.

Soon the candles were nubs, the table cleared, the wine bottles empty, and Fred and Ruth rose to leave. No one offered to take them home, and for once they didn't ask, nor did they fret aloud about driving in the dark. They simply hugged each of their children in turn, climbed into their truck and left.

Jesse and his sisters remained on the porch, withstanding the November nip in the air until their parents' taillights disappeared.

"Whiskey," Trixie announced.

They all murmured agreement, and ten minutes later were arranged on the sofas in the living room. The wagon-wheel chandelier was turned low, and the fire Jesse started cast lively, orange reflections on their cut-glass tumblers.

"That went well," Billie remarked.

"That went great," Trixie rephrased.

Mae sank lower against the cushions. "Teamwork makes the dream work."

His twin's flippant comment struck Jesse like a swinging door.

Kenzie was right. He wasn't just ruthless and deceitful.

He was goddamn arrogant.

Sure, he was the one with an MBA, who understood earnings and taxes and profit margins better than his sisters. But why the hell did he think he needed to shield them from the truth? Or that he alone should bear the burden of Lee's legacy?

His sisters were smart, canny and tough. Mae was a doctor, for God's sake, and Billie and Trixie effectively ran their own small businesses within Singer Pro Rodeo. Look how they'd stepped up to take care of their parents—take care of him.

Their random drop-ins weren't random at all, he realized with dawning admiration. Now that he thought about it, he bet they had a rota, taking turns to show up unannounced and make sure he'd slept and eaten and bathed. They weren't his bored sisters who wandered over when they were at loose ends—they were conducting welfare checks.

All this time he thought he was protecting them, and it had been the other way around.

Deep down, he'd known they could handle the real story. He told himself he was preserving their unblemished memories of their older brother, because the truth was too unpalatable. Too frightening, too damning.

Jesse thought if they knew the full extent of the damage, they'd blame him.

Like he blamed himself.

If you want to be just like him, then congratulations. You're succeeding.

That sentence, more than any other, had reverberated in his skull since Kenzie sped down the same path his parents had just taken. Since the day he'd taken over, that was exactly what he'd done—tried to be just like Lee.

Friendly. Approachable. Loyal. Likable. The total opposite of the cold-blooded corporate villain he'd left behind.

He'd also held everyone at arm's length. Suffered in silence and refused to ask for help. Lied to the people he loved most by pretending everything was fine, and he had it all under control.

Jesse loved his brother fiercely, and he always would. But lying to himself about Lee's choices was as much a betrayal as hiding them.

Lee wasn't all good, but he wasn't all bad, either. He was complicated. Imperfect. Deeply flawed, and deeply lovable.

Like Jesse wanted to be.

Time to accept that the only person he was capable of being was himself. He wasn't his brother, he never would be, and that was okay. He didn't have to fit neatly into Lee's vacant chair. He could pull up his own.

He'd been what Kenzie wanted, for a while. Maybe he could be more. Maybe he'd be enough for her, one day.

"Earth to Jesse," Billie said in a singsong voice.

"Yes. Sorry. I'm listening."

"Wherever you've been tonight, I hope it's warmer than here," Mae said.

Trixie arched a brow. "Something's up with you, and you should know by now we have ways to make you talk."

"It's just the Custer thing," he said, instinctively redirecting the conversation.

Then he changed his mind.

He leaned forward to place his glass on the coffee table. His sisters stirred to alertness, as if they could sense the weight of the revelation he was about to unfurl.

He glanced at Mae, whose expression softened in comprehension. She gave him the tiniest of nods, and he turned back to Trixie and Billie.

"I'm going to say this, and you'll probably be really angry with me, and that's okay."

His sisters traded wary glances.

He took a breath and let it out slowly. "I haven't been honest about the overall state of the business. It's bad. Really bad."

Trixie and Billie exchanged a look of confusion, then returned their attention to him.

"Lee screwed up," Jesse told them. "He lost control of the expenses, and he kept digging the hole deeper and deeper. I don't know whether—no, he must've known. He had to see the bottom line, even if he couldn't figure out how to fix it. Maybe he had a plan, and maybe he would've turned it all around. But when I stepped in, Singer Pro Rodeo was months from bankruptcy."

Billie gasped. Trixie drained her whiskey. Mae just watched him, sympathetic and encouraging.

"That's why I fired Kenzie Wallace," he continued. "The budget Lee gave her was outrageous, and she was overpaid. The wage bill is still higher than we can afford, but I've spent the last two years trimming every possible cost so we can keep paying our people. We're stable, now—we should break even this year. But we have a steep hill to climb before we're profitable again, and the first step will be Repeat Offender winning the purse for Bull of the Year."

His sisters stared at him in stunned silence. The old house creaked and yawned, as if the floorboards were flexing under the footsteps of the four generations of Singers that preceded them. Jesse imagined his grandfather leaning in the doorway, his arms crossed. Pictured Hugo staring out the window with his hands clasped behind his back. Imagined Fritz, the penniless Austrian leatherworker who'd started it all, smiling his approval.

I'll protect this family, he promised them—but he didn't need to.

They knew. They trusted him. He'd made them proud.

"But how?" Billie asked. "Where are you cutting all these expenses? I can't think of anything we're doing differently."

"I've lied to you. A lot," he confessed. "Said things were on back order when I canceled them. Pretended we dropped a vendor because they put up their prices, when really they're holding our unpaid invoices. Haggled and negotiated and weaseled my way around every supplier, every veterinarian, every farrier… Basically anyone who's ever done business with us has been on the receiving end of a pretty slippery phone call."

He cleared his throat, shifting in his seat. Now for the worst part. "I owe you all an apology, and not just for being dishonest. I didn't know Lee was struggling. I doubt he ever would've told me, but I could've involved myself more. I might've seen something, or put two and two together—except I didn't. I focused on my career, and my life in New York, and I never offered to help. I should've been here for him. I should've been here for all of you. I wasn't, and I'm sorry."

When he finally found the courage to meet his sisters' gazes, he found every single one of them warm and loving.

"You don't have to apologize for living your life," Mae said.

Billie nodded. "Trixie and I were right here, working with Lee every day, and we didn't see it. We didn't know anything until this very second. Right, Trix?"

"Absolutely no idea. We pushed him to involve us more, and to keep us updated on the business, but he always waved us off, or promised he'd get to it tomorrow. At some point we stopped asking, and Lee let us believe everything was rolling along as normal."

"So did I," Jesse pointed out.

"Which was a mistake," Trixie replied. "But you had your reasons."

"Overprotective big-brother reasons," Billie clarified.

Jesse rubbed his hands on his knees, struggling to process this total absence of the condemnation and disappointment he'd expected. "I didn't want y'all to worry, and I didn't want y'all to think badly of Lee. We'd all been through so much, and I thought I could fix it without anyone needing to know. Repay Lee in death for what I didn't do while he was alive."

Billie tilted her head. "Do you have any idea how much Lee loved you? He adored you, Jess. He thought you were so smart, so funny, so amazing to be making it out there in the big city, yet still able to come home and rope a calf or toss a bale. He never would've told you what was going on—not in a million years. You could've camped in his damn office, and he would've found a way to hide the books."

"You never owed him anything," Trixie agreed firmly.

Mae smiled wistfully. "You were a joy in his life, Jesse. Just by being yourself."

He felt it then—felt it for real. His brother's hand on his shoulder, steady and warm. Lee's soul squeezed his own, and for a fraction of a heartbeat, Jesse knew he was there. That he'd always be there—but not like this. Not anymore.

This was goodbye, Jesse realized in the same instant the pressure on his shoulder disappeared. With his affairs settled at last, Lee would return to God, his memory a reminder to those who loved him of their fleeting turn on this earth, and of the mitzvot they had yet to perform.

Peace descended over Jesse with a completeness he hadn't had since childhood.

He had forgiveness. From Lee, from his sisters, from his ancestors. From himself.

But not from Kenzie. The thought was a jagged hole in his happiness.

"Let's sit down tomorrow, the four of us, and go over everything," Billie suggested. "I know you're just a doctor, Mae, but we'll explain the big numbers so you can follow along."

"Excuse me, I counted all the way to eleven yesterday," Mae retorted.

Trixie came to sit beside him and slipped her arm through his. "We love you, and we're all in this together. Okay?"

"Okay," he echoed.

She smiled, then tightened her hold on his elbow and leaned in close. "How you?"

"Relieved. How you?"

"Curious."

"About what?" he asked.

"About *who*." Billie joined them on his other side, and Mae perched on the nearby armrest.

He was surrounded. "Is this an intervention?"

"Depends. What's going on with you and Kenzie Wallace?" Trixie asked.

Jesse gaped at his sisters. "How'd y'all know about that?"

"Women's intuition," they recited in sardonic unison.

He wondered again just how often he'd been discussed without his knowing. Did they hold regular meetings? Was he a recurring agenda item?

"Seriously, how did you all find out?"

Billie rolled her eyes. "Her truck was parked here at like two o'clock in the morning."

"Why were you driving past the house at two o'clock in the morning?"

"To make sure you weren't falling asleep in the office again."

"I wasn't."

"No, we agreed you probably weren't getting much sleep at all." Mae smiled.

Jesse pressed his hands over his face, unable to decide which was more mortifying: his sisters' discovery of his fling with Kenzie, or having to reveal that it was over.

Trixie waggled her brows suggestively. "Guess you two buried the hatchet."

"Is she very fond of it? Your hatchet?" Mae asked with exaggerated primness.

"Handle with care," Billie added, and the three of them cracked up.

"How was I born to this family of perverts?" he asked the

ceiling, then dropped his gaze to his sisters. "As much as I appreciate what we'll call y'all's compassionate surveillance, it won't be needed. Kenzie and I are done."

Trixie winced. "Mutually friendly done or bad done?"

"Bad done."

His sisters sobered.

"It's fine," he began—and stopped himself.

No more hiding. No more guarding his problems in the name of guarding others.

"Actually, it sucks," he amended, and spilled the whole, sorry story.

Jesse flicked on the light in Lee's office—*his* office. His sisters were asleep upstairs, their save-Jesse's-relationship council of war having stretched so far into the early hours they'd opted to crash at the ranch house rather than drive home.

At least he didn't have to worry about one of them cruising past and logging that the office lights were on, he thought as he took a seat behind the desk.

But he hadn't come here to work. His complicated financial balancing act could wait until tomorrow, when he'd unveil it for his sisters' scrutiny and advice.

Jesse still marveled at how calmly and nonjudgmentally they'd received everything he'd told them. His biggest mistake was not trusting his sisters, not his failure to help Lee.

He'd change that. And he'd do whatever it took to win Kenzie's trust, while he was at it.

That was where he'd landed after an hour of rehashing what happened between him and Kenzie, and how she'd ended it. She hadn't trusted him not to blame her for the Broken B joining Supreme Rodeo, and so she'd gone on the offensive—and he'd swallowed the bait.

That was on him. Not just rising to the argument, but failing to make her feel safe. He'd hurt her when they first met. He'd blamed her and tossed her aside, just like Jay McCutcheon.

Although Jesse had made efforts to repair the damage, he hadn't appreciated the threat his love implied, and he hadn't worked hard enough to show her he'd never hurt her again.

Jesse opened the bottom drawer and reached all the way to the back. He kept the most alarming paperwork there, where it was least likely to be found. Now he pulled out manila folders by the handful and stacked them on the desk, ready for the morning light.

Then he pushed to his feet with a grin, recalling his sisters' suggestions for making amends to Kenzie. Their ideas were all grand, wildly expensive, and more likely to make a woman like Kenzie slam the door in his face than burst into happy tears, but he appreciated their input.

He'd make a plan. But he had to do something else first.

Jesse took one last look around the office, committing this snapshot of his brother's life to memory. He considered taking a picture, but decided there was no need. Lee lived within him, and always would. The rest was just stuff.

He hauled in the stack of empty cardboard boxes he'd stashed outside the door.

Then he started packing up.

Chapter Eighteen

"Hey, watch where you're going."

Kenzie looked up into the angry glare of a woman wearing stiletto-heeled pink boots and a tiny pink cowboy hat glued to a headband.

If they'd been on a back road in Perry… If she hadn't been holding a tray of snacks for her boss… If her whole damn career wasn't riding on this dumpster fire of an event…

Kenzie set her jaw and kept walking.

Barely nine o'clock and already this Saturday was in contention for the worst night of her life. She'd never been so miserable at a rodeo, and that included the short go in Dodge City when she had food poisoning.

But this wasn't a rodeo, was it? Weaving her way back to the pens from the concession stand in the lobby was like descending through layers of hell. The impatient fans hoping to see a wreck. The sterile venue with none of the intimacy of small-town arenas. The bizarre backstage setup, which managed to be understaffed and overcomplicated at the same time.

And because she'd evidently been a serial killer in a past life, the Broken B's first appearance at the Supreme Rodeo Series happened to coincide with the introduction of a calf scramble, with stock provided by none other than Oklahoma's own McCutcheon Ranch.

Thus far logistics had kept her apart from her father, but Kenzie knew that wouldn't last long. Soon they'd both be idling through the bronc riding, forced to choose between the two evils of small talk or obvious avoidance.

Not that her boss would notice either way, she reflected as she found him beside the pens. Bob Boyd was having a blast, delighting in his newfound role as stock-contracting big shot, and lapping up the VIP indulgences Custer poured on him.

Excluding the VIP-lounge food, of course. Bob had sniffed at what he'd termed rich-people pickings and sent her out for corn dogs and curly fries, which she now handed over.

"Finally. I'm starving." He shoved three fries in his mouth.

She started to ask a question, then rephrased it as a statement, recalling Jesse's accusation for the millionth time—and weathering the millionth stab of despair that accompanied it.

"I'm going to shift that bull into the pen with the others. I know they wanted him separate, but he's not happy by himself."

Bob shrugged, biting into his corn dog.

Kenzie looked around for Richie, the backstage manager she'd met in Philadelphia, who still single-handedly ran the show behind the scenes. She started down the side of the pipe-fence maze and nearly tripped over Tucker Ramsey, one of the bull riders who'd found her and Jesse in the trees in Nebraska, back when Custer was a vague threat and Jesse was her sworn enemy.

Back when she had no idea how much she might love him—or how much it would hurt to lose him.

"Sorry, Tucker, I didn't see you there."

He nodded tightly, and on second glance she realized he was doubled over and breathing hard.

She crouched down beside him. "What's wrong?"

"Took a hoof in the gut on this last one. Didn't think it was a big deal, but I'm hurting."

"Let's get the medical team and make sure you're okay."

Kenzie knew full well that rodeo athletes were some of the most reluctant patients on the planet, yet the forcefulness of Tucker's headshake surprised her.

"I have to do this next round, or I'll lose my contract."

She frowned. "Your contract?"

"With Supreme Rodeo. If we don't hit a minimum number of rides, we don't get paid. I'm already behind from being injured last month."

"Hold up, are you saying that if you don't do a certain number of rides, Custer won't pay you for the ones you did do?"

Tucker nodded.

Kenzie's heart sank.

She didn't bother asking him why he'd signed up for such a ridiculous deal. Bull riders were known for their grit and their guts, not their ability to interpret legalese. Custer knew that, too. He probably counted on it.

"Let's at least ask the medics if they can set you up for this next go-round," she suggested, silently planning to tear Custer into strips if he forced Tucker to ride injured. "Maybe they can wrap your ribs."

Tucker glanced around to assure himself they were alone. "I don't trust those guys, Kenzie. Custer put together his own medic team. There are medical exemptions in the contract, and they'll find a way to make sure they won't apply. Happened to Chris Steeple, I heard."

Kenzie shuddered as she remembered Chris's runover—and Jesse facing down a bull to protect him.

"Then call Mae Singer. Tell her how you're feeling. You know she won't breathe a word to Custer."

Tucker smiled. "She hates him."

"And she doesn't want you to get hurt. You got her number?"

"I got it."

"Tell me what she says. I'll drive your ass to the hospital myself if I have to."

"Thanks, Kenzie," Tucker replied.

She helped him to his feet and watched him limp toward the exit, her concern deepening with each of his hobbling steps. She started to follow him, then stopped short when Jay McCutcheon stepped into her path.

Kenzie averted her gaze, silently rerouting. In her peripheral vision she saw him continuing toward her, so she took an intense interest in the calves clustered on the other side of the fence, willing him to pass on by.

He did not.

"I see you found my Angus calves. Nice-looking, don't you think?"

Incredulity momentarily overrode her discomfort as she took a second, clearer look at the calves.

"These are for the calf scramble?"

"Sure are," McCutcheon replied.

"They're too big."

His smile collapsed. "You think so?"

"We're in Atlanta. These are city kids. They've probably never touched a cow outside a petting zoo. They won't try to catch these guys and pull a ribbon off their tails—they'll run away, screaming. And if they don't scream, their freaked-out parents will."

"But in Perry—"

"In Perry the kids are from farms, and they're not afraid of a five-hundred-pound calf. You should've brought smaller ones. Custer didn't tell you what weights he wanted?"

McCutcheon shook his head, his expression drooping. "Just how many to bring. This is the size we use at home. Didn't occur to me that we were catering for a different audience."

"Everything about Supreme Rodeo is different."

McCutcheon brooded on that, and it occurred to Kenzie that this exchange wasn't stressing her out at all.

Not that she wasn't stressed—she was. Stressed about Tucker, her animals and her career, on top of her ever-present, gnawing despair about Jesse.

Maybe she didn't have room to be stressed about her father, too.

Or maybe her self-inflicted loss had put everything into perspective.

Either way, when he turned to her with a broad, friendly smile, she wasn't warmed. It didn't fill a hole, or complete a puzzle.

She was wary, impatient and a tiny bit exasperated.

"I know things haven't been easy between us, and that's mostly my fault. But I'll admit, I was glad when I saw the Broken B on the lineup tonight. I'd like to get to know you, Kenzie. Rebuild our bridges. I hope working together will give us the opportunity to do that."

Kenzie careened through every emotion she could name. She was flattered, grateful, resentful, furious, sorrowful, melancholy, resigned. She wanted to stomp her foot and scream at him and bask in his interest. She imagined boxing up this moment to keep forever, then stuffing it in the trash, never to be examined again. She was dizzy, and hopeful, and sad, and she could do nothing but stare at him, legs trembling, heart racing.

"I'm new to all this, and it'd be a privilege to have someone as accomplished as you guiding me through the industry. You've achieved so much, Kenzie. I'm proud of you."

I'm proud of you.

Kenzie had fantasized about hearing those words from her father for years. Now he'd finally spoken them, and she was completely unprepared.

She prodded herself, assessing her wounds like a bull rider in the receding shock of a buck-off. Was she healed? Was she happy? She had what she wanted. Was this the moment her life changed for the better?

She let her heart fall wide-open, waiting for his approval to penetrate. Waiting to feel complete.

Jesse.

He was all she thought about, the only face she pictured. His smile was sunlight on snow, melting her defenses and welcoming the growth beneath. When he touched her, she was precious and irreplaceable; when he kissed her, she knew she was loved.

Her father's opinion, by contrast, seemed…meaningless.

She woke up to the self-serving gleam in his eyes and the need in his posture. He wasn't proud of her, and he never would be. She'd become an asset, that's all. A knowledgeable ally in a commercial venture where he had little experience.

The dream she'd clutched since childhood slipped from her fingers and shattered on the floor. She would not have a loving relationship with her biological father. He would not make space for her in his family and in his heart.

She would grieve. Tonight, or tomorrow, or in some unexpected private moment, she'd feel the sharp edge of this ending. She'd mourn the wish that would never come true.

For now, though, she felt light. Liberated. And deliriously happy.

She didn't need her father's love. She had Jesse's.

Or she would, once she found a way to clean up the mess she'd made.

"Sounds good," she told McCutcheon, not sure whether that made sense in the context of their conversation, not caring either way. He'd dropped so far down her list of priorities, she could barely remember how he'd gotten on there, so preoccupied was she with the urgency itching up and down her limbs.

She had to talk to Jesse.

Kenzie tossed McCutcheon a random excuse and hurried away, pulling out her phone as she rushed toward the back of the pens.

She'd explain everything. She'd apologize. She'd tell him she loved him, and he'd say he loved her, too. He'd been about to do just that at the ranch house.

Hadn't he?

She skidded to a halt, staring at his number in her phone.

The number she'd blocked.

Kenzie took a breath. This was a big deal, the biggest of them all. She couldn't barge in with guns blazing, not after she'd intentionally hurt him. She had to think about this. Plan what she wanted to say. Find a gift, maybe, something small but…

Her gaze landed on Richie, standing on the other side of a pen. He raised something that glinted in the gloom. She squinted to get a better look.

Was that a syringe?

It was, she confirmed as he plunged it into the bull's side. The two-thousand-pound animal didn't blink, but alarm bells pealed in Kenzie's skull.

Richie gathered up the cardboard box the shot came out of. She rushed forward, intent on getting a look. There was every chance this was an innocuous dose of necessary medication—but her instincts screamed otherwise.

"Richie, hey. What're you up to?"

He flashed her that big, admiring, grateful smile that made her want to whisk him out of here whenever she saw it. "Just giving these guys their preshow vitamins. How're your animals settling in?"

"Oh, fine. Here, let me get that for you—oops."

She reached for the cardboard box, then deliberately dropped it on the floor, buying time to inspect the label. She didn't recognize the long, chemical-sounding name, so she committed it to memory as best she could before passing the box back to Richie.

"I better make my rounds. See you later, Richie."

He waved a cheery goodbye and Kenzie kept walking, typing her approximation of the name into a search engine. She pressed Enter, and a string of results appeared on the screen.

She stopped dead.

"Steroids," she hissed.

Kenzie scanned the backstage area, feeling like she was in one of those dreams where she was screaming and no one could hear.

No wonder the bulls were agitated and restless, their bucking more reactive than skillful. Custer had ignored decades of breeding and training techniques and pumped them with drugs to make them mean.

Kenzie put her hand on her queasy stomach.

Everything about Supreme Rodeo was a disgrace. Custer knowingly put unprotected riders on unsafe animals and got rich doing it.

Even the most grizzled, cantankerous stock contractors turned into ferocious mother bears at the prospect of their cattle being harmed. Bucking bulls were hand-raised and pampered their entire lives, from their first steps to their lazy retirements. She'd thought Custer cared about his stock, even if he didn't care about the humans who rode them.

She was wrong.

Jesse would've punched the air at this damning evidence. But he might've punched Custer, too, so maybe it was just as well he wasn't here.

Evidence. Of course—her word wouldn't be enough. She needed proof, and she'd better get it fast.

She darted back to where she'd seen Richie, but he was gone. McCutcheon was gone, too, no doubt terrifying the children of Atlanta with his oversize calves. Her own animals would be in action soon, right alongside Custer's, and she'd be busy at the chutes for the rest of the night.

She jogged through the pipe-fence maze, sweeping her gaze back and forth, not sure what she was looking for. Did Custer keep records of dosages? Could there be a prescription somewhere? Or worse, was he buying this stuff without veterinary supervision? She had to find something that tied him to the drugs, and the drugs to his bulls, and she only had five minutes to do it.

Kenzie snatched up a clipboard hanging on a rail, but it just had a copy of the lineup. She rifled through a backpack stowed against a wall, but she only found men's clothes and a pair of sneakers.

She tossed the backpack down with an irritated huff and

glanced around. Cement walls, metal fencing, cattle regarding her curiously. Nowhere to hide anything back here, and she realized with a sinking feeling that whatever Custer had was probably miles away, at his ranch.

She sagged against the wall. How much more defeat could she take? Just being here was total failure.

Then she spotted the trash can.

Kenzie sprang forward, gripped the sides of the cylindrical metal bin, and stared down the circular hole in the top.

The steroid box rested perfectly in the center, like a diamond ring in a velvet box.

She snatched it up and clutched it to her chest, spinning to see whether anyone noticed. She was alone, which on second thought, wasn't ideal, either.

A random cardboard box wouldn't be enough to shut down Custer. She needed to show these drugs were being given to his bulls.

And as she heard Richie whistling on the far side of the pens, she knew how.

Kenzie approached him with a loose, easy gait. She held her phone, her recording app activated, ignoring a stab of guilt at Richie's guileless grin.

She'd help him find another job. She'd make sure he came out of this with his reputation intact.

"Can I ask you something?" she began.

"'Course."

"This box, here—this is what you were injecting the bulls with, right?"

"That's it."

"What's it for, exactly?"

Richie shrugged. "Mr. Custer says it's vitamins. Helps 'em perform more than once."

"He personally told you to give these injections?"

"Yes, ma'am. Why, did I do something wrong?"

"Sounds to me like you did exactly what you were told to do."

"That's all I ever do."

Kenzie subtly moved her thumb to stop the recording. "Thanks, Richie. That's what I wanted to know."

He paled. "Am I in trouble?"

"Not with me, you're not."

Richie looked troubled, but she couldn't waste her precious minutes worrying about that. The muffled announcements rang overhead, declaring the calf-scramble winner—a fourteen-year-old who evidently hadn't heard the event was for kids aged eight to eleven. Never mind—she didn't have much time left before she'd be summoned to the chutes.

Kenzie sprinted back to the front. Ramon was beside their pen, his lightweight, fiberglass flag stick in hand, ready to swat the bulls into position. Bob stood just behind him, surveying the proceedings with his arms crossed.

"Boss," she called, turning the corner as fast as her boots would carry her.

"There you are. Let's go, Kenzie. It's showtime."

"Wait—I have to show you something."

She held out the box.

Bob frowned. "What's that, some kind of growth hormone?"

"Steroids. I found one of Custer's staff injecting his bulls."

Bob's eyes widened and his lips thinned. The calves thundered back into the holding area, the echoes of their thudding hooves and the ranch hands' whistled commands making discussion impossible.

With them came Jay McCutcheon. He stalled, creating a conversational triangle—or he would have, if the sudden tension between her and her boss hadn't warned away the greeting poised on his lips.

"That's quite an accusation, Kenzie. You sure you want to make it?" Bob asked.

She pressed Play on her recording and held out her phone.

In the span of her exchange with Richie, her boss's expression shifted from skepticism, to dismay, to a grim resolution she didn't like the look of. She glanced at McCutcheon, but he was watching them both, trying to gauge which way the wind would blow as clearly as if he had his finger in the air.

"What's your point?" Bob demanded.

She blinked, wondering if he'd heard the same thing she just had. "This is a serious animal welfare issue."

"Not our animals."

"The animals they're about to buck alongside, in an event we'll be associated with."

"The Broken B will be associated with, you mean. You keep forgetting you don't run this operation."

Despite her acute awareness of her father's hyperattentive presence, Kenzie resisted the urge to glance his way, keeping her focus squarely on Bob.

"My name will be out there tonight, same as yours. We need to take a stand against what Custer's doing here. It's unethical, and it violates the core principles rodeo was built on. We have to withdraw from the event."

McCutcheon sucked in a breath. Ramon stilled, ceasing the rhythmic tap of his stick.

Bob regarded her levelly, wheels turning behind his eyes.

"I'll take this up with Custer later," he said. "Quietly, and in private. Making a scene won't help anyone. Not me, and not you."

His last two words were low and hard, his threat made plain. He wanted her to shut her mouth and get on with the show. To buck up and back down.

No.

She was Kenzie Wallace, goddammit. She'd elbowed her way through the stock-contracting boys' club and risen to the top, not because of her last name or her family's network, but because she was smart and tough and *better.*

And she sure as hell was better than this. Better than the

mockery of the sport she'd dedicated her life to, better than a job made worthless by her boss's self-serving interests.

Kenzie wasn't sure what would happen next, and she didn't care. She didn't care that her father was watching, or that she was risking her career, or that she'd lose the roof over her head.

She knew what she had to do.

"I can't be part of this, Bob. It's wrong."

His eyes narrowed. "What are you saying?"

"I'm leaving."

Bob's face twisted in anger, his cheeks reddening. "You listen to me, girl, and you listen good. You walk out of this arena tonight, you're walking out of your whole damn job. You will no longer be employed by the Broken B, and you'll need to be out of your house by the time I get back. Do you understand?"

Kenzie waited, giving him space to change his mind. To realize his mistake and correct himself before it was too late.

His glare only hardened.

Irritated voices rumbled behind them. Ramon stepped forward.

"We're running behind. Custer's crew is stressing. Am I loading in these bulls?"

Kenzie saw Bob's flicker of indecision, the briefest waver in his stubborn posture. He looked at her, at Ramon, at the bored-looking bulls standing idly in the pen.

Make the right choice, Kenzie urged him silently. *Stand up for this sport. Stand up for yourself.*

"Load 'em." The authority in Bob's words didn't quite reach his eyes.

Ramon shot her an apologetic glance, then turned to push the animals forward.

"I enjoyed working with you, Bob. I hope our paths will cross again." She stuck out her hand.

Bob stared at her hand, then at her. "You're really doing this?"

"Rodeo means more to me than a salary and a place to sleep. It's my way of life, and I won't stand by and watch it be destroyed."

Bob seemed poised to say something else—something regretful. But he was a proud, obstinate man, and without another word he shook her hand, then turned on his heel and headed for the platform.

Kenzie watched him walk away, taking with him so much of what she'd dreamed about. The job she'd always wanted. The second chance she needed. Redemption in the eyes of the man who'd for so long refused to notice her.

The man standing three feet away.

McCutcheon gaped at her, open-mouthed, wide-eyed, and that was when she saw it. Right there in his face, threaded within the shock and disbelief, glimmering and bright and unmistakable.

He admired the hell out of her.

Kenzie smiled, and she hoped he saw her forgiveness, because she didn't stay to talk. She needed nothing from this place, nothing from him. She was her own woman, and she had everything she wanted.

Almost.

Kenzie walked out of that arena with her back straight and her head high. She pushed through the heavy exit door and stopped on the sidewalk, welcoming the quiet, drinking in the cool autumn air.

She tilted her head back and looked at the stars—or what she could see of them, this deep in the center of the city. She used the constellations to point herself slightly north, then west. Toward Oklahoma.

Toward home.

She tugged her trucker hat lower and left it all behind.

Chapter Nineteen

There was a man on her porch.

Bob's porch, Kenzie corrected as she parked beside the all-too-familiar pickup angled toward the side of the house.

There was a man on her porch, and he was asleep. Back propped against the post, hat tilted over his eyes, arms crossed, long legs stretched out in front of him.

Jesse didn't wake up when Kenzie killed the engine on her mom's sedan, so she took another minute to sit and watch him, wondering what this meant. It was six thirty in the morning and cold, the slow-rising November sun not yet over the horizon. Only forty-two degrees according to the dashboard display. How long had he been here, to be sleeping this deeply? And why hadn't he just called?

Probably for the same reason she wouldn't have answered if he did. She wasn't ready to talk to him yet. She wanted to get her thoughts in a row, put the best words in perfect order. She'd only have one chance to fix this, and she had to get it right.

Which made her consider driving away. She still hadn't decided what she wanted to say. She could reverse the car right now and buy herself more time.

But that wasn't the point, was it? She didn't need to be perfect, not for a man camped outside her front door, hunched in his coat. His presence was encouragement enough.

Kenzie slipped out of the car and eased the door shut. She crossed the frost-crisp grass and took a seat on the top step.

He was beautiful. The brim of his hat was low, the early-morning light still dim, but she could see his dark lashes fanned on his cold-reddened cheeks. The stubborn set of his mouth. The dark stubble shadowing his jaw. The elegant lengths of his fingers.

She put her hand on his knee. He stirred, slowly at first, then jerked awake, catching her in the laser-bright beam of those impossibly blue eyes.

He smiled, and it took her breath away.

"Hi." His voice was gravelly and rough.

"Howdy."

"What time is it?"

"Six thirty."

"In the morning?"

"Pretty sure."

"Y'all break down or something?" He rolled his neck and stretched his arms.

"How long have you been out here?"

"About twelve hours."

"Twelve hours?" she echoed.

Jesse shrugged. "More like thirteen."

"I can't wait to hear this one." She folded her arms expectantly.

He swung his legs over the step, sitting beside her. "I needed to talk to you."

"Ever heard of a phone?"

"Wasn't sure you'd answer."

That was fair.

"I figured you'd get back from Atlanta last night, so when I showed up and you didn't answer the door, I decided to wait."

Kenzie tried to roll her eyes, to dismiss what he'd just told her, but she couldn't. That simple explanation lodged in her heart, soft yet unyielding.

He'd decided to wait.

For thirteen hours, outside, in the cold, in the dark.

For her.

"You must've been freezing. Why didn't you sit in your truck, at least?"

He wrinkled his nose. "Seemed creepy. Like I was lying in wait. Felt more honest to stay here, out in the open, so you could turn around and drive off if you wanted."

"You're an idiot, you know that? A half-frozen fool."

"I don't know about that. You're talking to me, aren't you?"

She smiled. "I'll give you that."

"I have a lot more to say, too. Could I trouble you for a cup of coffee, first? I'll even make it, if you point me in the right direction."

Kenzie sobered, recalling how far out of the loop he was, and catching him up meant rehashing every ugly detail out loud.

"I don't have my coffee maker inside. Don't have cups or milk, either. Just the few boxes I came to clear out. Then this house will be empty."

His smile vanished. "You're moving? Where?"

"Perry."

His shoulders dropped. "I thought maybe you'd been poached down to Texas or somewhere."

She shook her head. "No, I'll be here in Oklahoma for the foreseeable."

"You want to be closer to your mom?"

She had to laugh at that, thinking of Irlene's tolerant but pinched smile as Kenzie stacked boxes into what had been the craft room.

"Looks like I'm going to be, whether I want to or not."

Jesse said nothing, leaving space for her to explain.

She sighed. "You're right, the Broken B convoy got back from Atlanta last night. I wasn't with them, though. I flew in yesterday morning, and by the time you got here I'd packed up most of the house and toted it over to my mom's."

She lifted her gaze to his, reminding herself not to be ashamed. She'd done what was right. Jesse of all people would understand.

"I don't work here anymore, Jesse. Bob fired me."

His expression hardened. His hand moved on his thigh like he wanted to touch her, but wasn't sure whether he'd earned it, yet.

She wished he would. But she needed to earn that, too.

"I have something to show you." Kenzie handed him her phone. "Custer is injecting his bulls with steroids. I saw it, and I can prove it. I recorded his backstage operations guy admitting it."

Jesse stared at the photo, his jaw tightening. He gave her back her phone.

"We'll ruin him," he swore, his voice low and dangerous.

"Should we send these to the other stock contractors?"

"Later. First we'll send them to the press."

"Like, the newspaper?"

His smile turned cold, and she remembered all he'd been—all he'd left behind when he chose his family. In that instant, she knew if he chose her, if she could still be that lucky after everything that happened, it would be forever. She would never need to question his devotion or his intentions.

He was nothing like her father.

If he chose her.

"I may not have Lee's network—or yours, for that matter. But I still have a few friends in useful places, and I'm owed a lot of favors."

"I'll send you what I have. Do whatever you see fit."

"Thank you." His tone softened again. "This is exactly what we need, Kenzie. You might've just single-handedly taken down Custer's empire."

She concentrated on the screen, forwarding him the images and the recording. She hoped he was right, and when that day came, she'd be happy.

Now, though, it was hard to see past the trees of the consequences to the handsome forest beyond.

"What happened with Bob?" he asked.

"I showed him what I've shown you and told him we should withdraw from the event. We couldn't be associated with misconduct like this—or I couldn't, at least. He refused. Said if I walked, I was walking out of my job. So I did. Oh, and I had an audience. My dad was there, and he watched the whole thing. Now I'm here, homeless, unemployed, trying to figure out why the man I said such mean things to waited all night in the cold to talk to me." Her voice wavered on the last syllable, the pent-up emotion of the last few days hitting her fast.

"Kenzie," he said, the word an ache come to life. He studied the ground between his feet, his brow furrowed. "Can I hold your hand?"

She dug her teeth into her lower lip, willing back tears of longing, and regret, and dangerous optimism as she held out her palm. He knotted his fingers with hers, warming her all the way through, despite the chill lingering on his skin.

"You made the right choice. I'm sorry I ever doubted you. What I said about you standing up to Lee, and standing up to Bob—that wasn't fair. You're the strongest woman I know. And you've met my sisters."

She smiled, shaking her head. "No, you were right. There've been too many times I should've backed myself, but instead I backed down. I spent so long fixating on what my dad might think. What you said made me realize that's exactly what my mom did, too. I don't know if at the beginning she held out hope they might get back together, or if she just wanted to prove she could raise me without him. Either way, he lived in her imagination like he lived in mine, and it cost her dearly. It would've cost me even more if you hadn't given me that push."

"You didn't need a push."

"I did," she insisted. "Maybe that's wrong—maybe I should've figured it out on my own. Or maybe it's okay to get help. To need an outside perspective on something you're so deep within, you can't see the way out. That's what you gave me, and that's why I realized something in Atlanta."

Kenzie sucked in a steadying breath, bracing to finally say this out loud.

"My dad doesn't love me. He probably never will. All those years I spent thinking about him, performing for him—he wasn't watching. He didn't care."

Jesse squeezed her hand. "I'm so sorry, Kenzie."

"It's okay—really. I needed to see his rejection and accept it. I had to stop looking for his love before I could find love with someone else."

She looked at him then, and knew she'd given herself away. She'd spread her cards on the table, and they were all hearts. She could do nothing now but hold her breath and wait, and pray to God he didn't rip them to pieces.

His gaze bored into hers, his grip on her hand tight. He looked like he wanted to say a thousand things at once. As the seconds wore on, she wished he'd just pick one and blurt it out, because every unreadable, unspoken sentence flashing behind his eyes made her confidence falter that little bit more.

"I told my sisters," he said.

Kenzie jerked, that particular statement not even on her long list of possibilities.

"I told them everything," he continued. "About Lee, about the business. About us."

She was frozen—she couldn't even nod.

He'd done it. He'd listened to her. He'd understood, and he'd *done it.*

"How are they?" she asked.

"Fine. Good," he amended. "Supportive, and not mad at all. You had it right. I did my best when Lee was alive—we all did. I didn't need his forgiveness, but I needed my own. And I'm there, now. I'm okay. I don't have to protect anyone."

"You could protect me." The words slipped out, quiet and unbidden.

He smiled. "You don't need protecting. I know it probably feels that way right now, sitting here in front of this empty house, but it'll work out. Trust me. You're tougher than I've ever been."

"Maybe I don't always want to be tough, Jesse. Maybe I want that one person who'll catch me, and wrap me up, and make me feel safe."

He stared at her, and after one too many silent, perplexed beats she rolled her eyes. "I'm talking about you, jerk. I freaking love you. Haven't you put that together yet?"

He blinked, then broke into a grin so radiant it rivaled the steadily climbing sun. "Kenzie Wallace, I've been out-of-my-mind in love with you for weeks. Maybe longer. Maybe since you damn near pushed me off that platform in New Mexico, come to think of it. You're so smart and good and honest and if you'll let me, I'll catch you every dang time."

"Yes. Please. I want you to," she told him, taking his other hand in hers. "I love *you*, Jesse—I want you to know that. Not the corporate hotshot, not the rodeo boss, not the heir to the Singer throne. You. Just you."

"Kenzie." Her name was a plea, a decision, an enchantment all at once.

Then he kissed her, and everything vanished—the uncertainty, the despair, the sense of being unwanted that had simmered in the background of her entire life.

She loved him. He loved her. That was it, and it was more than enough.

They kissed like they had all the time in the world. Like it wasn't a cloudy, chilly, autumn morning. Like they weren't sitting on the cold, hard, timber porch. Nothing mattered but the man in her arms.

The man she loved.

Epilogue

"There you are."

Jesse stood by the gas pump when Kenzie rounded the back of the truck to find him. He'd filled the tank, then remained with his hip propped against the bed and his arms crossed, enjoying the view.

He took one of the coffees she held, then he took her, too, wrapping his arm around her shoulders and pulling her into his side. He welcomed the warmth of her body in the chilly desert air, which cooled rapidly as the sun dropped toward the horizon.

She leaned into him. For a moment they stood in contented silence, watching the line of animal rights protesters encircling the arena where a Supreme Rodeo performance was due to take place that evening.

And because Custer had scheduled Supreme Rodeo to be in Vegas at the same time as the Pro Rodeo League finals, they weren't the only ones enjoying his downfall. A regular stream of dirty pickups with out-of-state plates slowed as they passed the protesters, honking in support.

Jesse's call to one of his old media contacts had worked in more ways than one. The reporter uncovered layers of financial irregularities and morally dubious contracts that he and Kenzie never could've found, prompting fierce backlash against Supreme Rodeo. Custer had already canceled multiple dates and hadn't scheduled any new ones.

That call hadn't only unseated his biggest competition—it rooted Jesse in his decision to return to Oklahoma. When their conversation turned personal, and the reporter prodded him about ever coming back to New York, there was a fresh firmness in Jesse's *no.*

This was his life, now, and it was better than he'd ever imagined. Bringing his sisters into the business operations had taken an enormous weight off his shoulders. He was less stressed and more energized, having more fun than he'd thought possible, even on the days he found himself doing damage control for whatever Trixie had just said or done.

Turned out four heads were better than one, too. Not only did his sisters help him find places to trim costs, having them in the loop let him make big, sweeping moves, without hiding or tiptoeing around them. He'd even freed up enough cash to make a strategic hire—one he still wasn't sure he deserved.

Kenzie had a new job now. It didn't pay nearly as well as her old one, but it came with room and board, home-cooked meals, and a few other late-night, between-the-sheets perks he liked to think made it worth her while.

She must think so too, considering how quickly she'd ended Bob Boyd's pleading phone call, desperate for her to come back.

He looked at the smile curving her lips, and the purple-dyed ends of her hair sticking out of her trucker hat. He loved having her by his side.

He loved her, full stop.

Even when she jammed her elbow into his ribs.

"Enough gloating. I need to shower and change before it all kicks off tonight."

They drove back to the hotel near the arena where the finals were hosted. His sisters were crammed into a single room, but he'd sprung for one of his own. As they stepped inside, he had renewed gratitude for the kindly check-in clerk who'd given them a free upgrade to a king-size bed.

Not that they needed the space. Not when every time he flickered to consciousness he rolled over and pulled her in tight.

He reached for her as soon as the door shut, unbuttoning her jeans.

Her smile undermined her eye roll. "Did you not hear what I said? I need to get ready."

"I know. I'm helping you undress." He pulled her shirt over her head.

"At this rate we'll have to shower together to save time."

"Is that a promise?"

"Of course." She slid her hand down the back of his jeans and squeezed his ass.

When they emerged from the bathroom forty minutes later, they were spent.

And late.

Kenzie was still hastily buttoning her Singer Pro Rodeo shirt when Mae pounded on the door.

"I've been sent to collect you," she called through the thick wood. "Your sisters seem to think my medical degree means I'll be the least traumatized by witnessing my beloved brother mid-coitus, but I'm telling you now, if—"

Jesse wrenched open the door. "Dang, Mae, there's rodeo people in every room on this floor. Can we keep the sex references to a minimum?"

"Got you to open up, didn't it?" She smiled past him. "Hey, Kenzie. You ready?"

"I'm ready," she confirmed.

They had a hell of a night. Trixie set an arena record in the barrels, and Billie's broncs outperformed all the other bucking horses. Repeat Offender wasn't on the roster, but two other Singer bulls had glorious buck-offs, tidily unseating top-ranked cowboys like it was just another day at the office.

There were still three nights left in the finals series, but as the competition ended and the crowd filed out, the atmosphere among the stock-contracting staff ramped up. They abandoned the usual gossipy, after-show lollygagging, feeding and putting up roughstock with ruthless efficiency. Even the laziest ranch hands were in a hurry.

In less than forty-five minutes the winners of the year's roughstock awards would be announced, and no one wanted to miss it.

"I fretted about this moment all year, but now that it's here, I feel weirdly calm," Kenzie remarked as they walked hand in hand to the ballroom.

Jesse saw through the open doors that chairs were set up, facing the row of tables at the far end of the room. "Because you win either way. Not Nice is yours, and Repeat Offender is yours, too."

"He's only sort of mine."

"He's yours," Jesse said. "You raised him, you trained him. All I did these last couple years was keep him healthy and happy."

"Understatement of the year."

"Don't think that's one of the awards they're handing out."

"Good, since you just won it."

Billie waved them over as soon as they stepped inside. They joined her, Mae and Trixie in the third row, and a minute later Billie's fellow pickup rider, Wyatt, slid into the last vacant seat.

"Y'all nervous?" He rubbed his palms together.

Kenzie shrugged. "Either way, it's all good."

"The prize money would be nice, but we'll survive without it," Billie added.

Wyatt shook his head. "Shoot, *I'm* nervous and it ain't my animals. Y'all Singers have nerves of steel."

"We're not all Singers," Kenzie pointed out.

"Yet," Trixie said.

Jesse glanced at Kenzie, hoping Trixie's comment hadn't

freaked her out. Instead she smiled at him contentedly, and he sat back in his chair, relieved.

It took more than a throwaway comment to push Kenzie Wallace off-balance—but the heirloom ring he'd taken from the family's bank vault last week just might do it.

He held that secret tight and held her hand tighter as the lights dimmed and League executives filed into the seats behind the tables.

Whatever happened in the next half hour didn't matter. He'd already won.

They began with the broncs. Billie's horses missed out in the bareback category, but she took second in saddle bronc, and her grin as she posed with the League CEO was worth more to Jesse than the check that came with the plaque.

He stood up to hug her when she got back to their seats. So did Kenzie, and as he watched the two of them embrace, he thought this night couldn't get any better.

He was wrong. Bob Boyd slipped into an empty seat across the aisle, angling to catch Kenzie's eye. When he did, he smiled apologetically, and Kenzie nodded in response.

Bob would accept the plaque if Not Nice won, and this was his way of acknowledging he didn't deserve it. She relaxed beside Jesse, her fingers threading through his as the CEO moved on to Bull of the Year.

"This was the most hard-fought category we've had in years," the CEO said. "The quality was outstanding, and I want to make it clear that the first, second, and third place winners were separated by fractions of points."

Kenzie squeezed his hand.

"Third place goes to… Southern Gothic, Occupy Rodeo."

Jesse released Kenzie's grip to clap for Nat Ware, whose smile lit up the room as he accepted his plaque. When the applause died down, the CEO again picked up the microphone.

"In second place, we have… Not Nice, Broken B Cattle Company."

Kenzie's chin dropped. He moved to put his arm around her, ready to support her as she watched someone else take credit for her achievement.

But she was gone, tugged out of her seat by Bob Boyd. He shoved her up the aisle, then planted his feet as he clapped, blocking her way back to her chair.

Kenzie hovered uncertainly, unsure whether to move forward or back. She caught Jesse's eye and he smiled. Then she smiled too, and walked up to the table to claim her rightful prize.

The CEO lifted his brows, but said nothing about the fact she was accepting an award for the Broken B while wearing a shirt with Singer Pro Rodeo embroidered above the pocket. The applause heightened as she received the plaque, then warmed even more when she gave Bob a hug before handing it over.

Kenzie dropped heavily into the chair beside him. He tilted up the brim of her dark gray cowgirl hat so he could see her face, and she gave him a shaky smile.

"You okay?" he whispered.

She nodded. "Overwhelmed."

"It's all good. I've got you."

"I know. I love you, Jesse."

His heart stirred, hale and hopeful and impossibly happy. "I love you, too."

"And now, it's my honor to announce the winner of Bull of the Year. The top-scoring bull in this year's Pro Rodeo League season is…"

The whole room held a collective breath.

"Repeat Offender, Singer Pro Rodeo."

Now it was Jesse's turn to stumble to his feet, Kenzie's hand the only thing anchoring him to earth. He'd gotten what he'd wanted, but not what he'd known he'd wanted. He marveled again that he'd convinced Kenzie to be by his side as he walked to the front—and that she intended to stay there.

The CEO's smile was enormous, the crowd's applause raucous, but in the split second before he reached the table Jesse turned, certain he'd caught movement out of the corner of his eye.

He was there, slipping out the back entrance, the breadth of his shoulders unmistakable, his gait inimitable, his cowboy hat as familiar as Jesse's own face in the mirror.

Lee.

Then the man turned around. It wasn't Lee at all. Lee was gone.

And yet he was here, too. Present through Jesse's choices and his triumphs. Through his love for his family, and the love he'd found with Kenzie.

Lee was here, and he was proud. He was smiling.

"Ready?" Kenzie looked up at him.

He nodded, and they continued forward.

The CEO held out the plaque, letting them choose who took it. They each put a hand on one edge. Whistles and hollers added to the din in the room, and when they turned to face their community the noise doubled, echoing off the walls.

Kenzie smiled at Jesse, and he smiled back. Then they raised the plaque in victory.

Together.

* * * * *